control

Also by

kayla perrin

OBSESSION
GETTING SOME
GETTING EVEN

Look for Kayla's next book

GETTING LUCKY

coming in 2011 from Spice Books.

control

kayla perrin

Recycling programs
for this product may
not exist in your area.

Spice

CONTROL

ISBN-13: 978-0-373-60547-7

For questions and comments about the quality of this book
please contact us at Customer_eCare@Harlequin.ca.

www.Spice-Books.com

Printed in U.S.A.

For Helen and James
I'm glad you both found each other,
and I wish you a lifetime of happiness together!

prologue

Oh, shit.

That was the first thought I had when my eyes met his hazel ones across the expanse of my shop. A man I had never seen before. He was the kind of man who sent a rush of heat through your body the moment you laid eyes on him. The kind of man who, with one look, made you think about getting naked.

The kind of man who inspired you to slip your left hand behind your back, hiding the visible sign to the world that you were married.

I had never done that before. Not once during the eight years that I'd been married.

He walked into my store on a Friday in late February. His tall frame—at least six foot two—was all muscle. Something about him oozed sex appeal, even though his eyes were dark and he looked as if he carried a burden

on his wide shoulders. I could tell that something serious was going on in his world. He wasn't in my shop
to buy flowers for a happy occasion.

And he wasn't interested in small talk, either.

He bought a ready-made bouquet with a Get Well
Soon balloon. So I knew someone in his life was sick.
And sick enough that he was very worried.

Then he left. There was nothing remarkable about our
interaction, and yet I couldn't forget him. I'd checked
his left hand and found no wedding band there. That
didn't mean he wasn't married, of course, or seriously
involved with someone.

I didn't know why I cared.

But I would come to think about him a lot over the
next several weeks, to the point where I was disturbed
by the unexpected direction of my thoughts.

Was it a sin to daydream about having sex with
someone other than your husband? Not just a simple
daydream, a quick flash of two naked bodies wrapped
together. But a fully fledged, detailed fantasy about
another man pleasing you in the way that only your
husband should. Vividly picturing another man with
his fingers and tongue all over your pussy, while you're
in the middle of fucking your husband. Imagining the
moment you slide over a stranger's cock and take him
fully into your body.

Something about him awakened a sexual part of me
that had been dormant for a long, long time. But it
came roaring back to life that day, shocking me with
its intensity.

What scared me was how easily thoughts about

another man invaded my brain as a married woman. Don't get me wrong—I loved my husband. And until that man walked into my floral shop, I never expected I would ever cross the line and fantasize about sex with a stranger. At least not to the point where it was no longer about the fantasy, but about the other man.

Seeing him and reacting to him were the beginning of a turning point for me, even though I didn't know it that day. It wasn't just lust that had been awakened in me, but something that my marriage had killed. I wouldn't put all the pieces together until later, but when I did, I could look back on that day when the sexy stranger with the hazel eyes came into the store as the beginning of my rebirth.

The beginning of me reclaiming my life.

part one

1

I gave myself a once-over in the bathroom mirror and smiled at my reflection. I looked *good*.

Sexy. Hot.

Hot enough that my husband wouldn't be able to resist me.

I'd flat-ironed my hair, giving my shoulder-length ebony locks the razor-sharp straight look I didn't wear often. Robert typically liked it softly curled. The straight hair, combined with the dress and dramatic makeup, gave me more of a high-fashion model or actress look. My hair had taken a good thirty minutes to perfect, but I was extremely pleased with the result.

I smoothed my hands over my black sheath dress. It was tight, hugging my curves. I'd put on a push-up bra to give me more cleavage, and the dress's V-neck exposed a teasing amount of flesh. A little too much?

I shook my head. No, I didn't think so.

I wasn't trying to be subtle in my sex appeal, though I was trying to be tasteful. What I wanted was my husband thinking of getting me home—and naked—during every moment of our dinner.

We needed something to get us into baby-making mood.

"Elsie, what's taking you so long?" I heard Robert call out to me. His voice was close, which meant he was in our bedroom. I'd left him downstairs watching CNN in the great room as I'd come to the master bathroom, locking the door so he couldn't inadvertently see me before I wanted him to. This was the second time he'd come up to check on me.

"I'm almost—"

"We have a seven-o'clock reservation," Robert said sternly. "It's six-twenty."

"I'm sorry, sweetheart," I said. "We'll get there. We've got enough time."

"We're going to midtown."

The doorknob rattled, but with the door locked, it didn't budge. "Open up, Elsie."

"Just give me a few more minutes." I wanted my look to be a surprise. We were going to The Melting Pot, a popular fondue restaurant in midtown Charlotte that always got rave reviews, and I wanted to look chic and sexy as I walked in on Robert's arm.

He knocked on the door now—fast, impatient. "Open the door, Elsie."

He was irritated. I could tell by his tone. He probably

thought I was going to take another twenty minutes to finish getting ready. "Okay, I'm coming."

I applied my deep red lipstick, picked my LuLu clutch up off the vanity—and then spotted the necklace I'd forgotten to put on. Robert liked classic pearls, but they weren't right for this look, so I had decided on a six-strand beaded black necklace that I rarely wore.

"Jesus, Elsie!"

"I'm just putting my necklace on." I secured the clasp at the back of my neck. Then I slipped into my Jimmy Choo black patent shoes. *Yes,* I thought. *Perfect.*

"I'm coming," I called, and hurried to the door. I hoped Robert's tone was an indicator of his impatience, as opposed to a bad mood. I'd been looking forward to our first visit to The Melting Pot for ages, and I didn't want anything to sour our romantic evening.

I swung open the door and spread my arms. "Ta-da."

It took only a second for Robert's eyes to widen in surprise. That I expected. This wasn't my typical demure look. His gaze roamed over my face and hair first, then went lower, stopping at my breasts. "What are you wearing?"

My husband's expression was far from appreciative—not the reaction I had expected. "You don't like it?"

"I thought you were going to wear the red dress I bought you last week."

"I preferred this one. We *are* going to that hip fondue restaurant." *And I want you thinking about getting me naked. Creating a baby inside me.*

"Restaurant. Exactly. Not a club with your friends."

Once again, Robert's eyes landed on my cleavage. Then they moved upward. "And what on earth did you do to your hair?"

I raised my hand, fingering some of the strands. "I tried something different."

"I don't like it."

"Oh." I had hoped he would. I'd worked so hard on coming up with a hot, irresistible look. The kind that would have my husband whistling with appreciation, not staring at me with scorn.

Robert glanced at his watch. "We're cutting it close, but you should have enough time to change. The red dress is more appropriate for dinner. Even if we're a little late, I'm sure they'll hold our reservation."

"Oh," I said, feeling deflated. "You think I should change."

"Do hurry."

"I'll, uh, need a few more minutes to get ready then." I spoke as evenly as possible, trying to hide my disappointment.

"I'll be downstairs."

Robert turned and walked out of the bedroom. There was no more discussion. He'd made his wishes clear, and if I went downstairs in anything other than the red dress, he would be miserable the entire night.

Closing the bathroom door, I tried to ignore the swell of unhappiness rising inside me. I tried, as I had done so many times before, to put the unpleasant feelings in an emotional box. It had taken him two years to agree to take me to The Melting Pot, and I didn't want to ruin an evening I had been looking forward to.

I went back to the vanity table and looked at myself in the mirror one more time. The spark in my eyes had disappeared. The sexy, excited woman didn't look sexy and excited anymore.

The his-and-her closets were connected to the bathroom by a carpeted hallway. I suppose the suite had been designed that way to make it easier for people fresh from the shower to be able to get dressed. Everything in a house like this—nearly ten thousand square feet—was about making life easier for the owners. If you wished to watch your favorite television show in the bathtub, you could do that. If you didn't want to go downstairs to your home office, you didn't need to; the master bedroom was so large, it had a desk and computer in a corner by the bay window. My closet was big enough to have shelves upon shelves for hundreds of pairs of shoes, plus racks to hang hundreds of outfits. So was Robert's.

I took the red dress off the hook where I'd hung it after deciding I'd wear the black one instead. There was a mirror in my closet—two floor-length ones, in fact—so I didn't need to go back to the bathroom to see what the gown looked like when I held it up against my body.

It was a perfectly nice dress. Classic. Elegant.

But it wasn't the look I had wanted for tonight.

I pushed that thought aside. Time was ticking away. I had to tone down my dark makeup, which would be too dramatic for the red dress. I went back into the bathroom, dampened a face towel and tried to smudge off as much of my dark eye shadow as I could—then grabbed a tissue to dab at the tears that filled my eyes.

"Why are you crying?" I asked my reflection. "So what if Robert wants you to change? What's the big deal?" I unzipped my black dress and wriggled out of it. "If he thinks the dress isn't right, it's because he knows more about this stuff than you do."

My husband was the former head of a Fortune 500 company. Having lived most of his life in privilege, he knew much more about etiquette than I did. Maybe he thought I looked trashy, and as the wife of a wealthy and prominent citizen, I couldn't bring any shame to him.

The words made sense to me, and yet I found myself thinking something that had flitted into my mind many times over the past couple of years. *Robert doesn't think I fit into his world. Even after all this time.*

And then I had another thought: *When you dress too provocatively, it screams to the world that you're a trophy wife. Everyone will always see you as the woman who married up.*

Robert had said that to me more than once when we'd first gotten married. I'd understood his point then, and I understood it now. Eight years ago, I'd married a wealthy man thirty years my senior. I know that most people would believe I did it for financial reasons. But that wasn't true.

I married for love.

Before walking down the aisle, I signed a prenup entitling me to one million dollars if our marriage ended before the ten year mark. My lawyer had wanted to renegotiate for a higher amount, arguing that Robert was enormously wealthy, but I had refused. My goal wasn't how much I could get should we divorce, but rather on living happily ever after with the man I adored.

Reaching a hand behind me, I was about to unclasp my bra, figuring something more conservative would be better. But then I glanced at the clock. It was already 6:33. I could imagine Robert downstairs, sitting on the chaise in the great room, impatiently glancing at his watch.

So I kept the bra on and got into the red dress, a delicate number with a much higher neckline. The gown cinched below the bust with a black ribbon band, and from there flowed down to my knees. With the combination of the push-up bra and the ribbon detail, my breasts really popped.

But at least they were covered. It was one element that made me feel sexier, and I was grateful for that. I still wanted to be irresistible to Robert.

The only other issue was my hair. Robert had said he didn't like it. I did. But again, I wanted to be turning him on, not off. I searched my vanity for a black clip. Instead of wearing my hair down, I swept the back of it up off my neck and styled it up with the clip. I arranged some loose tendrils around the sides of my face, giving me a softer look.

The black ribbon on my dress went well with my black clutch and shoes, and also my necklace, so at least I didn't have to change my accessories. I wrapped a cashmere shawl around my shoulders and was ready to go.

One last time, I checked myself out in the mirror. I wasn't the vixen I'd been a while earlier. But I was still attractive, hopefully in a way that would make my husband happy.

Because I still hoped that Robert and I would end up in our bed later, making love.

And making a baby.

2

By the time we got to The Melting Pot, we were ten minutes late. But I had called ahead, ensuring that they'd hold our table, while Robert drove.

He pulled up to the valet stand in front of the restaurant. An attendant came over immediately. They usually did when the car was a Porsche.

Moments later, we were inside The Melting Pot. The restaurant was warm and inviting, done in a combination of dark beige and burgundy. Intimate, curved booths lined the walls. Unique lighting fixtures hung above the tables, reminding me of blown-glass designs I'd seen in Venice.

I liked the place. A lot. My mood instantly brightened.

The restaurant was full of chatter. Happy people all

around us were laughing and talking and dipping various items into pots of fondue.

"I hope we made the right choice," Robert mumbled.

I glanced at him as we approached the hostess stand. He didn't make eye contact with me. I didn't bother asking him what he meant.

The hostess sat us at our table in the center of the restaurant. I took my shawl off and placed it and my clutch on the seat next to me.

Robert was looking around. Not a casual glance inspecting his surroundings, but more of an intense, evaluating look.

Some of the diners were throwing curious glances our way, as well.

I suddenly understood why Robert had muttered that comment. The crowd was young—late twenties to late thirties, mostly. Young and attractive. You didn't have to be a rocket scientist to figure out that Robert was uncomfortable here.

Uncomfortable because of our age difference.

I reached across the table and took his hand in mine, letting him know that *I* wasn't uncomfortable. After eight years of marriage, I was used to the second glances we got from some people. At first those looks had bothered me, but not anymore.

I was with my husband, and if the rest of the world didn't like it, they could go to hell.

In the beginning of our relationship, Robert had had no problem going out with me in public. He'd been a fit and attractive fifty-nine. And when he colored the gray in his hair, he looked more like fifty. So while there was obviously an age difference between us, he hadn't been bothered by it.

But over the last few years, his face had aged considerably and his posture was no longer as imposing as it had once been. Because of knee replacement surgery last year, his gait wasn't the strong, confident stride it had been when we'd met.

Once, Robert had been able to walk into a room and have heads turn—that's the kind of attention he commanded. Not anymore.

The physical changes, capped off by a full head of gray hair he could no longer be bothered to color, troubled my husband. Oh, he never said as much, but I could tell. He was sixty-seven and looked it—his body defying his ageless spirit more and more.

"This place is beautiful," I said, hoping to distract him from his thoughts. "The ambience, the decor..." I glanced up at the goldish-orange light fixture above our table, which sort of resembled a large, upside-down wineglass with a very long stem. "Remember that shop in Saint Mark's Square—the one where we almost bought that chandelier before we realized it wouldn't look good in our place? I wonder if these light fixtures came from there."

"Perhaps." Robert released my hand to withdraw his reading glasses from his jacket pocket.

"Thank you for bringing me here," I said, hoping that being extra sweet would help his discomfort dissipate. "I keep hearing how fabulous the food is, that the menu is second to none."

"Let's hope so," Robert stated.

He lifted his menu. Even with his glasses on, he squinted slightly as he read.

Something tugged at my heart as I watched him. A little sympathy. I was sorry about the changes age was bringing about that neither of us could control. I wasn't thrilled about heading toward forty. I could only imagine how Robert felt, nearing seventy.

He needed something else in his life. Something positive to concentrate on, as opposed to life's ticking clock. We both did.

Which was why I was hoping we'd get pregnant sooner rather than later.

"Good evening." A man's voice drew our attention, and I glanced up. The waiter who had arrived at our table wore a crisp white shirt, black tie and burgundy apron neatly tied around his waist. There was an air of confidence about him that said he'd been doing his job—and doing it well—for a long time.

"Good evening," I replied. Robert continued to peruse the menu.

"Have you been here before?" the waiter asked.

"No," I said. "We haven't."

"Then welcome. I think you'll be very pleased. Our cheeses are aged to perfection to create the best possible fondue. You can enjoy them with bread or fruit. We have salads as well, if you prefer. And all of our entrées are cooked in our popular fondue styles."

"Mmm." I looked at Robert before meeting the waiter's gaze again. "Sounds delicious."

"The dinners for two are very popular, and come

with a cheese fondue, salad, and one of three entrée items." He pointed to the page on my open menu.

"Ooh, the surf and turf looks good." I glanced at Robert. "What do you think, sweetheart? Lobster tails?"

"I think that we need a few more minutes to make up our minds," he said.

"Certainly." The waiter smiled cordially at both of us before his gaze landed on me. "My name is Alexander. And madam, the surf and turf is one of our more popular items. You certainly won't be disappointed if you decide on it."

"All right." Robert's tone held a tiny note of impatience. "You've done your job. Now run along and give us some time to make up our minds."

Now run along?

My eyes went wide as I stared at him, shocked by the demeaning words. "Robert," I began when the waiter was gone, "that wasn't a very nice thing to say."

"You would say that, wouldn't you?"

I was confused by the comment. "Do you expect me to approve of you being rude to our waiter?"

"It was like he didn't even know I was at the table," Robert went on.

"That's because I was the one doing the talking. You barely gave him a second glance."

"I saw how he was looking at you."

What was Robert getting at? That the waiter had been out of line? "He was looking at me like he was our waiter."

"Right," Robert said, his tone dripping with sarcasm.

I didn't understand what was happening. The waiter had been professional and cordial. He hadn't ogled me or anything like that. So why was Robert making an issue out of nothing?

Because he never wanted to come here.

Was that what this was about—Robert making an issue because he didn't want to be here? He hadn't been interested when I'd suggested the place time and time again, and the moment he'd seen the crowd, there'd been a visible change in him.

"It's that dress," he said.

"The dress?" Again, I was confused. "This is the one you wanted me to wear, remember?"

"But what did you do to your *breasts?*" His expression was one of disdain as he lowered his eyes to my chest. "You're wearing some kind of bra that makes them look larger. As if you got breast implants."

Certainly that couldn't be the issue. Even though I was annoyed that he seemed to be trying to sour the mood, I forged ahead gently. "What's wrong? Is there something else bothering you?"

Robert pretended he didn't hear me. Pretended to be absorbed in reading the menu.

It was probably best to let the matter drop. I lifted my own menu. "Do you want to do one of the entrées for two? Or decide on a cheese fondue and maybe a couple other items?"

"I'm trying to make up my mind."

I nodded. "Okay."

As we both perused the menu in silence, I decided I would let Robert choose our meals. Everything looked great, so it wasn't as if I'd be disappointed. He was clearly irritable, and I wanted to keep him happy.

It was something I did a lot.

Why shouldn't you decide? a tiny voice inside me asked.

Before I could even contemplate the question, Alexander arrived again, a warm smile on his attractive face. This time I noticed that he did stare at me before turning to Robert. But he had to look at *someone* first. Just because it was me didn't mean he wanted to fuck me.

"We've hardly looked at the menu," Robert all but snapped.

"Take your time." Alexander clasped his hands together. "But may I start you off with a drink? Some wine or a cocktail?" He looked at me. "Or perhaps a martini."

"Or perhaps my wife."

My eyes grew wide with shock and horror. I gaped at my husband before looking at the waiter, who appeared absolutely mortified.

"Excuse me?" Alexander asked.

"Jesus, you're salivating over her like she's an item on the menu."

"Robert, stop it."

"It's true," he insisted calmly. "Isn't it, Alexander?"

Embarrassment mixed with my horror. I pushed my chair back and stood. I was certain that people around us were overhearing this ridiculous conversation, and I could no longer stay here.

"Sir, I apologize if I somehow—"

"You're not the one who needs to apologize," I said, cutting Alexander off. I gave Robert a pointed look, barely keeping my fury contained. And to think I'd been concerned about keeping *him* happy. I picked up my clutch and my shawl. "We're leaving."

"Good idea," Robert said.

Worry creased the waiter's brow, almost as if he suspected Robert was the type to lodge a complaint with the manager. If that was his assumption, then he'd read my husband correctly.

Alexander held up both hands, a sign of submission. "If I was disrespectful in any way, I apologize."

"Next time, look at a woman's face—not her tits—when you're speaking to her."

I heard the words and cringed. For the first time in our marriage, I wanted to slap Robert.

I didn't dare look around for fear everyone within earshot had heard his crude words. I wanted to meet the waiter's dejected eyes and tell him that my husband's high blood pressure medication was making him act like an asshole. But all I could do was head for the door before the embarrassment killed me.

I didn't stop until the cool evening breeze hit my face. With Robert moving more slowly these days because of his knee, I made it outside before he did. And once there, I wanted to scream.

But I didn't. I couldn't. Not with the valet attendants and other patrons nearby.

Robert had been rude on other occasions, more often than I liked these days, but his behavior tonight was completely uncalled for.

Was it his age, his medication, or his growing insecurity? Or was this the real Robert? Had I overlooked his true nature all of these years?

Yes.

The answer sounded in my mind—and it scared me.

3

I wrapped my shawl around my shoulders as I stood outside waiting for Robert. I didn't turn back to see how close he was, or if he'd stopped to complain to the manager. It was just the kind of thing he would do.

Several agonizing seconds passed and no Robert. My curiosity getting the better of me, I turned. He was a couple steps from the entryway.

People were staring in his direction with the kind of interest reserved for tabloids and reality shows.

Despite my anger, I reached for the door and opened it for him. It was something I did all the time, the kind of thing a younger wife did to take care of her elderly husband.

"Thank you, sweetheart," Robert said casually, as though he hadn't created a public spectacle inside.

I didn't respond. Just watched as he approached the valet stand and handed in our ticket.

A few minutes later, our yellow Porsche 911 Carrera pulled up to the curb. The young valet who'd brought it held the driver's door open for Robert, then made his way around the car and opened the passenger door for me.

Not going to accuse him of staring at my tits? I thought sourly.

No, Robert just handed the young man a ten. Then he revved the engine and began to drive.

Angry, I stared ahead blankly. I was going to give Robert the silent treatment if he spoke to me, but he didn't say a word, either. After a couple of minutes, I glanced his way to gauge his mood. On his face, I saw a contented expression—and if I wasn't mistaken, a hint of smugness. Not at all the look of a man who'd acted so outraged that a waiter had been inappropriately ogling his wife.

If he truly believed that ridiculous claim.

Robert hit a button to turn on the stereo, and classical music filled the car. He thrummed his fingers against the steering wheel like a man who didn't have a care in the world.

"I say we head to the country club. You can count on professionalism there."

I turned my gaze from his face to my window. *To the country club...gee, what a surprise.* Suddenly, I couldn't help thinking that Robert had orchestrated the whole ugly incident just so we would leave The Melting Pot. He hadn't wanted to go there in the first place, and what a perfect plan, to make the experience so uncomfortable there was no way we could have stayed.

Did you do it on purpose? I wanted to ask him. *Did you humiliate our waiter just so you could get your way?*

Yes. You know he did, Elsie.

And I did. That was exactly his style. Passive-aggressive bullshit so that he could always get his way.

After a few minutes, Robert asked, "Are you not going to speak to me again?" He sounded almost cheery.

I said nothing.

"Elsie…"

"You embarrassed me," I said. "Not to mention that poor waiter."

"That poor waiter needs to learn some respect."

Now I faced Robert. "What are you talking about? He wasn't looking at my *tits,* as you so crudely put it."

"He was."

"I didn't see it."

"You never see it, do you?"

Knowing what Robert was referring to, I once again turned to look out the window.

"I don't want a repeat of Hawaii," he said.

"Hawaii?"

"Yes, Hawaii," Robert stated curtly. "Don't play dumb when you know exactly what I'm talking about."

Nothing had happened in Hawaii—though Robert wouldn't believe it. During our last vacation there, over Christmas, he had been convinced that one of the pool attendants was hitting on me. The man had made pleasant conversation, brought me extra towels, reserved our lounge chairs every day. Robert had point-blank asked the man if he'd been trying to get me into bed.

He hadn't been, of course—even if I can admit he was flirting. Robert and I weren't the only May-December couple who went to the spectacular St. Regis Resort in Kauai over Christmas, year after year. Hollywood producers and their young wives also packed the place over the holidays. Men with power and money and trophy wives. The hotel staff knew how to cater to just that kind of clientele. How to pander to them and even kiss their asses when necessary. But this attendant, Richard, was new, and didn't keep the same kind of "professional" distance that men like Robert expected. He'd talk to you about the weather, your interests, where you were from—that sort of thing. And sure, he probably stole a few excited glances of me in my two-piece.

That was to be expected. Guys the world over checked women out, not caring if they were married or not. And wasn't that supposed to be the perk of having a beautiful woman on your arm—that other men were openly envious of your catch?

Unfortunately for Richard, Robert had been so offended by his "lack of professionalism" that he'd complained to the hotel. There was no way that management wanted to risk losing any of their high-end customers, especially not Robert Kolstad, so Richard had been made to apologize to me and Robert—and then he'd been fired.

"Our waiter was nothing but courteous and professional," I said.

"He's lucky I didn't speak to the manager."

"I'm glad you didn't."

"I'm sure you are."

I sighed. "Robert, can you just let it go? Please, you're making an issue where there is none."

He had never been jealous. Not early in our relationship, anyway. But in the last few years, I think, as the realization that he was getting older, while I was still comparatively a young woman, hit him, he had become far less secure in our marriage.

That had to be the reason for his odd behavior. Which was why I felt he needed something else to make him feel more secure. Something that would show I loved him and was committed to him.

A baby. I wanted a baby more than anything.

"Maybe I did overreact," he admitted. "I guess I need to accept that I have a wife most men would love to steal from me."

Then don't push me away, I thought silently. It was a sentiment I'd felt more than once over the last year— that Robert's behavior was eroding the relationship we had. There were other men out there, maybe someone who was perfect for me.

Like the man with the hazel eyes who had come into my shop a couple weeks before.

But I said to Robert, "I'm not going anywhere."

"Good." He paused a beat. "Shall we go to the country club?"

"Sure," I said. *You got your way again.*

When I was out of town or on vacation, and anyone asked me where I lived, I always said Charlotte. But

Robert and I actually lived just north of Charlotte in an exclusive community called The Peninsula. Situated on Lake Norman, The Peninsula was a country-club community with so much to do, you didn't have to go anywhere else if you didn't want to. There was a yacht club, a championship golf course, swimming, tennis. Casual and fine dining. We were members of both The Peninsula Yacht Club and The Peninsula Club. Though we had our own pool at home, we sometimes used the pool at the yacht club when we socialized.

On most days, Robert could be found on the greens at The Peninsula Club. It was his home away from home. We ate there much of the time when we chose to dine out, which was why I had wanted to try someplace different.

But that's where we went, and Robert was a much happier man. After a casual dinner and a couple of drinks, we headed home—where I still hoped to end the night the way I had originally planned.

I tried to get Robert in the mood after we pulled up in front of the house. Reaching across the seat, I lazily skimmed my fingertips over his hand before taking it in mine.

Robert squeezed my fingers in return. Then he met my eyes.

I stared at the man I had married. He was getting older, yes, but he was still so distinguished. Still looked like Harry Belafonte, a man who no matter how old he got would always be attractive.

"I love you," I told him. "Only you."

Robert's mouth curled in a small smile, one thing

that despite the years was as dazzling as it had been the first day I met him.

Leaning forward, I pressed my lips to his. A lingering kiss that said we would continue this in our bedroom.

"I love you, too, Elsie," Robert whispered as we pulled apart.

We exited the Porsche, which he had parked at the front of the house. A series of pod lights and spotlights illuminated our grand, Italian renaissance manor. It truly was a spectacular place, complete with a Roman-style fountain on an island of grass in the center of the long circular driveway.

I looped my arm through Robert's as we made our way up the steps. Once inside, I kissed his cheek. The double front doors led to a huge great room with a plasma television mounted on the wall, a fireplace, sofa, love seat and lounge chair. There was plenty of room to make love right there, and Olga, our housekeeper, was long gone for the day. But I knew my husband. He would want to wait until we were comfortably settled in our bedroom, as opposed to getting hot and heavy on the sofa.

Holding his hand, I led him up the curved staircase, across the portion of hallway that overlooked the great room below, to the double doors at the end that led to our bedroom.

The moment we crossed the threshold, I turned to face Robert, snaking my arms around his neck, my mouth on his, slowly coaxing his lips apart. Slipping my tongue into his mouth, I held him tighter. Robert began to kiss me back and I moaned, the sound ripe not just with desire, but with desperate need.

Robert's hands went to my upper arms. He held me for several seconds, kissing me. Then he tightened his grip and forced my body away from his.

"I haven't taken my pill, Elsie."

"You can take it now." I moved forward to kiss him once more, but he held me away.

"I want to make love to you—I do. But tonight—"

I planted another kiss on his lips. "Please, sweetheart. Please…"

I continued to kiss Robert, not ready for our night to end like this. He allowed it to go on for a few more seconds before pulling away again.

"I'm sorry, Elsie." His eyes roamed over my face. And I thought I saw, just for a moment, a flash of disapproval.

"What is it?" I asked him.

"It's…" He fingered the loose locks of hair around my face, almost as if examining the strands. "I'm tired, sweetheart. I'm sorry."

I got the feeling that Robert had been about to say something else. That there was another reason he didn't want to take me to bed.

But it *was* late for him—nearly eleven—and he'd had a couple glasses of that expensive cognac at the club, which always made him a little drowsy.

"Okay." I gave him a soft kiss this time, trying to quell my disappointment. "If you're tired, you're tired. Why don't you go get ready for bed, then? I'll do some reading in the great room."

"I'm sorry," Robert repeated.

"It's okay." I gave his hand a reassuring squeeze.

I turned and exited the bedroom. Halfway down the hallway, I felt tears fill my eyes.

What am I doing wrong?

Robert and I hadn't made love in nearly two weeks. There'd been some crisis at the office, Kolstad Systems, and he'd stepped in to help sort the problem out. I'd been busy with work. With all that had been going on, we hadn't carved out any time for us.

This was the first evening in a while that we had spent any significant time together. I hadn't wanted it to end like this.

Because I was pretty certain I was ovulating.

I went downstairs to the kitchen and made some tea and put on some smooth jazz. I hoped it would wash away my disappointment, but it didn't. Two years I'd been off the Pill. Two years I'd been trying to get pregnant.

Robert's rejection—even if he *was* tired—stung.

And then I asked myself why the night was necessarily over. Sometimes one partner had to do some coaxing to get the other in the mood. It wouldn't be the first time I'd seduced my husband.

My drive renewed, I made my way back upstairs. I would take off my clothes and crawl into bed with him. All he needed to do was get erect. I would climb on top of him and do the rest of the work.

As I neared the bedroom, I unzipped my dress. I pulled it over my head and tossed it onto the floor. Then I unclasped my bra and let it fall, as well. It was an idea that came to me, and I acted. Surely when I entered the room, naked except for the pumps and necklace, Robert would become aroused.

Outside the door, I paused to strip off my thong panties.

The lights in the room were doused, except the lamp on my night table. Robert was lying on his side with his back to me. He didn't hear me approach.

"Robert," I whispered.

No answer.

Time for plan B.

I kicked off my pumps and pulled the covers back on my side of the bed. Then I slipped under the sheets, their coolness caressing my skin. I slid over to my husband, running my hand down his left arm. He didn't react, so I leaned closer, nuzzling against his neck.

That's when I heard his deep, steady breaths—and realized he was sleeping.

Still, I ran my hand over his hip and stroked him through his silk pajamas, hoping to wake him. Robert didn't react.

I was defeated. I lay back on my pillow, sighing. It wasn't just that I wanted to make a baby. I was sexually frustrated, needed sexual release.

As I lay in the dimly lit room listening to my husband's steady breathing, I rested my right hand on the lower edge of my belly. I ran my fingertips over my skin. It was my own touch, yet my vagina thrummed in response. It needed to be stroked.

My hand went lower, over my pubic hair and to my

center. I spread my folds. Lazily let my finger stroke my clitoris.

Angling my head slightly, I glanced at Robert. He hadn't moved. He was still asleep. But even if he woke up and found me touching myself, I wouldn't stop.

If he saw me, hopefully he would become aroused and make love to me.

I circled my finger around my clit, each stroke making me hotter. Raising my left hand to my breast, I tweaked my nipple. It hardened instantly.

I played with my nipple. Played with my clit. Looked toward Robert and saw that his back was still to me. He was clueless.

Closing my eyes, I started to imagine my husband's hands on my pussy. But the fact that he was sleeping beside me, that he'd turned me down... It left me cold.

So I began to imagine someone else's hand playing with my pussy. A man who, if I climbed into bed naked beside him, would wake up. He would wake up, lower his head over my chest and lick my nipples with his tongue. He would lick and suck, pull at them with his teeth....

My clit flinched in response to the image playing out in my mind. I moved my finger more quickly over my sweet spot, then dipped it into the soft folds. I was wet.

I used two fingers to play with my pussy now, but in my mind it was a tongue. A wet and hungry tongue that couldn't get enough of me.

The tongue belonged to the man with the hazel eyes. And he was merciless with it. He circled it around my clit, over and over and over. Oh, God, I needed this. And he needed it, too, this lover of mine. He was young and virile and would fuck me all night long...eat my pussy all night long, if he knew I wanted that.

I spread my legs wider and arched my hips upward, giving him more of me. He buried his fingers inside of me and drew my engorged clitoris into his mouth and suckled me so damn sweetly....

An orgasm shuddered through my entire body. I arched my back, pushed my fingers deep into my pussy as I rode the wave. The pleasure was so intense and overdue that I couldn't suppress my moan. I let myself enjoy every last bit of my orgasm.

As it subsided, I glanced to my right again. Robert's back was still to me. He was still asleep, unaware that I'd brought myself to climax.

And for just a moment, I wished the man with the hazel eyes was beside me in this bed. That I could climb on him right now and slide onto a hard penis. One that could stay hard for a very long time.

Just as quickly as I thought it, I pushed the idea away. Guilt ate at me immediately. It wasn't the first time I had fantasized about him—but I hoped it would be the last.

It was wrong, I knew. Wrong to have such an explicit fantasy about someone other than Robert.

I got up and went to the bathroom, where I started the shower. I stayed in there for a good long time, letting the cool water splash over my body.

Letting the memory of my fantasy wash away, like the soapsuds disappearing down the drain.

4

All the next week, Robert was preoccupied by business. There was some complication with a company out of Germany that Kolstad Systems wanted to buy—a software firm with some sort of graphics technology that would aid in the computer systems Robert's company created. The German owner was suddenly stalling, and Robert believed he was trying to solicit other bids. If this acquisition didn't go through as planned, Robert feared that Kolstad Systems' stock would fall.

With all of this weighing on his mind, he wasn't interested in sex—not in the least. But I was able to coax him to erection one morning with a blow job. Excited that he was hard—and without the aid of Viagra, at that—I had straddled him, then moved slowly and steadily over his penis until I made him come.

I hadn't come, but that didn't matter. My husband's sperm was inside me, and I was elated.

"What are you doing?" Robert had asked when he came out of the bathroom and saw me lying on my back on the bed, my legs bent at the knee. What he couldn't see was the pillow beneath my hips, positioned to angle my pelvis on a downward slope—something I hoped would give Robert's sperm the advantage of gravity.

"I read somewhere that lying on your back for thirty minutes increases the chance of conception," I told him. "I've got fifteen minutes to go."

"Oh." He raised his eyebrows. "All right. I'll be downstairs, having breakfast."

"If I don't see you, I hope all goes well at the office."

When I was sure Robert was downstairs, I closed my eyes and began to stroke my clit. A couple minutes later, my body was shuddering with an orgasm.

What I didn't tell Robert was something else I'd read—that a woman's orgasm also aided her chances of conceiving.

I didn't know if that was true, but I wanted to give myself every advantage in getting pregnant.

Nothing else had worked thus far.

I didn't typically masturbate, yet I did twice more that week. Both times when Robert wasn't home. My body had needed release—release I wasn't getting from my husband. And as I touched my pussy I found myself thinking about the man with the hazel eyes, not Robert. Each fantasy was becoming longer and more vivid.

On Thursday morning, as another earth-shattering

orgasm ripped through my body, I gazed at Robert's side of the bed. It was empty. And I realized why I was consumed with this phantom lover: I was lonely.

Or was there more to it than that?

Even though Robert had retired from his position as CEO of Kolstad Systems, he was still involved in the company's operations as a board member. He had been in the office every day this week, dealing with one problem after another regarding this German acquisition.

His absence reminded me of the early days of our marriage, after we'd returned from our honeymoon and Robert had gone back to work. I'd had fantasies of the wonderful life I would share with my distinguished and successful and charming husband. But it hadn't quite played out the way I had dreamed.

After Robert proposed, I'd quit my job as a waitress, so I wasn't working when we got married. He, of course, had his business to run. Robert would be at the office sometimes twelve or fourteen hours a day. Even longer on some occasions. I had missed him terribly, and didn't like being in my new, oversize home with the housekeeper as my only company. Especially when he went out of town.

I'd occasionally accompanied Robert on his longer business trips to Europe. He promised we'd steal some romantic time to see the sights when his work was done. But on more occasions than not, I would sit alone in my hotel room in London or Paris, longing for my husband's touch, but having to settle for a glass of wine as I watched a movie in our lavish suite.

Convincing Robert to fund my own business venture

had been not only the fruition of a dream, but a godsend in terms of my mental sanity. I needed something constructive to do—much more than shopping and lunching with other wealthy men's wives.

Before Robert and I married, he'd promised to make my dream of opening a floral shop a reality. Ask any of my friends from childhood and they'll tell you how I would always pick dandelions and wildflowers and arrange them in a bouquet. If they had a bad day, I would make them something special. Ditto if they got a good mark on a test. My teachers probably got bored with all the homemade bouquets I brought in for them. And I got in trouble more than once for picking tulips and roses from a neighbor's garden.

Meeting and marrying Robert had enabled me to open Distinct Creations, a shop in downtown Cornelius, just north of Charlotte.

We had a beautiful house, luxury cars, lots of money in the bank. We'd traveled on yachts, and to exotic and exclusive places all over the world.

And yet something was missing.

I hadn't given a second thought to what it would mean to marry a considerably older and powerful man, or that anything would ever go wrong. Yet the fact that he'd been married and divorced twice was testament to the fact that money and security didn't guarantee a lasting marriage.

No matter what happened, I would always be grateful to Robert for the life he had given me. But I couldn't deny the reality that we didn't seem to be on the same page anymore. There were times I wondered if we were even in the same book.

It wasn't about his age. I loved my husband the day I married him, and I still loved him now. And yet there had to be some reason I was so vividly making love to a stranger in my mind.

Maybe it was because the passion with Robert had undeniably faded.

I'd married him for better or for worse. I'd known that "worse" would be the age issue—and I had never expected that we would be able to fuck like bunnies. That kind of passion hadn't mattered to me then, and it didn't now.

It was the intimacy I craved most.

I almost wouldn't mind if Robert chewed guys out for staring at me, if he followed up that proprietary attitude with some genuine attention. Some romance and affection.

Something that showed he viewed me as more than a possession.

I wanted Robert to hold me and kiss me, even if he couldn't make love to me. I wanted him to assure me that he wanted a baby as much as I did, even if it meant adopting. He never said those words, and there were times I got the feeling that he didn't care at all if we had one.

It was one of the things that made me wonder if we were on the same page—and with that thought came the question as to whether or not there would be a happily ever after for us, after all.

Don't think it, Elsie, I said to myself as I stared at the ceiling. *You did not get married to get divorced. You married Robert because he was the first man who made you feel that he could give you the emotional stability you needed.*

He wasn't a man interested only in hot sex. I'd had hot sex with the younger men I'd dated, but had always felt cold in those relationships. Probably because sex was the first thing—and seemingly most important thing—they wanted from me. Being seen as desirable should have made me feel confident, but instead it brought out my insecurity.

Because it reminded me of my childhood with my mother.

My mom had treated sex like a sport, breaking my father's heart over and over again as she engaged in meaningless rendezvous with man after man. As a young child, I didn't understand what was going on. I would overhear heated arguments between my parents and know that something was wrong. And there were days I would come home from school to find my mother gone, and my dad crying. Even the bouquets I made for him didn't help to cheer him up.

As I got older I understood what caused most of their marital conflicts. In the bits I overheard, my mother always claimed the other men meant nothing to her, that for her sex didn't mean love.

I don't know why my father stayed with her. Much later, I began to suspect there was some emotional issue about my mother he understood that I did not. But I always felt for him, was brokenhearted for him.

I was fourteen when my father asked one day how I would feel about going with him to Texas for a long visit, just me and him. He had a sister there. I had been elated by the idea. It was a chance to get away, escape my parents' arguments for a while.

Two days later, my mother hurriedly made me pack some things while my dad was at work. She ushered me into the cab of a Mack truck between her and some guy I didn't know, and suddenly we were off to God only knew where.

The trucker, as it turned out, was my mother's boyfriend. He took us to Philadelphia, where we moved into his small apartment. They fought, too, but I heard them screwing every night in the bedroom next to me.

I was devastated at the way I'd been uprooted. And knew I would never be able to forgive my mother for leaving my father behind.

I had always known that I didn't want sex to be the first priority in any relationship of mine, no doubt because of my mother, and that's why I'd grown wary of men my own age. Robert was older, far more mature than any of the men I had dated, and genuinely seemed to want to make an emotional connection with me first, instead of a sexual one.

It hadn't taken me long to realize I could have emotional security with him—something I desperately wanted after my parents' fucked-up marriage….

My bedside phone rang, startling me from my thoughts. I rolled over to my night table and plucked the cordless handset off its base. "Hello?"

"Morning, Elsie. I hope it's not too early to call."

"Sharon." My spirits lifted. Her call was the distraction I needed. "No, it's not too early. How are you?"

"So-so. I've been mostly up. I really have. But last night I was way down."

"Oh, sweetie."

"It gets to me sometimes, being in this big empty house."

"Of course it does."

"Maybe I need to get out and volunteer. Do something so that I'm not home alone so much."

"You know your doctor said you'll have to take it easy for this pregnancy. You don't want anything to jeopardize carrying your baby to term."

Two months ago, Sharon's husband had been tragically killed in a plane crash on his way back from a business trip. As if that wasn't devastating enough, Sharon had just learned she was pregnant. She'd been able to share the thrilling news with Warren over the phone, and had been looking forward to celebrating with him upon his return. Only his company's private plane had gone down shortly after takeoff in Virginia, killing all on board, including three members of the firm's executive team.

"I know…and I want this baby more than anything. Warren and I both did. I keep trying to look on the bright side. I'm financially set and I don't have to travel to a job every day, which means I can take it nice and easy and make sure to carry this baby to term. I'll be able to hire a nanny, which will be great—as much for the company as for the help. But the truth is…the truth is I keep thinking about what a wonderful father he would have been, and how much he wanted this baby. I miss him so much, Elsie. I can't believe I'm finally pregnant and he's not here…"

Sharon was one of my closest friends, and she sounded as if she was about to fall apart. "You want me to swing by your place on my way to work?"

"No. No, I'll be fine. But I was thinking that I wouldn't mind getting away this weekend. If Robert can spare you, will you go to South Carolina with me? We could drive to Charleston, or Myrtle Beach. Stay from Friday to Sunday. It's not quite bikini weather yet, but I might put one on anyway—before my stomach gets too big." Sharon laughed, but the sound morphed into a whimper.

"Shh," I soothed. It broke my heart what she was going through. She had mentioned being financially set, but all the money in the world couldn't ease a loss like this. "Maybe I should stop by."

"No…you have to go to work. I just want you to give me something to look forward to. But if you can't because of the shop, I'll understand."

"I'd love to go away," I told her. "I can get Spike to run things for a couple of days." Spike was my righthand man at the store, and I didn't anticipate any problems with him heading up operations for Friday and Saturday. My shop was closed on Sundays. The only issue would be Robert, and whether or not he would have a problem with me going away.

That was another thing that bothered me about my husband on occasion: as much as he had his own life and traveled a lot on his own, he didn't like me to travel without him. He didn't outright tell me I couldn't go somewhere, but when I returned he would complain incessantly about how much he'd missed me, how the house hadn't been the same without me, how there was an event in Charlotte he would have liked to have taken me to—if only I'd been home. It used to drive me crazy.

I learned to seek Robert's approval first, and not just tell him I was planning to go somewhere with a friend. More times than not he would find some reason to object to my plans. And more times than not, I ended up staying home because I didn't want to disappoint him.

But this weekend Sharon wasn't the only one who could use some time away.

"If you can, that'd be great," she said, sounding better already. "I need a change of scenery, you know?"

"Of course you do. Robert's been in the office all week, but I'll run it by him tonight. I know a great place in Charleston we can stay, this quaint bed-and-breakfast where he and I stayed the last time we were there."

"I'll wait to hear back from you."

As I hung up, I mentally prepared myself for broaching the subject with Robert. I'd take him to the club tonight, where we would have a nice dinner and he could unwind. If I could get him to relax and be happy, then he'd be more likely to say yes to me going away.

I climbed out of bed and headed for the shower, a niggling thought bothering me.

That I was Robert's wife, not his child—and I shouldn't have to get his permission to take a short trip with a friend.

5

I called Robert at lunchtime and told him I'd made reservations at the club for seven. "You've been working hard all week and I've hardly seen you. I'd love to have a nice dinner with you tonight."

"That's a great idea, Elsie. Thank you."

Robert looked harried when he arrived at home, but once we were seated in The Peninsula Club's dining room, I could see the stress begin to fade from his face.

Good. The better his mood, the more likely he would be favorable to what I was going to suggest.

Everyone knew us here, and shortly after we were seated, Robert's usual glass of Remy Martin Louis XIII was brought over—an outrageously priced cognac considered to be one of the best in the world. There was also a glass of Santa Lucia Highlands pinot noir for me—much more reasonably priced by comparison. This is how we always started our order, so the staff knew there would be no complaints.

Robert took a sip of his very pricey drink, and I could almost see more of his stress dissipate. He felt comfortable here, his home away from home. Perhaps also because—unlike The Melting Pot—it was full of people he could relate to: rich older men with wives who knew their place.

Wives who didn't want to lose, by way of a nasty divorce, the luxuries they'd become accustomed to. I saw some in the dining room who I believed should have left their marriages ages ago. Ruthie Davenport. Agnes Long. They were older, in their sixties, but it was long rumored that their husbands had had affairs with several younger women. Ruthie's husband apparently had gotten not one, but two mistresses knocked up.

Felicity Williams was in her early thirties, and her husband was a philandering pro athlete. They'd been college sweethearts, and the word was that she wasn't going to let some "skank-ass ho" steal her man.

There were even a couple rumors of physical abuse. But through it all, those wives had stayed.

I had always pitied the wives of such husbands. And I'd never seen Robert as a man who would abuse his wife either emotionally or physically. And yet here I was, a little fearful of asking if he would be okay if I went out of town with a dear friend for a few days.

How had our marriage gotten to this point? For the first couple of years, I never would have been afraid to ask Robert anything. He had been thoughtful and patient—at least with me. I'd heard him argue with his ex-wives on occasion, and had always thought it odd that he could be so cruel with them, yet loving with me. Once, when wife number two was dropping off their teenage daughter, she'd murmured, "Enjoy Robert while he's nice. Because once he turns…"

She hadn't finished her statement, but I'd dismissed her warning as a comment from a bitter ex-wife.

Now, as I looked around the busy dining room, I couldn't help wondering if anyone there pitied *me?* The wait staff? The managers? The other wives? Had any of them seen something in my marriage that I had missed?

Robert smiled brightly and waved at someone across the room. He *was* charming and pleasant. Definitely likable. Successful.

Though I'd been having some doubts about my marriage over the last several months, I now found myself flip-flopping. Robert's irritability, and his occasional rude behavior, such as he displayed at The Melting Pot— they had to be effects of getting older. Either emotional or physical—or both.

Approaching seventy, he could no longer ignore his mortality. And maybe there were changes in a man's body that made him more irritable as he hit a certain age. If there was some physiological reason for Robert's behavior, how could I hold it against him?

And there were so many happy memories from early in our marriage that I clung to.

Like the time we were in Paris, and I was in the hotel suite alone while Robert was at a business meeting.

There was a knock on the door and I'd opened it to find Room Service delivering a cart with three trays on it. The waiter wheeled the cart into the room and lifted the silver lids to reveal fresh fruit slices and chocolate fondue.

I'd assumed Robert had simply sent the fruit to the room as a treat for me—but the real surprise came when he suddenly appeared in the doorway as the waiter was leaving.

Robert had ordered the fondue platter not so much for the fruit, but for me. For my body. He put the chocolate on my nipples, licked it off slowly. He put it on my ass, then ate it off with his tongue and his teeth. And he made me come—over and over—when he'd licked chocolate off my clit with tender, hot strokes....

"Cindy," Robert was saying warmly.

At the sound of his voice, I was jerked from my memory. I glanced upward at Cindy, a waitress we knew well. He greeted her by squeezing her hand. "How are you?"

"Better now that you're here."

A flirtatious comment? Perhaps, but I didn't take it seriously—and I certainly would never get mad at Robert for it. Unlike how he had treated Alexander.

Robert chuckled. He proceeded to joke with Cindy and make conversation about her studies. She was putting herself through UNC, the University of North Carolina at Charlotte, and one day hoped to become a lawyer.

Cindy smiled as she answered his questions—and yet I would never consider her anything other than professional. She was being nice to a customer. The same thing the waiter at the other restaurant had been doing.

Cindy or any of the waitresses here could easily have designs on some of the rich regulars at the club. And they'd be in a far better position to try and undermine a marriage than a waiter we were likely to see only once in our lives.

Forget what happened at The Melting Pot, I told myself.

But the hypocrisy bothered me—even if I could forgive Robert's behavior.

I glanced around as he continued to chat with Cindy. And when my eyes landed on a pair of wide shoulders beneath a black blazer, my heart pounded in my chest.

The shoulders…that golden-brown skin…the shaved head.

Oh, my God. Was it *him?*

My pussy began to throb.

"Elsie," Robert said urgently.

I jerked my eyes back to his. "Sorry."

"Cindy wants to know if you're having the steak."

"Yes. Yes, the steak is fine."

My eyes ventured across the dining room again. Disappointment came crashing in.

It wasn't him. Lord, it wasn't him.

The guest had turned, and now I could see his face. He wasn't the man I'd been fantasizing about.

As Cindy walked away, I brought my wineglass to

my lips and sipped. But the wine didn't wash away my discontent.

I tried to push the sexy stranger out of my mind as we enjoyed our dinner. Tonight was about getting Robert to agree to my trip with Sharon.

By the end of the meal, two glasses of cognac had had their effect on Robert. His business problems forgotten, he was smiling and laughing and telling me stories about the early days of his company.

It was the perfect time for me to ask him about my trip.

"Darling." I reached across the table and covered his hand with mine. "There's something I want to talk about."

Robert swirled the dregs of cognac in his glass. "Yes?"

"You know Sharon's been having a hard time ever since…ever since Warren's death."

Sharon was one of the first women I'd met in the neighborhood after marrying Robert. A stunning, dark-skinned beauty, she could have easily passed for a high-fashion model. I'd been pleasantly surprised to find her completely down-to-earth. She was a couple years older than me, and had married Warren the month after their college graduation. Warren had gone on to start an Internet business, which he'd sold for millions and millions before the dot-com bust. He took part of that profit and began a telecommunications company, which was also a huge success.

Like Robert, Warren had been a self-made million-aire. But the difference between Sharon and Warren's relationship and mine and Robert's was that they'd met and fallen in love before either of them had any money. And from everything Sharon had told me, Warren always treated her as an equal in their marriage.

"Yes, of course. Such a tragedy."

That was an understatement. The one thing that had kept them from being one hundred percent content was their inability to have a baby. Sharon had been pregnant six times, but miscarried each one. For a few years she'd gone on the Pill, giving up her dream altogether. Then they'd decided to try again. Six months after going off the Pill, she miraculously got pregnant.

And then she'd lost her husband.

"Understandably, Sharon is feeling glum. Oh, she's putting on a brave face. She's been incredibly strong since losing Warren." I knew she was trying to be extra strong, not wanting anything to cause her to miscarry again. "But she could use a change of scenery. And who could blame her?"

I paused. Swallowed. Asking my husband if I could go away with a friend for a weekend shouldn't have given me such anxiety, but it did.

"She wants to go away?" Robert asked.

"Just for the weekend," I quickly said. "Probably drive down to Charleston, or Myrtle Beach. You know. To get her out of that big, empty house."

"And she wants you to go with her," Robert stated.

"Yes."

"When?"

"This weekend. Tomorrow until Sunday."

"So you've already planned it," Robert said.

"No." I tried to sound casual. "Nothing is planned. I told her I would run it by you first, but that as far as I know we have no plans, so hopefully..."

"I think Charleston would be the best option," Robert said. "I don't think a pregnant woman has any business at Myrtle Beach. There are too many horny college kids there. It's not a good scene."

My anxiety ebbed away. I tried to mask my surprise when I met Robert's eyes. "So, you don't mind that I go with her?"

As Robert sipped the last of his cognac, I wondered if it had magical powers. For the price, it certainly should. And in this case, if it had put him in such a good mood that he was offering no objections, it was well worth the money.

"Why would I mind?" he asked. "I'm sure you've been bored all week. I've been working more than usual. And you're Sharon's closest friend here. Of course she would want to go with you."

I felt a smile break out on my face. "Thank you, Robert. She'll be very happy."

"What about the shop?" he asked. "It's not a busy weekend?"

"Not particularly. Spike can handle all orders, and Tabitha is always asking for more hours. I'm sure between her, Maxine and Olivia, the store will be appropriately staffed."

"Sounds like it's all set. You should stay at that wonderful bed-and-breakfast where we went the last time we were there."

"The Barksdale House Inn. I'll call them to see if they've got room."

"Very good, then."

My lips curled in a soft smile as I stared at Robert. This was the man I'd fallen in love with—the kind and considerate man.

My doubts about our marriage seemed to float away.

Robert had his flaws, sure.

But no one was perfect.

6

I had always believed that I was not motivated by sex. That for me, an emotional connection was paramount, first and foremost. So I was very surprised to find myself having another hot dream about the stranger from my store later that week.

In the dream, I was sitting at the bar, looked to my right—and suddenly he was there. My body had an immediate reaction to him, as if an electric current were hitting me.

He said no words, just smiled at me, the kind of smile that oozed sensual heat. Then, abruptly, we were no longer in the bar, but in a bedroom somewhere, with only one lamp on.

He was sitting on the large bed. I was standing in front of him.

"Take your clothes off," he said.

The words aroused me. The thought of undressing for this stranger, of fucking him, excited me beyond anything I had ever known.

So I pulled my dress over my head, revealing my nude body. I stood in front of him for a long while, his hazel eyes feasting on my nakedness and almost burning me with desire.

I'd never stood naked like this in front of a stranger before, and yet I didn't feel self-conscious. Instead, a delicious rush coursed through my body.

"Touch your pussy," he said.

I ran the tip of my finger over my clit, something I had never done in front of a man I didn't know.

"Are you wet?"

"Yes," I said, feeling an erotic charge at the admission. "Very."

Slowly, he rose from the bed and came to me. He kissed me, deep and hot, while his hands covered my breasts. As he squeezed the soft mounds, tweaked my nipples, he moaned—a low, hot growl that made me feel a surge of feminine power beyond anything I had ever experienced.

I gripped the edges of his shirt, anxious to see him naked, as well. As his tongue tangled with mine, I pulled his shirt out of his pants and splayed my hands on his abdomen. He was all hard ripples and muscles, with the body of an Adonis.

Tearing his lips from mine, he lowered his head to my breast and drew one of my nipples into his mouth. Prickles of pleasure and pain shot through me. He suckled me hard, hungrily. This was raw, primal. About lust and need with a man whose body spoke to mine in a language all its own.

I arched my back, moaned. Stroked his cock through his pants.

As his tongue worked its wicked magic on my nipples, he cupped my pussy. I melted. Had anyone's touch ever felt this good?

When his fingers slipped into my layers of flesh, I gripped his shoulders and threw my head back, whimpering from the exquisite pleasure. "Oh, my God. Oh, my God."

"Yes, baby," he whispered against my ear, and penetrated my vagina with a finger, pushed it in deep. "I love how your pussy feels." His digit still inside of me, he went down on his haunches. "Now I want to see how you taste."

He flicked his thumb over my clit, and then his tongue—and a shudder roared through my body. Then he spread my folds and suckled me with exquisite gentleness until I was coming and screaming.

I woke up to find my hand between my legs, my pussy throbbing and wet. I rode the wave of my orgasm from my dream state to consciousness.

After my pleasure subsided, I was satisfied but perplexed. I had just come while *dreaming*.

Me—someone who hadn't had these kinds of arousing fantasies even as a teenager.

Something was changing in me. I was having sexual needs and urges I wasn't used to.

And I was liking them.

★ ★ ★

On Friday around ten, Sharon and I left for Charleston. She wanted to drive, and that was fine, so she came by my place and picked me up in her Cadillac Escalade. Robert had once again left for the office early that morning, but before he went, he'd kissed me deeply and told me to have a good time.

I had expected him to be busy with the board, with conference calls to Germany and whatever else he needed to do in order to seal the acquisition deal. So I was surprised when my iPhone trilled before Sharon and I even made it Charleston.

"I had a break, so I thought I'd call," he explained when I picked up. "I phoned the bed-and-breakfast. They said you hadn't checked in yet."

"That's because we're just getting into Charleston now."

"It's nearly three o'clock," Robert said.

"We didn't leave until ten, and there was must have been a wreck on I-77, because we were backed up for a good hour."

"Oh. So how far are you?"

"Ten minutes from the B and B, I think. Maybe fifteen."

"Call me when you get settled," he told me.

But before I could, he called again, just as Sharon and I got to the room.

I put the phone to my ear. "Hi, sweetheart."

"Just making sure you've arrived."

Or checking up on me? "We're here."

"Are you going to go get a bite to eat?"

"A snack, most likely. I already made reservations at Hyman's."

"The seafood place. Ah, very nice. For what time?"

"Six-thirty."

"What's the weather like?"

"Pretty nice. About seventy-one, right, Sharon?"

"Yeah, that's what they said on the radio," she concurred. "I might bring out that bikini yet."

"What?" Robert asked. "What was that about a bikini?"

"It was a joke," I told him. "We're definitely not going swimming." I paused. "Can I call you back? We just got up to the room, and we want to get settled—"

"No problem. I'll talk to you later."

Hanging up, I faced Sharon. "He wanted to make sure we arrived okay."

She smiled and looked away. But I got the feeling there was an opinion behind the grin.

It might not have been warm enough to swim, but it was warm enough for ice cream—at least as far as Sharon was concerned. So, two hours later, after getting a manicure, we went into an ice cream shop in historic Charleston. I got a cone. Sharon got a hot fudge sundae.

We were walking down the street two minutes later when my phone rang again. I pretty much knew, before looking at the display, that it would be Robert.

I lifted my phone from my purse. Somehow, I refrained from rolling my eyes when I saw his number on the display screen. I didn't know what had gotten into him.

"Give me a second, Sharon," I said, stopping. "It's Robert."

"Again?" she asked.

I answered my phone. "Hello?"

"Where are you?"

What kind of greeting was that? "Sharon and I are taking a stroll."

"Oh. I called the room, and you weren't there. And then your phone went straight to voice mail. I thought you might have headed to Myrtle Beach."

"What? Myrtle Beach is two hours away." I wondered why Robert was calling so much. He was acting like a paranoid parent checking up on a kid who'd gone off on her own for the first time. "We were getting our nails done, so I turned my phone off."

"Of course. Of course. Are you having a good time?"

I looked at Sharon, who was making quick work of finishing off her sundae. "Yeah, we are. So far, so good."

"Don't let Sharon drag you into anything scandal-ous," Robert said. "Like scoping out a new father for her baby."

"What?" I asked, stunned by such a ridiculous question.

"Bad joke," he admitted. "I was out of line."

Bad joke was right.

"I suppose you're tired of me calling, but I just miss

you, that's all," Robert said. "I kind of feel a little...
off."

"What do you mean?"

"Oh, nothing in particular. A little woozy. Some
aches and pains."

"How serious?" I asked.

"It's probably stress," he replied. "It's been a long
week. Nothing a nap won't cure."

"You have been very stressed this week. Any success
with the acquisition?"

"Finally, I think so." Robert sounded relieved. "The
deal should go through by Monday, as planned—so this
is very, very good news."

"I'm so glad to hear that, darling. I know how much
of a headache it's been for you."

"It has been, but the end is in sight." He paused
briefly. "So, Hyman's, right?"

"Yep."

"Six-thirty?"

"Yep. Six-thirty."

Sharon narrowed her eyes at me. I could read her
thought: *What's with the twenty questions?*

"Excellent," Robert said. "I love you, sweetheart. I'll
call you later."

"Love you, too," I replied, then pressed the button
to end the call.

I sighed loudly, playing up my own frustration with
Robert's many calls. "Sometimes it's like he can't survive without me."

"That's sweet," Sharon commented, and she seemed

sincere. "At least it can't be said that he doesn't love his wife."

"That's one way to look at it."

She made a wistful sound. "I miss that. The calls to see where you are, even if they're annoying. I miss it so much."

"Oh, Sharon." I put my arm around her shoulders and squeezed. For the most part, ever since Warren's funeral, she had kept her feelings locked inside. It was a rare moment when she even talked about missing her husband. So for her to be doing so now made it clear to me how much she was hurting. "I'm so sorry."

"It's okay." She placed a hand on her belly. "I have our baby. I'll be okay."

"You want to go back to the room and relax for a bit before dinner?" I asked, releasing her.

"Actually, I wouldn't mind another hot fudge sundae."

We both smiled.

I was surprised she'd finished off the first huge one. But I said, "Who am I to keep a pregnant woman from what she craves?"

We made it through dinner without Robert phoning again. I was relieved. Despite what Sharon said about Robert's calls proving he loved me, she had to be wondering the same thing I was.

If he was checking up on me.

"What are you thinking?" she asked.

I looked up at her. "Hmm?"

"You've hardly touched your key lime pie."

And before I could speak, my phone rang.

If this was Robert calling for an itemized list of what we'd eaten...

Instead, the display showed the name Felicity Williams.

"It's Felicity," I announced, almost happily. I put the phone to my ear. "Hey, Felicity. What's up?"

"Wondering where you are tonight. A few of us are going to head to NV Lounge to kick back and have a couple of drinks, and wanted to know if you'd like to join us."

"I can't. I'm out of town right now."

"Oh."

"With Sharon."

"Ohh." Felicity's tone fizzled. "How is she?"

"She's good. Doing well, all things considering."

"So sad, what she's going through," Felicity said, but she didn't quite sound sincere.

"I'm gone for the weekend, so I'll call you when I get back to town," I told her.

"Where are you?"

"In Charleston."

"Well, have fun. Ta-ta."

"Bye," I said, and ended the call.

"Did she actually ask about me?" Sharon inquired, looking dubious.

"She asked how you're doing."

"Funny—she could call me herself to find that out."

"You still haven't heard from her?"

"Ha ha ha. That's a good one."

Up until the time Warren died, Sharon and I used to get together on Sundays after church with a few other wives "to lunch." Felicity was one of the women we regularly met with, as was Carmen, the wife of another Carolina Panther. It was what society women did, and we'd discuss what was happening in our worlds, charitable efforts and, of course, gossip.

Unlike Sharon—whom I truly connected with—there seemed to be a wall of glass around Felicity and Carmen. As if you could see them on the other side of the table, but couldn't touch them. Couldn't get close.

I'd taken to Sharon the instant I'd met her, seen her as a real person. Felicity and Carmen always put on a bright smile and played like they were happy to see you, but I never felt either one was genuine.

The fact that they hadn't seen Sharon since her husband's funeral proved me right.

"I can't believe Felicity." I shook my head. "You haven't heard from Carmen, either?"

"You know those two are thick as thieves. What one does, they both do. And they suddenly have no use for me."

"Do you think they're staying away because they don't know how to…to deal with your grief?" I knew that some people were uncomfortable in the face of another person's pain.

"Yeah, *that's* it." Sharon rolled her eyes. "Let's get back to you and what's going on with you."

"Me?"

She gave me a pointed look. "You know what I'm talking about."

I did. And it was one of the reasons I'd wanted to go away with her—to use her as a sounding board for some of my doubts about Robert.

I cut my fork into the key lime pie, but didn't lift the morsel to my mouth. I did it to keep my hands occupied.

"What's bothering you?" Sharon pressed.

I sighed. "I just wonder sometimes."

She raised an eyebrow, waiting for me to go on.

"You and Warren were married for sixteen years. And I know you were college sweethearts and all that. But I just wonder...did you ever... Is it normal to sometimes feel that maybe you're not sure about your marriage? To wonder if it will last?" I finished with difficulty.

"Is it normal to have doubts about your marriage? Of course it is."

"So you had doubts at times?"

"Doubts?" Sharon made a face. "There were times I didn't know if we would make it."

"Really?"

"After my last miscarriage, I shut down. I had an emotional wall up that no one could penetrate. Warren threw himself into work as a way to avoid both my pain and his. For nearly a month, we hardly spoke."

"Wow," I said softly.

"I felt like a failure. We had a great life, and all I wanted was to complete our family with a baby." Sharon stopped. Inhaled deeply.

"I'm sorry," I said. "I didn't meant to...to be a downer."

"You're not. Of course I'm thinking about Warren."

A soft smile curved her lips. "Gosh, we would fight sometimes. Yell and scream at each other. But when we made up…"

I chuckled.

"So, yeah, it's normal to go through rough times."

Again, I moved my fork around on my plate. Then I leaned forward and whispered, "But is it normal to… to have fantasies about other men?"

Sharon didn't answer right away. She took a sip of her water first, which made me wonder if my question had shocked her.

But she said, "I think fantasies are fine. If they help your sex life, why not? It's a hell of a lot better than some of the things I've heard some of our neighbors have done to spice up their love lives."

I was about to ask if she would still feel that way if all the fantasies were about the same man, but the waitress arrived at our table right then.

"Are you still eating your dessert?" she asked, nodding toward my half-eaten key lime pie.

"No. Please, take it away. I'm stuffed." I pushed the dessert plate toward her.

"Can I get you ladies anything else?"

"We're fine, thank you," I said. "Just bring me the bill, please."

"Actually, you can bring *me* the bill," Sharon said. "It'll be my treat."

"That's not necessary, Sharon," I told her. "I can take care of it."

"Lucky for both of you," the waitress interjected, "the bill's already been settled."

I stared up at her in confusion. "But I didn't give you my card."

"Are you Elsie Kolstad?" she asked.

"Yes," I replied.

"Your husband called in." Now the woman smiled. "He gave us his credit card and strict instructions to charge the bill to him."

I looked across the table at Sharon. She shrugged.

"Oh," I said lamely. "So it's already been paid."

"Yes, ma'am," the waitress replied. "I wish my husband was so thoughtful."

"Yeah," I responded, making sure to keep my voice cheery.

It wasn't the first time Robert had called ahead to pay my dinner bill, even if I was just out for the evening with friends. The first time he'd done it, I'd considered the gesture chivalrous.

Not today. Today, it seemed like control.

7

Despite my lack of appetite for dessert, Sharon and I sat on the sofa munching on popcorn and watching a teen slasher flick that we'd picked up from a variety store—a movie that neither of us had heard of, starring no-name actors. The special effects were so pathetic and the story line so incredible that the movie wasn't scary in the least. In fact, it was laughable.

We were watching a shower scene now, with a big-busted woman who seemed more interested in touching herself than getting clean, lathering soap over her breasts and ass in what was meant to be an erotic display.

"All right, all right, we get it," Sharon mumbled. "Can we move on with the plot, please?"

"What plot?" I asked, laughing.

"Why are there never any naked guys in these movies?" she asked.

"Because the writers and producers are men. And they obviously don't think that women enjoy seeing a nice male ass, too."

Sensing a noise, the actress paused with her hands on her nipples, which she had caressed to an erect state. The music's tempo had picked up, indicating that danger was imminent. The blonde-haired beauty asked, "Who's there?" and then playfully, "Donnie, is that you?"

Though Sharon and I had to know what was coming, that when the woman pulled back the shower curtain she would face the masked killer, we screamed when it happened. The woman's eyes went wide with terror, and the killer raised a large butcher knife. She started to scream, but it was too late, and a moment later blood sprayed all over the bathroom.

Or tomato juice.

The gruesome murder completed, the killer muttered, "Nice tits."

"*Right,*" Sharon said in an exaggerated tone. "That's realistic."

I started to laugh. So did she. The movie might have been stupid, but it was just what we needed—something so far from reality that it wouldn't remind Sharon of the loss of her husband.

The scene went from the gruesome one in the bathroom to a college campus. I picked up a handful of popcorn—extra butter as Sharon had requested—and had just begun to munch on a mouthful when the room phone rang.

"I know it's not for me," she said.

"I guess Robert's calling to say good-night."

I got up from the sofa and hurried to the phone. Sharon paused the DVD.

"Hello?" I said.

"Oh, darling." He seemed a little breathless. "I'm glad I reached you."

Instantly, I was alarmed. "Robert, what's the matter?"

"I don't know...but I haven't been feeling well for the last couple of hours." He sounded as if it hurt to talk. "I..."

"What hurts? Your head? Is it stomach pains again?"

"My...chest."

"Oh, my God."

Sharon flashed me a look of concern.

"All the stress of this week... I think it's gotten to me."

"Oh, Robert."

"I need you, Elsie."

"Of course." My heart pounded against my rib cage. "Oh, my God." I spoke hurriedly, my own breathing ragged. "You have to hang up and call 911. Get to a hospital, Robert."

"All...right...I will."

Sharon got up and moved to stand beside me. "You'll be fine, sweetheart," I told him. He had to be. "You'll be fine."

"I need you, Elsie."

"I'll leave right now. Have the hospital call me when you get there, so I know which one you've gone to."

"Elsie… If anything happens, I love you. I want you to know that."

"Don't talk like that! You're going to be fine. But please call for an ambulance. Now."

My hands were shaking as I replaced the receiver. I met my friend's concerned gaze. "We have to go. Right now." My hands began to shake. "Oh, Sharon."

"What?" she asked. "What's going on?"

"I think Robert might be having a heart attack!"

Fear unlike any I'd ever experienced before gripped me for the entire drive home. Even if I'd taken my car to Charleston, Sharon would have had to drive back. I was far too shaky to control the wheel.

With each passing second, I grew more and more terrified. I'd called every hospital in the Cornelius area, and even within Charlotte proper, but couldn't confirm that a Robert Kolstad had been admitted to any of them. If he wasn't in the hospital, did that mean he was dead on the floor of our house?

"Why does *no* hospital have any record of him being admitted?" I asked. My voice was shrill, laced with panic.

And I was also feeling guilty. Guilty that I'd entertained, even for a minute, the idea of leaving Robert.

"Maybe it's too soon," Sharon said. "Or maybe there was an error when they put him in the system."

"Or maybe he's dead on the floor!"

"He's not dead." Sharon reached for my hand and gave it a comforting squeeze. "I know he's not. Don't start thinking the worst."

"I should call Olga!" I exclaimed, remembering our housekeeper. "She's not normally in on the weekends, but—"

"Olga's out of town for her daughter's wedding this weekend, remember?"

"Oh, shit. That's right." I pressed a palm to my forehead. "Shit, Sharon. He mentioned he wasn't feeling the best. I shouldn't have left him. I shouldn't have…"

"Don't blame yourself. He's okay. I know it. And we're almost there."

My phone was sweaty in my hands. "I'm going to try the hospitals again."

Calls to all area hospitals produced no results. I would make the rounds of every one if I had to, but first I needed to go home and see if Robert was there.

If he was…

No, he's not. He can't be.

As Sharon pulled into my driveway, I drew in a gaspy breath and wiped away tears. I wasn't sure how she'd been so strong after the death of her husband, but I was already an emotional wreck, anticipating finding Robert's lifeless body in the house.

"Don't do that," she said. "Don't fall apart yet."

I nodded. "Thank you, Sharon." I reached for the car door. "Thank you."

"You think you're going inside without me? Not a chance."

I pulled on the handle a couple of times, wondering why it wouldn't open.

"It's locked, sweetie," Sharon said. "Give me a second."

Of course.

I let go of the handle, and she hit the button to release the locks. I all but fell out of the car when I opened the door.

Sharon had to unlock the front door to my house because I was too jittery to do it. She stepped inside first. I took a deep breath and went in after her.

The great room was empty, but I had expected that. If Robert was anywhere, it was going to be our bedroom.

I rushed for the staircase. Darted upstairs. At the top I turned left and ran down the long hallway.

The double doors were slightly ajar, and I pushed them open. The light on Robert's night table was on, illuminating his still form on the bed.

I gasped. Started to cry.

"Robert!" I ran toward him.

And that's when something amazing happened. He lifted his head and looked at me.

Utterly surprised, I stopped dead in my tracks. It was as if I had so expected the worst that my brain couldn't process what I was seeing.

"Elsie…"

The sound of Robert's voice broke the spell. Happiness bubbled out of me in a relieved breath.

"Thank God!" I quickly looked at Sharon. She clasped her hands together, clearly overjoyed. Then I made my way to the bed, where I sat beside Robert and took his hand in mine.

"You're here." He sounded weak.

"Oh, baby. I was so worried." I pressed his hand against my cheek. "What happened?"

"I'm fine now. That's all the matters."

"You went to the hospital?"

Robert's eyes flicked in Sharon's direction. I got his meaning. He didn't want to discuss the situation with her here.

I eased off the bed and crossed the room to the door, where Sharon was standing, respectfully keeping her distance.

"Well, he's not dead," I said, stating the obvious. I heaved a weary sigh. "Thank you so much for getting me here safe and sound. I couldn't have done it alone."

She waved away my comment. "There's no need to thank me."

"I'm sorry we had to cut our weekend short," I told her.

"Gimme a break. There's no need to apologize for that."

I nodded, then gave her a hug. "I'll call you tomorrow. Update you on Robert's progress."

"Go take care of your husband."

"Let me see you out."

I walked downstairs with Sharon, saw her to her car, then went back inside. Before rejoining Robert, I went to the kitchen and put on the kettle to make some tea for him.

The kettle on, I headed upstairs. Robert was still lying in bed.

I climbed onto the bed beside him and gently stroked his face. "How're you feeling?"

"I'm good now." He reached for my hand. "I'm glad you're here with me."

"I called every hospital. No one could tell me if you were admitted. I was going out of my mind with worry. I thought I'd come here and find…and find…"

"I'm sorry, darling. I didn't mean to put you through that."

"Where did you go? University Hospital?"

"I went to Lake Norman."

"Weird," I said. I'd phoned Lake Norman Regional Medical Center first. "I called there. A few times. They said they didn't have you in their system."

"Perhaps because I was in Emergency."

"Perhaps," I acknowledged. After a beat, I went on. "Obviously, you didn't have a heart attack."

"I didn't." Robert chuckled softly. "You'll think this is silly. It was gas pains."

Three years ago, I'd rushed Robert to the hospital when he'd been having chest pains. We'd feared a heart attack, but we'd learned that he actually had a gas bubble in his chest that was causing the pain.

"Like the last time," I said.

"Yes." Again, Robert chuckled. "Just like the last time."

"Well." I planted a kiss on my husband's soft cheek. "Thank God it wasn't a heart attack. I really freaked out, Robert. All the way driving here, I was…"

"I'm sorry about your weekend."

"Don't apologize. Of course I had to come home." I

gazed down at him, once again feeling guilty for thinking that he and I might be headed for divorce. Biting
back that thought, I said, "Look, I've got the kettle on.
Would you like some peppermint tea?"

"Oh, that would be nice."

"All right. I'll be back up soon."

Downstairs, I prepared tea for both of us, and arranged the cups on a silver tray, along with two spoons
and a jar of honey.

"Here you go," I said, setting the tray on the large
night table closest to Robert. We had a four-poster
bed, with oversize nightstands and dressers. I'd thought
the tables too large when I'd first seen them, but the
marble surface did come in handy when extra space was
needed.

Robert eased himself up and reached for a cup.
"Thank you."

"I didn't put any honey in it."

"Oh, it's fine like this."

"By the way, how did you get home?" I asked.

"Pardon me?"

"From the hospital. You called for an ambulance,
right?"

"Oh. Right. Yes, yes I did."

"So how did you get home?"

"I...I took a taxi."

"You could have waited for me at the hospital. I
would have picked you up."

"It was no bother."

I glanced at the bedside clock. "You made it through
the E.R. in very good time." It was a little after 2:00 a.m.,

and Robert had called me just before ten. Sharon and I had wasted no time in checking out, but it still took us about three and a half hours to get home.

"A man my age who goes to Emergency with chest pains… The doctors don't want to take any chances."

"Of course not. And I'm glad. I just wish I'd been here for you."

Robert sipped more of his tea. He finished about half of it before putting the cup back on the tray. "I hope you don't mind, but I'm very tired. I'd like to get some sleep."

"It's very late. We both need to get some sleep." I gave my husband a lingering kiss on the lips. I collected the tray and cups and took them down to the kitchen.

By the time I came back upstairs, Robert was asleep, his lips parted as he snored quietly.

I went to the master bathroom. Seeing my reflection in the mirror, I groaned. I looked awful. The worry had had its effect on me, but that was to be expected. Thank God the crisis had passed.

The last time Robert had gone to the hospital for chest pains and learned it was gas, the E.R. doctor had given him a prescription for lactulose—a thick, sugary liquid that he'd complained about taking, though it had worked wonders.

I didn't see a bottle of lactulose on the bathroom counter, or any other prescription bottle. I searched the medicine cabinet, but once again saw nothing other than the regular medicines Robert was already taking.

Something made me head downstairs to the kitchen again. I couldn't remember if the prescription Robert had been given last time was supposed to be stored in the fridge. But there was no lactulose in our refrigerator, either.

Was Robert lying?

"No," I replied aloud to my silent question. "Robert wouldn't have lied about something so serious."

But he was in and out of Emergency so quickly.

The time we had gone to the hospital for the same issue, it had taken more than four hours, what with the myriad tests he'd gone through. They'd given him an EKG, X-ray, blood tests. Breathing tests.

Even if I could understand him getting through Emergency in under three hours, I found myself wondering about his current physical condition.

When he'd had the heart attack scare the first time, there had been shortness of breath and intense pain every time he inhaled. The agony had lasted for hours before the medicine kicked in. But this time, Robert wasn't exhibiting any of those symptoms.

What if this whole incident was an elaborate scheme to get me to come home?

I'd been wary of broaching the subject of going away. Robert didn't like me to leave him, and definitely not for a few days. In fact, I'd been a little surprised that he'd been so agreeable to the idea of me and Sharon taking off for the weekend.

But then there had been the constant phone calls. Him paying our bill at the restaurant. I hadn't been able to shake the feeling that that was Robert's way to check and see if I was actually there....

Maybe I was overreacting.

"Or maybe I'm not," I whispered. It wasn't the first time he had done something to subtly—or not so subtly—convince me to change my mind about something.

Like the time a year ago when my father had invited me to Texas for a visit. After my mother took me away when I was fourteen, I didn't see my dad for four years. There were no cell phones back then, so no easy way for me to sneak a call to him without my mother finding out. But I'd called my father collect from a payphone on my first day at my new school. I'd been relieved to reach him, and quickly told him where I was so that he could come and get me. I'd been stunned to learn that he already knew where I was. My mother had called him days after we'd arrived in Philadelphia. I didn't understand why he hadn't come for me, but he explained that he'd wanted to do exactly that, that he'd contacted the authorities to try and find me. But my mother had convinced him that she was in a better position to take care of me. My father worked long hours as a janitor at two different office buildings and didn't make a ton of money. Who would see me off to school in the morning, or make dinner for me when he worked late? He also explained that while his desire was to fight for custody of me, he knew that the courts favored the mothers the majority of the time. Besides, going to court would cost money—money he didn't have. He promised we would stay in touch via phone calls and hopefully visits when the opportunity arose.

I'd had to accept what he'd told me—I didn't have any other choice. But I secretly believed that he hadn't pushed the issue of custody because he didn't want to fall out of favor with my mother. That after everything she had done to hurt him, he still hoped she would come back to him one day.

Their relationship may have been dysfunctional, but he'd loved her.

True to his word, my father and I did stay in touch. We talked on the phone about once a week in the beginning, then tapered off to about once a month. When I was eighteen and legally an adult, I borrowed money from a friend to go see my dad. I thought maybe I could live with him. But a week into the visit, I knew it wasn't going to work out.

There'd been an expression in my father's eyes all week that I couldn't quite place. A sort of sadness in his gaze as he regarded me, even though he'd been glad to see me. When he'd called me by my mother's name, I realized what the issue was. He couldn't look at me without seeing my mother.

And that was painful for him. Not because he didn't love me, but because I looked so much like the woman he had adored with all his soul and lost. He had been crippled by the loss. Like a person unable to move on after the death of a loved one.

Four years apart, and I no longer knew how to relate to him. I couldn't help him out of his melancholy. I went on with my life, moving to North Carolina with my best friend, Treasure.

I'd only seen my father a handful of times after that. Once a year, maybe. And we didn't speak on the phone all that often, either.

My dad hadn't been a consistent figure in my life for many years, but I'd been trying to come to terms with the unhappiness of the past, trying to find a way to move beyond the disappointment of my childhood. So going to Texas to see him had seemed like a great opportunity to strengthen our relationship. Robert, however, had thought that seeing my father would be a bad idea, that it wouldn't go the way I had hoped and maybe even send me into depression.

I understood his concerns. I had shared the truth of my troubled upbringing with my husband, as well as the fact that I'd experienced bouts of depression at times in the past. But when I made the decision to go to Texas anyway, and had booked my ticket, Robert "surprised" me with a trip to Paris. It was one of my favorite cities on the planet, and I'd been looking forward to the day when we could go back and explore it as a couple, rather than me shopping alone while my husband did business. Robert had conveniently forgotten to tell me that he'd booked the trip for us.

It had been a surprise, he'd reasoned.

But I couldn't help wondering if the trip had been a surefire way to make certain I didn't visit my dad. Robert didn't like him—and he especially despised my mother—and felt any contact with my parents would negate all the progress I'd made in moving to an emotionally better place in my life.

So I'd gone to Paris, where Robert had wined and dined me and treated me like a princess—and reminded me of the time when my father, after two years of not hearing from him, called to ask me for a loan. Robert had me doubting my father's motives. I'd returned from Paris and hadn't gotten back in touch with my dad, convinced that my husband, who loved me and wanted the absolute best for me, was right.

My father died of liver disease three weeks later. I hadn't known he was ill. He'd wanted to tell me in person, but never got the chance.

8

My legs were spread wide over the arms of a love seat, my lover's face buried in my pussy.

He was looking up at me from his position on the floor, his eyes locked with mine as his tongue ran circles over my clitoris. He had three fingers inside me, fucking me with his hand to heighten my pleasure. He plunged his fingers in, withdrew them and greedily lapped at my essence, then thrust his fingers deep inside my pussy again.

I watched as his teeth grazed my clit, knowing I was on the verge of a wicked orgasm. And when my clitoris disappeared into his wet, hot mouth, the erotic charge was so electric that I came violently, shuddering hard.

There was a hand on my breast. But whose? Something wasn't right.

My eyes popped open. I saw not my hazel-eyed lover,

but Robert beside me, his hand stroking my nipple through my nightshirt. I was momentarily stunned.

"Looks like someone was having a very interesting dream," he said.

My face flushed. "I...I was?"

"No need to be embarrassed." Robert slipped his hands beneath the fabric and placed his warm skin on mine. "It turned me on."

"Turned you on?" I repeated.

"I know it's been a while, but I want to make love, sweetheart."

"But...but your heart."

"It wasn't my heart, remember?"

I came fully awake. My husband wanted to make love. I pushed the image of my fantasy lover from my mind and concentrated wholly on Robert. I was already wet— ready to take advantage of this rare sexual advance.

"I haven't taken my pill, but I think I'll be okay," he said, and kissed my lips.

I eased my body upward, leaning into his kiss. He moved his hand slowly over my breast, gently. I moaned and pressed into his palm, trying to encourage him with my response to be less gentle. I wanted excitement and passion and I-need-you-now kind of sex.

I opened my mouth, deepening the kiss while I placed one leg over his. "Yes, Robert. Touch me harder. Suck my breast, please."

He lowered his head and began to lick my nipple. I gripped his head and held him to me, wanting him to take me completely in his mouth. But he continued to flick his tongue over my breast in steady thrusts.

Teasing me, but not quite exciting me the way I wanted him to.

I reached for Robert's penis as he continued to lick my nipple. I wrapped my hand around him and pumped his erect cock, hoping to make it harder before I spread my legs for him.

And then he was groaning and gripping my arms. I felt his cock pulse beneath my hand. He buried his face in my shoulder.

Oh, shit. He'd come.

"I'm sorry," I said. "I shouldn't have…" I didn't finish my statement. I was too disappointed. I'd wanted my husband excited, but not so much that he'd ejaculated prematurely.

I needed him to come inside me.

"Well, that didn't turn out as I'd hoped." Robert rolled onto his back.

"Don't feel bad. It's my fault."

"I should have taken my pill."

Feeling defeated, I watched as Robert got off the bed and headed for the bathroom.

You've got to find a way to loosen up, I told myself after a minute of wallowing in misery. *You're putting too much pressure on yourself, and on Robert. If you're ever going to get pregnant, you need to loosen up.*

It's just that I wanted a baby so badly. I was beginning to feel what Sharon said she had felt after so many miscarriages: that I was a failure as a woman.

It was a silly thought. In my heart, I knew that. Some things in life were out of our control.

But still… I wasn't ready to throw in the towel yet. I

truly believed that a baby was what Robert and I needed to fill that void in our lives, to give our relationship renewed purpose.

In the meantime, however, I needed to find a way to let myself enjoy whatever sexual interaction Robert and I shared, even if it didn't end with lovemaking. I was thirty-seven. There was no reason I couldn't have a baby in my early forties, if that's how long it took to get pregnant.

As the day passed, I contemplated getting Robert into the mood for lovemaking later, but I dismissed the thought. With his chest pain scare last night, there was no reason to push it.

That's what I told myself as the weekend passed, but that niggling doubt about the whole chest pain story didn't quite vaporize. Because I never did see Robert take any medication for his supposed gas pains. As he'd prematurely ejaculated, and his breathing had grown more rapid, he hadn't complained about any burning sensation.

He even played golf on Sunday.

He seemed completely back to normal, which was a marked difference to how he'd been the first time around.

But I let the matter slide. There was no point in be-laboring the point. It would only lead to conflict, and I didn't like conflict with Robert.

And who was I to say how long the discomfort should last? Each incident could be completely different.

I concentrated instead on how to spice up our sex

life. Maybe what Robert needed was extra stimulus. Something different and out of the norm.

Something new and exciting.

Hell, younger couples tried a variety of tricks to spice things up. Why shouldn't we?

By Wednesday, I had an idea.

As the owner of Distinct Creations, I always arrived at least half an hour earlier than my staff. Spike was my full-time employee, and I had a few part-timers as well.

Spike was scheduled to help me open this morning, while Maxine was due to work in the afternoon. She was a college student who fit in her part-time hours between classes. Like me, she had always loved arranging flowers for friends and family, and hoped to have a floral business of her own one day.

As I sipped my morning coffee before Spike arrived, I logged on to the computer and began to check a couple of options for how to spice things up with Robert.

The sound of footsteps surprised me. I looked up to see Spike approaching from the back of the store. He was decked out with his usual dramatic flair, in a royal-blue blazer, pink scarf wrapped neatly around his neck, and a multicolored hat.

He was gay and proud of it, and didn't tone down his flamboyance even in this conservative town.

"You're here already?" I asked.

"Good morning to you, too," he replied.

I smiled sweetly at him. "Good morning. I wasn't expecting you for another fifteen minutes."

He made his way around the counter, to where I was staring at the computer screen. "Whatcha looking at?"

I put a finger on the mouse, about to minimize the screen to hide what I was researching, but then decided not to. Having been judged his entire life for being gay, Spike was the last person in the world who would judge me for what I was considering doing. In fact, he'd probably get a kick out of it.

Besides, I needed to share my erotic plan with somebody.

"Take a look," I said.

He lowered his travel coffee mug and glanced at the computer screen. "Is that what I think it is?"

"Yep, it's a pole."

"You planning to open a strip club, doll-face?" he quipped.

"No." I sipped my coffee. "But I thought it would be fun to use one...to spice things up in the bedroom."

Spike's eyes grew wide. "You trying to give your husband a heart attack?" As soon as he asked the question, he realized his error in judgment. "Sorry. I shouldn't have said that."

"Robert didn't have a heart attack. I think his heart is stronger than most men half his age. It's his cock I want to work on."

"Girl...you are gonna hurt that man."

"You know how things get stale in a relationship sometimes," I said. "You fall into a routine. Or a rut—whatever you want to call it."

"No."

"All right, Casanova. You may not know personally,

but you know what I'm saying. Sex can get…boring. And when your husband is nearly seventy, it's hard to…"

"Keep it hard?" Spike suggested. "Oops. Did I say that?"

I gave him a look of mock reproach. "I want a baby," I said after a moment. "I'm ready. I'm more than ready. And yet it's not happening. I figure if I can add some excitement, maybe that'll lead to us having the kind of sex we used to before." Like we'd had that time in Paris when he'd smothered my body in chocolate. "And if we can let go and do that, maybe that'll help us conceive."

"Or you could find someone your own age. Someone who won't be dead as you raise your kids."

It wasn't the first time he'd casually suggested that I should leave my husband. We'd also had a couple of heart-to-hearts regarding my marriage. Spike, who was completely motivated by sex, didn't understand what the attraction was to a much older man.

"There are no guarantees in life," I told him. "Just ask Sharon."

"Touché."

"So here's what I was thinking," I went on. "Pole dancing is all the rage these days. Bachelor parties, divorce parties."

"Uh-huh."

"You can rent them for whatever function you want. So I'm thinking that I'll rent one, have it put in our bedroom. And then I'll put on a very special show for Robert."

"You know how to work a pole?" Spike asked.

"Not really. But I could figure it out."

"Why don't you go to a strip club?" Spike suggested. "Learn from the pros how it's done."

"Ooh." I nodded slowly. "I like that idea!"

He rolled his eyes. "I was *kidding*."

"But it's brilliant!" I knew nothing about strippers except what I'd seen in movies, and I had hardly been adventurous when it came to sex. I was ready to change all that. "And you could come with me."

Spike snorted—and damn near spit out his mouthful of coffee. "You want *me* to go to a strip club—the kind where *women* take their clothes off?"

"I'm not going alone."

"Girl, you're not serious."

"You would only be going with me so I don't feel uncomfortable. You don't have to watch if you don't want to."

"You've lost your mind."

"Think about it. It'll be fun. And for me it'll be a different experience. Maybe help loosen me up, too."

"You tryin' to unleash your inner ho or something?"

"Or something," I said, smiling wickedly. "Robert used to tell me that he went to strip clubs for 'business' meetings. Some out-of-town clients liked to be entertained that way. And I'm not stupid—I'm sure he enjoyed looking. I used to tease him that I wasn't enough for him…but I think this will be a fun way to turn the tables on him." My eyes went back to the Web site. "It says they provide a training video. Or personal instruction."

"Then there you go. Problem solved."

"Maybe. But if I'm going to do this, why not go all out? The outfit, the shoes. Ooh—the wig. I've got to find a store that sells all this stuff." I went to the search engine and typed in "adult stores in Charlotte."

As I waited for the various options to load, my gaze ventured to the store's front window. And that's when I saw a pair of familiar wide shoulders and a smooth bald scalp.

This time I was sure.

"Oh, my God," I muttered.

"What is it, doll-face?" Spike asked.

I didn't answer. Instead, I made my way to the door. The stranger with the hazel eyes had peered only briefly through the window before continuing on his way.

I unlocked the door as quickly as I could and rushed onto the sidewalk. I looked to the right—the direction he'd gone—but didn't see him.

I hadn't been imagining him. He'd been real.

He must have turned at the corner. It was the only place he could have gone.

A part of me wanted to follow after him.

"What's going on?"

I turned at the sound of Spike's voice. My heart was racing, and I was slightly breathless. Why did that man bring out this reaction in me when I didn't even know him?

"I thought I saw a friend," I explained. "But I was wrong."

I turned and went back into the store. Spike followed and locked the door behind him. We still had another ten minutes before we officially opened the shop.

My heart still pounding, I went back to the counter and the computer, ready to see the results of my search.

"So about this strip club thing," Spike began, "you really want to do this?"

"Yes." *Forget that guy. He's nobody. You're ready to get pregnant.* "I'll call Robert and tell him we're going out for dinner. Then we can catch an early show."

"An early show?"

"Or whatever they call it. I'm sure they must have shows throughout the evening."

I saw those hazel eyes again, this time in my mind. But I tried to block the image of the man I'd been fantasizing about.

Focusing on my plan again, I looked at the computer screen, at the list of stores where I could buy a sinfully delicious outfit. "Look at all these places. I've been missing out."

I clicked on the first link, and Spike's eyes widened as a barely clad woman appeared on the screen. "Girl, you really do want to unleash your inner ho."

"Uh-huh. And hey, you never did say yes," I said when I realized he hadn't confirmed whether he'd go with me to a strip club. I folded my hands together in a pleading motion. "Please say yes. I'd take Sharon, but there's bound to be cigarette smoke in these places and she's pregnant. But you—you'd be perfect. Please? Pretty please?"

Spike pursed his lips as he stared at me. I held my breath as I waited for him to answer. "Don't ever say I'm not up for adventure."

"Yes!" I threw my arms around Spike's neck. "Oh, thank you."

"Which club are you gonna hit?"

"Hell if I know. But you can find anything on the Internet these days."

I found the perfect spot.

It was an upscale gentlemen's club in south Charlotte, a part of town I wasn't hesitant to go to. I think I might have changed my mind if the only strip clubs around were in seedy areas.

The online reviews were great. Men commented that they'd been in town for business and decided to check the place out. That's exactly the kind of venue I wanted—one frequented by professional men. I called and asked if women were allowed. I was told that we were definitely welcome.

To my surprise, there were a number of women in line, all accompanied by men. Maybe going to strip clubs together was a hip thing to do these days. A bit of foreplay before you got home and fucked.

I slipped my arm through Spike's, willing to play the part of the girlfriend. I'd told him to tone down his flamboyance for the night. To try, if he could, to look a bit more manly.

We paid the cover and entered the club, which was large, with staggered levels. There was a lot of neon. Blues and purples and pinks.

"Look at the cellulite on that one," Spike said, eyeing the dancer on stage as we went to an unoccupied booth.

"You did not come here to be a critic," I said to him. "You're supposed to be a manly guy enjoying the view. Not a gay man who's going to critique outfits and hair."

"But look at that pink thing she's wearing," he protested. "Surely that's not meant to turn anyone on. And I thought you had to be skinny to perform in these clubs."

"Every guy has his type. And judging by all the applause, she's a crowd favorite."

The dancer had ample curves, thick hips and a huge ass…which she was now shaking at a speed that was both impressive and startling.

"I'm not sure I can do this," Spike said.

"Next time, we'll go to a male strip club," I promised him.

"Girl, you're on."

A waitress came to our table, her breasts bare. They were small and perky, a contrast to most of the other boobs I saw around the place.

She smiled sweetly at us, the kind of smile I was sure she plastered on her face for tipping customers. I wondered if she liked her job or just did it for the cash.

"I'll have a Bloody Mary," I said.

"Jack Daniel's on the rocks," Spike told her.

And then we settled in to watch the show. The Web site had said that the women here took off all their clothes, but I was still startled to see the woman come out of her bra and panties, piece by piece.

Totally nude, she lowered herself on all fours, her ass facing the audience. Once again, she did that ass-shaking thing, driving the crowd insane. Then she rolled onto her back and skillfully maneuvered one leg behind her head, exposing herself in a way I thought was reserved only for doctors. The audience satisfied, she collected the bills that had been thrown onto the stage and then sauntered off, her gait as confident and sexy as any I'd ever seen.

Our waitress returned just in time, because I needed a drink after what I'd seen. I took a good gulp of the Bloody Mary. Then I rolled my shoulders in an effort to loosen them. Now that I knew what to expect, I was prepared.

I'd never been to a strip club before, and this was a little shocking. But Robert had been many times, so hopefully my research would pay off.

The next dancer, a skinny redhead with massive breasts, came onto the stage in a nurse's outfit. The top of her uniform barely covered her chest—which I supposed was the point.

"What do you think about that outfit?" I asked. "You think Robert will like that?"

"It's kind of cute," Spike conceded. "But I see him as the type to go for a classier, slutty look."

"Like what?"

"I'll tell you when I see it."

The nurse headed straight for the pole, wrapping her right hand around the metal and doing a slow walk around it. Then she thrust her body forward, so it nestled between her breasts. She slithered down, cocking her ass outward, exposing a teasing amount of the flesh on her butt.

That got cheers from the guys.

"I like that move," I said. "Robert likes ass. That should get him hard in a hurry."

"This is the kind of shit you tell your shrink, not your best friend," Spike joked.

"That's why I pay you the big bucks!"

The waitress came back to the table, eyeing our glasses. We weren't ready for refills yet.

First, the dancer pulled off the cute nurse's hat she was wearing, letting her locks fall free. She shook her head, ruffled her hair with her fingers.

"I'm definitely going to get a wig," I said. "I think it'll add to the whole act."

Spike didn't answer. His eyes were glued to the stripper.

"Well, well, well," I said. "And I thought you only came for me."

"Are you gonna talk all night, or watch and learn?"

I watched. The stripper somehow maneuvered herself on the pole so that she was upside down, a move that took good arm strength. Holding the pole, she bent her legs—completely exposing her ass, save for the white fabric strip of her thong.

She came down from the pole, and with one easy pull, whipped her uniform off her body. Now she was in a bra—one that covered only her nipples—her thong, her thigh-high stockings and what had to be five-inch white stilettos. There were cries of "Take it off!"

She returned to the pole, curved one leg around it and bent her body back until her hair flowed to the ground. Then she climbed the pole using her legs and arms. Reaching the top, she held on with her legs only, bent backward again—and ripped off the bra.

The screams were hysterical.

I glanced around. Some of the female patrons were whistling and clapping. I began to do the same, not wanting to feel like the oddball in the place.

The way the first woman had shaken her ass so well, this one did with her breasts. When she came down from the pole, she did a few dance moves and then shook her upper body so that her breasts didn't just bob up and down, they swung around and around. I found myself jerking my shoulders, seeing if I could figure out the move.

I watched dancer after dancer. Spike got into the whole show, not as a man appreciating women's attributes, but as someone watching a form of entertainment. He even paid for a dancer to perform before us. She sat on his lap and gyrated against him. I watched not only how she moved her body, but the expression on her face. The oh-my-God-I'm-so-turned-on-by-this look.

The dance cost twenty dollars. We gave her forty.

"So are you straight now?" I joked when the dancer left our table.

"I still love me a hard cock," Spike admitted.

"Me, too."

"Have you seen enough?" he asked.

"I guess so." My seduction plan was coming together in my mind. I would find a place to get an outfit that would be supersexy and fun. The wig and the shoes would complete the look. "I can try to practice some moves when they drop the pole off tomorrow—see if my arms are strong enough to maneuver me up it the way these women do."

"Oh, to be a fly on the wall…" Spike's eyes lit up. "Hey, you can take a video of yourself."

I made a face at him. "I might be ready to get a bit more adventurous, but this show's just for my husband."

9

I put my plan into action the next day.

I knew that Robert would be playing golf in the afternoon, followed by an early dinner and drinks with his friends at the country club. Hopefully, when he got home he would be relaxed and in a good mood.

And ready to be seduced.

From my shop I called Olga and told her she could go home early. I didn't want her around to see what I was up to. I arrived home just after three to meet the deliverymen.

I learned more about poles than I ever thought I would. A lot of the options could be installed directly from floor to ceiling—provided the ceiling wasn't more than nine feet high. Our bedroom had ten-foot coffered ceilings, so I chose a pole that would stand on a platform.

The platform was a four-by-four-foot box of frosted acrylic with LED lights inside that would illuminate while I danced. It was sturdier than I'd expected, almost like a real stage, with a steel pole rising in the center.

Hours later, I was dressed and ready for my performance. I'd found the perfect outfit. I decided not to go for a tacky nurse or Playboy bunny outfit, but instead wear something more traditional. At Frederick's of Hollywood, I almost bought a beautiful lace corset, but thought better of it. A corset might pose problems when trying to get it off. So I opted for a sheer, red lace trimmed baby doll with matching thong. I made the outfit a little more racy with black fishnet stockings, four-inch black patent knee-high boots, and a long, black wig. The baby doll was covered by a black silk robe. I had white wine chilling in a carafe and had already helped myself to a glass. The stereo system was ready to play the music I would dance to. A spritz of Red Door perfume on my neck completed my outfit.

At six-thirty, I called Robert at the club. "Are you ready to come home soon?" I asked.

"Nearly."

"Good. What I want you to do is take one of your pills. You know the one."

Robert didn't like me to say "Viagra." He hated the reality of the word, and preferred for me to call it simply "the pill."

"But I don't have any."

"Oh, yes, you do. Check your wallet. You'll find it in the zippered compartment, wrapped in tissue."

"Really?"

"I'll see you soon," I said, hoping that my elusiveness hinted at what was to come.

By seven o'clock, I'd had two glasses of wine. That's when I heard the chime that sounded when the front door opened.

I put my wineglass on my night table and quickly stood. Drawing in a breath, I combed my fingertips through the wig.

"Elsie?" I heard Robert call from downstairs.

"I'm in the bedroom, honey." I plugged in the stage to turn on the array of neon lights. "Can you come up, please?"

My heart was pounding as I waited for him. When I saw the knob begin to turn, I struck a sexy pose.

Robert stepped into the room. His eyes widened as he regarded me. Then his gaze went to the pole platform in the center of the room.

I smiled. Took a step toward him, then stopped. "Good evening, sweetheart."

"You're taller." Robert's gaze lowered to my boots. "And your hair is longer."

"I know."

"What is this?"

I trailed my fingers along my skin where my robe fell open above my breasts. "It's a pole."

"I can see that. What's it doing in our bedroom?"

I strutted toward Robert, swaying my hips in an exaggerated motion. I placed my palms on his chest. "I'm gonna entertain you, baby."

"Entertain me? Oh, Elsie—you don't need that foolishness to entertain me."

The words stung a little. I wanted Robert to smile. I wanted to see a gleam in his eyes, some excitement that I would try something unique and different.

"I know we don't need this," I said, gesturing to the pole. "But I think it'll be fun."

I slipped my hands beneath his jacket and slowly pushed it off of his shoulders. Robert chuckled, but it was more of an embarrassed sound than one of expectation.

"Did you take your pill?" I asked.

"Yes, I did."

"Good." It normally took thirty minutes to take effect, and it was about half an hour since I'd called him. Which meant he was ready to be seduced.

"Music!" I exclaimed. "I'm forgetting the music. Why don't you sit down. Make yourself comfortable for the show."

"Why don't I take a shower first," Robert suggested.

"No." I pressed my hands flat against his chest. "No shower. I want you dirty...."

I giggled and twirled around, hoping that he was becoming inspired. I was sure he would be—once he saw what I was wearing beneath my silk robe.

I already had a CD in the Bose player, something bluesy and soulful. It was good music to prance around and gyrate to.

"I'll turn on the stereo," I said. "You sit down." I pressed my lips against Robert's and kissed him softly, a promise of what was to come. Then I urged him backward to the bed. He sat.

"So you're going to perform," he said.

"I know you've gone to some gentlemen's clubs in the past. But I hope this performance trumps any you've ever seen."

He made a face, almost as if I was being silly, but I wasn't deterred. I did my best sleazy walk as I went to the console on the far wall where we had our DVD player and sound system. I pressed the play button to start the music.

I was tipsy from the two glasses of wine I'd consumed, so had no problem shedding my inhibitions. I danced my way to the pole in the center of the room. I put one foot on the platform and displayed it there for a moment, showing off my leg in the pink neon light. Then I leaned forward, put both hands on my leg and trailed a path with my fingers up to the edge of the robe.

I stepped onto the platform, twisting my body seductively. Wrapping my fingers around the metal pole, I held on as I strutted around it.

Then I secured a leg around the pole and swung around it, as I'd practiced earlier. I tipped my head back, letting the wig's hair dangle as I spun.

Holding the pole, I drew myself to an upright position. Then I turned my body so that my back was against it. Each of my movements was timed to the sultry beat. Gyrating my hips, I slithered down the pole. My lips were parted, and I hoped I was pulling off a sexy pout.

When I was on my haunches at the bottom, I met Robert's gaze. I kept my eyes locked with his as I loosened the robe's ties. Slowly, I worked myself back up the pole, and when I was standing tall again, I slipped the robe off.

Robert's eyes widened with interest, and that simple reaction gave me an adrenaline boost. I picked up the pace of my hips and shoulders. Pushing my breasts forward, I played with my nipples through the delicate fabric of my baby doll.

The look of lust on Robert's face was my reward.

I pulled the fabric off one breast, exposing it completely. I licked my finger. Ran it around my nipple. Drew my bottom lip into my mouth as I continued to move my body erotically.

Slowly, I turned around so that my back was to Robert. I pulled the baby doll over my head and tossed it onto the platform beside me. Then I went down on all fours, giving him a view of my ass. I spread my legs slightly, knowing he would see the scrap of red covering my pussy. Maintaining that position, I started to shake my ass—hoping I could do it half as well as the dancer in the club.

Robert wasn't making any comments, at least not that I could hear above the music. Getting to my feet, with my back still to him, I slipped my thumbs beneath the sides of my thong. I slid the panty down my thighs and over my heels, then kicked it aside.

"Are you ready for me yet?" I asked Robert in a husky voice. When I turned around, I saw that his eyes were dark with lust. His eyes fixated on my nipples, which I was stroking. A jolt of desire shot through me when I saw the strain of his erection against his pants.

"Yes." The sound was low. Almost a ragged whisper escaping his lips.

Naked as the day I was born, except for the boots and stockings, I started down from the platform. Robert stood now, beginning to undress. While he watched me, I tweaked my nipples, feeling the same surge of excitement I had felt in my fantasies.

I kissed him deeply the moment I reached him, a kiss such as we hadn't shared in a long time. I forced his lips open with my tongue and pressed my mouth to his. I moved forward, forcing him back onto the bed.

"Did you like the show?"

"How could I not?"

Giggling with a sense of pride, I straddled my husband.

"Wow, you really do want it," Robert said against my lips.

"Mmm-hmm."

I gave him a shove—not too rough—and he got the point. He lay back on the bed.

"That's better," I purred. My body was ready, positioned over his cock. A few hip movements and he would be inside me.

"Hold on for a second," Robert said.

"What?" I asked.

"Can you take off those boots?"

"I bought these sexy heels just for you."

"Sexy they may be, but I don't want them to ruin the bedding."

I stared into Robert's eyes, wondering if he was serious. He was. I wanted to fuck with an urgency and passion we hadn't experienced in a long time.

He wanted to make sure that the bedding stayed intact.

"All right," I agreed, but his request was like a pin-prick in my balloon of desire.

I eased off my husband and unzipped the first boot. The music was still playing, but I was aware that our momentum was fading.

I got one boot off, but decided to stand as I peeled off the next one, bending forward so that Robert would have an unrestricted view of my pussy from behind.

"Sweet Jesus," he said. "You keep that up and I might come before I touch you."

His words were like a shot of adrenaline to my libido, and I turned to face him. He was lying on his back, and had his hand around the base of his cock.

"Come here," he growled.

I slithered onto the bed, still trying to emulate the moves of a stripper or a porn star. Robert snaked his hands around my waist and pulled me down beside him.

He pulled off my wig, saying, "That's better."

And then he began to kiss me. As he did, he edged me onto my back. One hand moved over my right breast. He moaned, played with my nipple. Then he moved his hand to my other breast and did the same.

I knew what was coming next before he did it. He slid a hand down my torso and cupped my pussy, all while continuing to kiss me. Then he broke the kiss and lowered his mouth to my breasts. He suckled one nipple for a few seconds before turning his attention to the other.

Right on cue, he pushed a finger into my pussy.

This was all from the how-the-Kolstads-fuck play-book. It was the same routine.

And I felt my desire ebb away, slowly but surely. Little by little, the excitement of having sex was replaced by familiarity. This was not how I wanted to be fucked.

Not today.

God, not today.

Not after I'd done my best to spice things up.

Robert kissed my belly—he really liked my belly button—but by the time he began stroking my legs, I was faking my moans.

He knelt over me now, his head just above my raised knees.

"Spread your legs, darling."

I let my legs fall apart. At once, Robert reached for my pussy, using his thumb—always his thumb—to dip into my folds and massage my clit. His deep groaning said he was enjoying this. And I tried, for both our sakes and the goal of getting pregnant, not to be disappointed that we had fallen into our typical lovemaking routine.

Robert slipped a finger inside me again, then two. And then he lowered his face between my thighs and started to lick my clit. His tongue was stiff as it moved up and down in rigid strokes. I closed my eyes, tried to enjoy the sensation. I moved my hips, faking a pleasure I wasn't feeling.

And then I found myself picturing another man be-tween my thighs. A man whose tongue wasn't stiff. A man whose tongue licked and flicked and went around my clit in soft circles. A man whose tongue dipped into my pussy. A man who drank my juices as if they were the sweetest nectar.

The man with the hazel eyes.

I imagined him suckling me softly and playing with my pussy, using both his hands and his mouth to bring me pleasure. That's when heat began to envelop me, and my moans became genuine again.

I grabbed my own nipples as my fantasy played out. I could hear Robert's groans, louder, more satisfied that he was pleasing me. But I imagined the groans belonged to the sexy stranger who couldn't get enough of my pussy.

My orgasm came out of the blue, shuddering through every part of my body. Crying out from the pleasure, I arched my spine, arched my feet. Tightened my thighs around my lover's face.

Easing upward, Robert eased his cock into my body. I wrapped my arms around him and nibbled on his jaw as he made love to me, still feeling wonderful from my orgasm. Minutes later, Robert came, and I squeezed my inner muscles around his cock.

For several moments we lay together, the sound of our heavy breathing mixing with the music. I moved my lips from Robert's jaw to his mouth and kissed him.

He broke the kiss quickly and rolled off of me. I turned onto my side and raised myself up on an elbow.

"So." I trailed a finger over his gray chest hairs. "Did you like the show?"

Robert met my gaze. "It was different."

"Different good?" I said hopefully.

"Well…" He sighed softly. "It wasn't what I expected."

"What—not as good as all the professionals you've seen?"

"You don't have to go to these lengths." He gestured toward the pole. "I love you as you are. Actually, I prefer you as you are. No wigs and stilettos and props."

I couldn't help it, I was hurt. Because I sensed what he wasn't saying—that he disapproved. "You didn't like it."

"Elsie—"

"No, tell me." I had turned him on, he had fucked me, but now that he was satisfied he was criticizing me.

"If you want the truth—no. I didn't. It was trashy. And…"

I drew in a deep breath. "And what?"

"It's not important, Elsie. Just know that you don't have to do anything like this again."

"And what?" I repeated.

"If you must know, it made me think of something your mother might do."

I bolted upright, my stomach tightening. "How could you say that to me? I was trying to turn you on. To spice up our sex life. How could you—"

"You wanted my opinion. I gave it to you."

"You sure did." I jumped off the bed and ran to the bathroom. Tears were already streaming down my face.

Robert *knew* how much his comment would hurt.

All my life, I had run from the stigma of my mother's behavior. To compare me to her...

Even though my mother had married my dad, she had never been faithful to him. She had slept with man after man. And then she'd left my father—moving from Ohio to Philadelphia with some truck driver she'd barely known.

That relationship hadn't lasted. A succession of men had come and gone through my life. Some for a few days. Some for longer. Some who seemed as love struck as my father, only to end up brokenhearted.

Once I'd been old enough to understand my mother's behavior, I had been able to separate her from her actions. I guess it was a coping mechanism. I loved her. She was my mom, even if she was emotionally vacant. Even if she was more concerned about snagging her next boyfriend than about taking me shopping, or to the movies. But when she'd left my dad and brought other men into my life in his place, I had grown to resent her.

All I could think about was the father who was no longer in my life, and how hurt he must have been after standing by my mother despite her behavior for so many years. I'd lost my dad—and it was all my mom's fault.

There have been many times when I've thought back to that day when I was fourteen and my father suggested we take a trip to Texas. My mother had run away with me only days later. Maybe she feared that my father wanted to make a clean break from her. Had that been his intention? Had my mother's running away with me been a panicked reaction to the thought of losing me, or had she been planning to abandon my father all along?

I would never know the answer. All I knew was that my life had only gotten more difficult.

At my new high school in Philadelphia, my mother slept with the principal and caused the breakup of his marriage. Word got out, and I was teased endlessly by other students. Humiliated by what they said about my mother. It was a truly awful time in my life. My mom had never been there for me emotionally the way other mothers were for their kids—cheering for them on the volleyball court, sitting in the audience, beaming, at the school play. I came to understand that it was my mother's emotional unavailability that had led me to suffer from low self-esteem, making me a prime target for bullies.

At least when my father was around, I hadn't felt as alone in my suffering. But without him, the bullies who teased me in high school, spreading rumors that I was easy just like my mother, succeeded in sending me running from Philadelphia as soon as I was old enough. I followed Treasure, my one good friend from high school, to North Carolina.

I dated, but I didn't trust men. Or perhaps it was myself I didn't trust.

I didn't want to become my mother.

Then I'd met Robert. And he'd offered me a whole new life.

He'd offered me safety. Security. A marriage that was nothing like my parents'.

But what had I sacrificed in the process?

10

Robert's comment about my mother cut me deeply. It was a wound that I wasn't sure would heal.

We were heading toward disaster. As the next couple weeks passed, I felt it my soul. Knew it even as a part of me desperately hoped we had conceived a child.

How had we gotten to this point? My relationship with Robert started off wonderfully. As I sat in the steam room the next morning, hoping the heat would melt my hurt, my mind drifted back down memory lane….

I rushed into the restaurant's kitchen, about to pull my hair out. Seeing my fellow waitress, I sighed loudly. "Jane, I'm about to lose my mind. I just got another table. Can you take it for me?"

Jane, who was piling plates of food onto a large tray,

met my eyes briefly before she answered. "God, I wish I could, but I'm so friggin' behind it's not funny. Sorry, hon."

Then, lowering her body to ease the giant tray onto her shoulder, she lost her balance. The tray tilted and plates slid onto the floor with a loud crash. Mortified, she burst into tears.

I couldn't help her. I had to rush past her and collect the two plates of pasta that one of my tables was waiting on. I balanced them on my arm and hurried back to the busy restaurant.

I delivered the meals to the waiting couple, then turned and headed to the new table with the four older men.

Though I was flustered, I offered them a smile, hoping not to show how stressed out I was. All their eyes perked up when they saw me—a reaction I was used to because of my looks—but I pretended not to notice. Good looks certainly helped get better tips, but I didn't believe they made me special. Maybe because men had fallen over my mother because of her looks, and I wanted a life nothing like hers.

"How're you all doing this evening?" I asked as I fished my notepad from my apron pocket.

There was a chorus of "goods" and "fines." And I noticed the lingering stare from one of the men at the table.

While I ignored him, I was surprisingly not offended the way I often was when other men ogled me.

He's older, I told myself. *Hardly a threat.*

"I'm sorry for keeping you waiting," I said. "I'm superbusy, and—"

"No problem." This from the man who had given me
the longer look. His attractive face wore a soft smile. He
had a full head of salt-and-pepper hair, and I figured he
was in his late fifties. Something about him reminded
me of Harry Belafonte at that age. The shape of the face,
the smile. The twinkle in his eyes.

"I could run through the list of drink specials," I
began, "but you don't strike me as the margarita or
frothy drink type." They all chuckled. "What can I get
for you? Beer? Whiskey?"

"A bottle of Glenlivet," one of the men said. "We're
celebrating."

I was ready to celebrate myself—a bottle of Glenlivet
Scotch would add a huge amount to the bill, meaning
a much larger tip for me. These men were well dressed.
I was certain they knew how to tip well.

And they did. They left me a one-hundred-dollar
bill.

With that bill came a note from the older gentleman who had clearly been interested. "I would love for
you to call me," the note read. And he left his phone
number.

I didn't call. But a week later, Robert showed up at
the restaurant again, requesting my section. And he
made it clear that he wanted to get to know me.

I guess because he was safe, I decided to give him a
chance. He was gentle and persistent. Charming and
romantic. Sending flowers and chocolates and notes to
brighten my day. When he came to the restaurant and

sat in my section, we enjoyed an easy rapport. It was clear to me that his attraction wasn't based on his desire to get me into bed.

And I fell for him. I thought we would have a story-book ending.

Eight years later, the story had somehow changed along the way. It had changed from a fairy tale to something else.

Something much darker.

"You're running late, aren't you?" Robert asked as I breezed into the kitchen. I hadn't even seen him sitting at the breakfast counter. I thought he'd left for the club half an hour earlier.

"I thought you were at the club already."

"I had a few phone calls to make so I came back." Robert brought his mug to his mouth and sipped. "How come you're not at the shop yet?"

"I promised Sharon I'd go with her to the obstetrician today."

"I see. You're a very good friend to her."

"She's got no one else right now," I said as I made my way to the coffee machine. A fresh pot was brewed. "Her family rallied around her after Warren died, but they live all over the country and simply can't be there for her as much as they'd like." Robert already knew this. Why was I explaining my desire to be there for Sharon?

"She should have gone to live with her sister," Robert commented.

"I'm sure her mom and Melanie will come closer

to her due date." Sharon's sister, Melanie, had invited her to move to Phoenix and live with her and her husband until the baby was born, but Sharon had declined. She didn't want to leave her matrimonial home. Even though the house was large and empty, she still felt close to Warren there.

"Good morning, ma'am."

I looked up as Olga, our housekeeper, came into the kitchen. "Good morning, Olga."

"Would you like me to prepare some breakfast for you?" she asked.

Olga was German-born, and despite having lived in America for close to thirty years, she still spoke with a fairly thick accent. She'd been Robert's housekeeper for fifteen years—while he'd still been married to wife number two.

"No, thank you." I took my travel mug from the cupboard above. "I'm just going to have coffee and run."

"Are you sure, ma'am?"

"Yes. I'm fine."

"Okay, then."

Olga crossed the kitchen and opened the dishwasher. I filled my travel mug.

"I just wonder if it's wise to go to this appointment with her."

Robert's words had me turning to face him. "Why?"

"Because." He glanced in Olga's direction, but she was busy filling the dishwasher. Satisfied that she wouldn't hear, he continued, "Because of our own inability to get pregnant."

I nodded grimly. After the pole incident a couple weeks earlier, Robert and I had made love only one other time. He'd killed my desire for him. One day, I hoped I would get over the hurt his words had caused— because I still wanted to get pregnant.

Robert already had three grown children and four grandchildren, and knew firsthand the joy of being a parent. I wanted to experience that joy, too.

"Actually, I think that going with Sharon will be good for me. Seeing her happy makes me happy. And seeing the baby move inside her belly...I can't wait. It's such a miracle, I know I'll feel only joy." I lowered my voice. "Besides, who says I'm not pregnant right now?"

I did hope that what I'd said was true, but there was another reason for my words. I wanted a reaction out of Robert. Did he want a baby as much as I did? Or was I in this alone?

He raised an eyebrow, then sipped more coffee. "Perhaps you are."

Perhaps you are... No excitement. No yearning.

"I was thinking perhaps we could plan a trip to Paris," Robert said.

"Now?"

"Why not? I know how much you love Paris."

Paris won't make me forget what you said to me.

"You know this isn't a good time for me to get away," I told him. "With all the graduations, and with Mother's Day coming up, I'm superbusy."

"Maybe in a few weeks, then."

"We'll see how it goes," I said noncommittally.

Because as I looked at my husband, I thought: *Do I even want your baby? Maybe I can start my life with someone else, someone who adores me. Someone who wants what I want.*

Maybe all my fantasies about that sexy stranger were a subconscious sign of something I hadn't dared to put into words.

"I have to go," I told Robert.

I didn't bother to give him a kiss before I left the house.

I watched the ultrasound monitor in awe.

"It's a baby." I held a hand to my chest. "Look at the legs and arms moving about. It's like she wants to get out and start ruling the world already."

"It's a he," the ultrasound technician pointed out.

My eyes flew to Sharon's. "A boy?"

She nodded, and her eyes welled with tears. "Warren would have been so happy."

"He is happy," I said softly. "He is."

"Let's just hope this little ruler waits another fifteen weeks before making an appearance," the ultrasound technician continued.

"Oh, he will," I said, as if willing it could make it true. "I'm going to make sure that baby stays inside until he's good and ready to take on the world."

That elicited a smile from Sharon. "Twenty-four weeks," she said. "I've never made it this far before."

Emotion hit me, instantly filling my eyes with tears. "This is the one. Warren's gonna make sure of that."

Sharon started to cry, but she was shedding happy

tears. As was I. I gripped her hand in support and we both smiled through our tears.

When the technician left the room, I said to Sharon, "I haven't asked you, but seeing the baby moving around inside of you, it's suddenly very real. Are you planning to have a natural birth, or are you going to schedule a C-section?"

"You mean a 'too posh to push' birth?"

"Is that what they call it?"

"Women opting for scheduled C-sections is a trend now. So yeah, there's a name for. And no, I'm not planning a C-section. Not if I can help it. I'll take the drugs. I'm no fool. But I'm going to try and have a vaginal birth, unless nature dictates otherwise."

"That's good," I said. "Or not. Whatever you choose."

Sharon smiled. "Now I have a question for you." She paused. Gave me a long look. "Will you be there with me in the delivery room?"

"What? You want *me* there?"

"I've been meaning to ask…. Now seems like the perfect time."

"You want me there?" I repeated, my eyes filling with tears again.

"I'll have other family here, come the time. But I want you there. And I'm going to need a Lamaze coach."

Giddy with joy, I started to laugh. "Definitely, Sharon. I'll be there for you. Of course I will."

I was honored, and touched.

As I got into my car in the parking lot, I was still in awe of what I'd witnessed. Seeing Sharon's son moving around was the most amazing thing. My own longing for a baby intensified.

I wanted to experience the joy Sharon felt. And like my dear friend, I knew that if I had to, I could raise a baby alone.

When I left the appointment, I decided to swing by my own doctor's office. I never showed up without an appointment, but today I was desperate. If Dr. Cairns could squeeze me in, I would wait as long as it took.

An hour and a half later, just before her lunch break, she was able to see me.

I went into her office with hope, determined to find out from my doctor if there was anything special I could do to help me and my husband conceive.

When I left, I was devastated by a truth I'd never expected to learn.

One that changed everything.

part two

PART TWO

11

I stood in the lobby of my doctor's office building, bracing my hands on the glass doors as I gazed out at the world before me. The leafy trees rustling in the wind looked the same. The towering pines beyond the parking lot looked the same.

And yet nothing about my world was the same. It never would be again.

Everything had been a lie. Everything Robert had told me. Our marriage. Our life together.

All of it.

God, I should have known. Should have realized the truth.

But how could I have? How could I ever have believed that the words my husband had told me were a bald-faced lie? That he had undermined me and my hope, likely right from the beginning?

Someone was approaching the front door. Breathing raggedly, I stepped aside, allowing the middle-aged man to enter the building. Then, numb, I slipped through the door before it could close, stepping into the warm spring air of what appeared to be a beautiful day.

But it wasn't a beautiful day. Not anymore. It was a downright dreadful one.

Like a zombie, I crossed the parking lot to my Mercedes SUV. Instinctively, I placed a hand on my belly.

The day had held so much promise just two hours ago. With Sharon, I saw the fruition of a dream she'd almost given up on. And I'd believed—foolishly—that I could have that dream, too.

Hope crept into my brain again. Hope that I'd held on to for the last two years in my marriage.

Could Dr. Cairns have been mistaken?

But the reality of her words sank my hope as surely as if it were tied to an anchor.

Mistaken—yeah, right. No doctor would make a mistake about that. The mistake had been in blurting the truth—a truth she clearly thought my husband had shared with me.

"Robert and I are ready. Ready to have a baby."

"Oh, how wonderful."

"I'd like to know what you think I need to do to help bring about a successful conception. Do you think there might be an issue with my husband's age?"

Warm chuckle. "No need to worry. You won't have to do anything special. Vasectomies are reversible, and there's no age limit on when men can impregnate."

I'd stared, dumbfounded, as the doctor's words had registered.

Vasectomies are reversible.

I hadn't played the "what are you talking about?" card. I think because even amid my shock, I hadn't wanted to embarrass myself. How could I let our doctor know that my husband hadn't shared a crucial detail with me—the one that had prevented the thing I wanted most?

I rested my hip against my vehicle as my head swam. Two years ago, I had told Robert that I was finally ready to have a baby. He'd agreed that I should go off the Pill.

God, what a joke. All those years on the Pill…

Robert must have been secretly laughing at me. Laughing at my stupidity.

"How could you do it?" I said aloud, but the rustling trees gave no answers. "How could you never tell me that you had a vasectomy?"

I got into the car, and the tears finally came. I let out a wail as they flowed down my face. I pounded the steering wheel. I screamed.

When I couldn't cry anymore, I spent the next couple of minutes trying to regain my control.

"What control?" I laughed bitterly. "Robert has controlled every single aspect of your life, of *our* life. Of our marriage."

Obviously, he didn't want a baby. And he obviously believed that if he couldn't give me one, I would leave him. So he'd kept me in my place by lying to me, by supplying me false hope.

Yes, I was always the one who brought up the topic of having a baby. But if he didn't want a child, he should have told me the truth. Given me the option to go on with my life without him, if that's what I chose to do.

A vasectomy… It didn't seem real. Didn't seem possible. Robert had seen my disappointment every time I'd gotten my period. He'd watched me try to predict when I might be ovulating. He'd heard the hope in my voice when my cycle was finished and I knew I had another chance to conceive.

After two years of trying, I'd been beginning to wonder if it was due to my husband's age, or some biological issue with me.

I'd like to know what you think I need to do to help bring about a successful conception. Do you think there might be an issue with my husband's age?

In the privacy of my car, I laughed again—but it was an angry, bitter sound.

Never in my wildest dreams would I have expected to learn that my husband had had a vasectomy without telling me.

I took my phone out of my purse and dialed Robert's cell.

"Hello, sweetheart," he said. "How was Sharon's appointment?"

"Are you home?" I asked.

"I'm at the club. Just sat down for lunch with George and Colin."

"I need to see you," I told him, my voice firm.

"I'll be home in a few hours."

"No. I need to see you now."

control   135

"What is it, Elsie?"

So much concern in his voice. It was bullshit. All of it. "I'll be home in about fifteen minutes."

"If it's that important, I'll be there," Robert said, clearly realizing that I meant business.

Damn right it was important.

The most important issue we would deal with in our marriage.

I was the first to get home. I went up to the bedroom, where we would have privacy from Olga's ears.

My hands were jittery as adrenaline pumped through my body. I was too wired to sit. Instead, I paced the bedroom floor.

I felt betrayed. And hurt.

But mostly I felt angry.

Robert opened the bedroom door five minutes later. A smile formed on his lips as he saw me.

But not a happy-to-see-his-wife smile. More of a patronizing what-could-be-so-important smile.

His smile withered as he saw the look on my face. "What's the matter, Elsie? What happened?"

What happened is that I hate you, I thought. *I found out your lie, and I hate you.*

"I learned something today, Robert. Something so disturbing I can't even believe it."

"What?" he asked, his concerned expression adding to my anger.

"I've been so stupid," I said, not sure if I was talking to Robert or to myself. "I thought a baby would…would fix things between us. Give us both renewed purpose, I guess."

He eyed me carefully, saying nothing.

"And then I find out that what I want the most is something you don't want at all." I paused, holding his gaze. I waited for a reaction from him as my words sank in.

But Robert showed no reaction at all.

"I saw Dr. Cairns today," I went on. "I asked her what she thought I could do to help us get pregnant. Imagine my surprise when she said that all we needed was for you to reverse your vasectomy."

Robert's jaw twitched.

"Obviously, you didn't want a baby. But why—" My voice cracked, but I forged on. "But why would you make me believe that you did? Why would you…"

Unable to look at my husband, I turned away. Turned away and tried to compose myself.

After a beat, Robert said, "I can see why you're disappointed."

"Disappointed?" I said as I whirled around. "Disappointed doesn't begin to describe what I'm feeling! Why would you do this? How could you lie to me about something so important?"

Robert said nothing.

"Answer me, damn it!"

"You didn't have the time for a baby."

It wasn't the answer I expected, and it stunned me. For a few seconds I couldn't speak.

"Didn't…have *time?*" I finally asked. "I've been want-ing a baby for two years, talking to you about that desire nonstop, and your excuse for lying to me is that I didn't have *the time?*"

"A new business takes a lot of work," Robert went on, seemingly unfazed by my brewing anger. "Don't you think I've seen how many hours a week you've had to dedicate to the shop? It wasn't the right time."

His answer pissed me off. "You're serious."

"Yes, I'm serious. That business occupies most of your time. Where would you fit in raising a child?"

I couldn't believe my husband—justifying his lie with an excuse that made no sense.

"And so you just decided—without informing me—that you would have a vasectomy? Is that what you're saying?"

Robert looked away.

"Answer me!"

"That's not how it happened."

"No? You didn't decide that you would have a vasectomy without telling me? While I was *trying to get pregnant?*"

"No, I didn't."

I stared at him, waiting for him to elaborate. And then it occurred to me. What if he'd had the vasectomy *before* we'd gotten married? Before we'd even met? Though I was angry, I could suddenly envision a scenario where Robert might have felt uncomfortable telling me the truth.

"Did you have the vasectomy before we got married?" I found myself asking. Was I, even now, finding a way to excuse a horrific lie?

It was something I'd done many times in my life

with my parents. Made excuses to justify their bad behavior.

I couldn't do it now. *Wouldn't* do it now. Not anymore. I wasn't the same meek, insecure person I'd once been.

Robert didn't answer right away, and again refused to make direct eye contact with me.

"Robert?" I prompted. I wasn't going to back down.

Now he met my gaze, his expression one of resolve. "Once you were involved with your store, and very busy with that, I assumed…I assumed you were no longer interested in a baby."

A shocked gasp escaped my lips.

"I'm not getting any younger, Elsie."

I felt a sharp pain at his words. An honest to goodness pain in my heart. Despite his promises, despite knowing that I'd reiterated on countless occasions that I definitely wanted children, Robert had decided to have a vasectomy *after* we were married—leaving me out of the decision completely.

"I *always* told you that I would want children one day," I said, seething. "I wasn't ready in the beginning of our marriage, and you agreed, but I maintained right from the beginning that I *would* want children."

"Honestly, Elsie, once you threw every ounce of your being into your business, I thought you'd changed your mind. You were getting older. And after five years of marriage, you still weren't ready for children. People change their minds all the time. I thought you had."

Many emotions began to swirl around within me—anger, disillusionment, hurt.

Revulsion.

"Bullshit," I snapped. Robert's eyes widened, shock and disapproval streaking across his face, but I didn't care. "Let's pretend for a second that what you're saying is true. You had a vasectomy because you *somehow* thought I'd changed my mind about wanting children. Why wouldn't you have told me? Hell, consulted me first? You're lying!"

"Calm down, Elsie."

"Don't tell me to calm down!"

"Elsie, what do you expect? I'm not a young man anymore."

Did I know him at all? Had he always been a son of a bitch? "If that was your issue, you would have said so before. You would have told me that you had concerns about being too old."

"What's the sense in getting you pregnant? I won't live forever. You want to be like Sharon, raising a child without a father?"

You bastard! Somehow I refrained from saying the words.

"And I already have three children, Elsie. Four grand-children."

"I just want to know if you lied to me from the beginning," I replied, barely keeping my anger under control. "If you never planned to give me a baby."

"I'm too old," Robert said, not answering my question—which was answer enough. "And at thirty-seven, you're likely too old, too."

I glared at him. If looks could kill, he would have dropped dead.

"I know you think this is what you want, my love." Robert's tone was gentle, as though he was speaking to a child who needed extra care in understanding something. "But when you have time to reflect, you'll see that it doesn't make sense."

Doesn't make sense... I heard my husband's words, stared at him in disgust. A part of me wanted to lash out at him now—scream, throw something. But another part—the part that had learned how to behave as Robert's wife—silently held in my resentment.

I watched as he turned and left the room, effectively putting an end to our conversation. No more discussion. It was over because he deemed it was over.

Angry as I was, as I sat on the bed, with a numb sensation spreading through my body, something clicked in a way it hadn't before.

I wasn't surprised. Of course I wasn't surprised. Because every decision in our marriage had been made by my husband. If I wanted to do something that he didn't agree with, he would simply change the subject, or do things the way he wanted. And I'd always accepted that.

When he was shopping for a new car for me nearly three years ago, we both knew it would be a Mercedes. Except for Robert's fancy sports cars, he didn't drive anything else. But I'd wanted the classic E-Class sedan, an updated version of the one we were turning in. Robert had insisted that I get the GL-Class this time—a sport utility vehicle. Even though I'd spoken to the salesman about the E-Class—smaller, and in my opinion, easier to manage—Robert had ignored me, telling the man that we would be leasing the GL-Class.

"Remember that fender bender you had," Robert pointed out. "You worried that you might have permanent back pain. Thank God that's not the case, but you'll be better off in an SUV."

When the salesman asked what color I wanted, my husband finally turned to me. That was when I was allowed my choice. In a detached voice, I told him that I wanted the Storm Red.

I'd gone home angry, but had reasoned my way out of the emotion. Why the hell was I angry when my husband was leasing me a brand-new luxury car? The model he'd chosen was more expensive than the one I'd wanted. Honestly, did I have a right to be angry?

That's what I'd told myself, but now I understood why it had bothered me so much at the time. It was the way Robert had made the decision for me, as though my opinion didn't matter.

As though I were his child, not his wife.

And boy, had I ever been used to excusing bad behavior when I was a child, of turning my anger inward, which resulted in my bouts of depression. I thought that Robert had offered me emotional stability and security. Instead, I was living the same kind of existence with him that I had with my parents, being controlled by him as if I were his daughter and not his wife.

It took me a full two months to feel comfortable driving the SUV. I'd told Robert before we even went to the dealership that I'd had an SUV in my twenties and was scared to drive them. I'd taken a corner too fast and the vehicle had rolled. For those couple of seconds as the SUV turned top over bottom at least twice, before stopping on the grass, I'd honestly thought my life was over. I'd promptly gotten a car with a lower center of gravity.

So while my husband thought the SUV was a safer car because I'd had a fender bender, my experience with one left me terrified.

But my fear hadn't mattered to him.

Just like my desire to have a baby didn't matter to him.

I was remembering everything now, things I had dismissed because I thought I was being ungrateful to a man who had given me so much. Robert had had to have the final say in where I set up my business. He insisted I choose a locale in downtown Charlotte. The idea was appealing, as I knew the market in Charlotte would be bigger, giving me more potential business. But I wasn't interested in a megashop where I spent practically all hours of the day working. I wanted a smaller store, one where I could offer personal service to customers. I wanted to grow my business one customer at a time.

But the big issue for me was the commute. Spending over an hour in traffic every morning and again every evening was far from ideal. I wanted a business closer to home.

Robert told me the only way I would make any serious money was to have a shop in downtown Charlotte.

As someone who'd run a successful company for forty years, he claimed he knew what he was talking about.

So I had acquiesced, deferring to his experience. I reasoned that I should have been grateful that he was willing to fund my dream in the first place.

Looking back, I realized I'd done that a lot. I expressed my opinion about something, perhaps something I wanted to do or someplace I wanted to go, but if Robert disagreed or wanted to go somewhere else, I gave in.

In my heart, I knew why: the sense of gratitude for him coming into my life and offering me a whole new world. I'm sure it's a feeling many women who marry wealthy men have. That you're never really on equal footing and don't have the right to complain.

I'd opened the shop in downtown Charlotte, but it didn't take Robert more than a few months to complain about the commute, the expense of the monthly lease versus the business I was bringing in. Then we were shopping for leases in downtown Cornelius, where I'd wanted to open Distinct Creations in the first place.

There were many, many times over the course of our marriage that I felt my view didn't matter to Robert, when it was his way or no way at all. He had this annoying habit of walking away from me in the middle of a conversation when he decided it was over. Every time, I hadn't bothered to push whatever issue I'd been discussing. Robert was the handsome older man I'd married, and I knew that many women would kill to be his wife.

The fancy cars, the fancy trips. The upscale restaurants. All the privileges that money could buy.

Well, another woman could have it.

I was done.

12

I was in no mood to go to work for the remainder of the day. Because I was going to Sharon's appointment, I'd already arranged for Spike to be at the store, along with Tabitha and Maxine. The shop was in good hands.

Our house, with its six bedrooms and five full bathrooms, was surely big enough for someone to get lost in, at least for a while. I went downstairs to the movie room and curled up on a big leather recliner.

There, in the darkness, I bawled my eyes out.

I didn't know where Robert was. If he was still upstairs. If he'd left the house. If he bothered to look for me in any of the rooms. But a few hours later, when I had to go to the bathroom, I finally left the comfort of the theater and quietly crept up the stairs.

I didn't see Olga, but I heard her humming. She was

in the kitchen cooking. A pot roast, if my sense of smell was correct.

I made my way to the upper level, then down the hall to the master bedroom. I held my breath as I opened the door, fearing I would see Robert.

He wasn't in there, and I gave a sigh of relief. I knew I would have to see him again at some point, but right now I needed my space.

I gathered my toiletries and pajamas, things I would need for the night, then crept out of the master bedroom and all the way down the hall. I was sneaking around like an unwanted houseguest.

Which was exactly how I felt. Like an unwelcome guest in a home that no longer felt like mine.

As much as I wanted to be anywhere but here right now, all I really cared about was being away from Robert. I wasn't even in the mood to face any of my friends. I still needed time to deal with what had happened—and what it meant—before I spoke to Sharon or Spike.

I chose a bedroom at the far end of the hall. Symbolically, it was as far from Robert as I could get on this floor.

Still in my clothes, I climbed into the bed. Then I lay there, staring up at the ceiling, unable to stop wondering about all that had gone wrong and how I'd gotten to this point.

Should I have known? Not necessarily that Robert would lie to me about the vasectomy, but that he would take advantage of my naïveté in some way? A few of my friends had warned me against marrying a man who had already been married and divorced, but I hadn't listened. They'd warned me that a much older, much wealthier man might end up controlling me. That for all I might gain, I might end up losing myself.

I hadn't listened, and those friends from the restaurant where I'd met Robert had slowly but surely disappeared from my life. At the time, I hadn't minded—I hadn't needed their negativity about my marriage. I'd slipped into a world that was me and Robert. A world that included evenings at the beach behind our house, sharing some wine and great conversation, and holding hands as the sun went down. A world that included lying in bed at night and reading the classics that we both enjoyed so much. Charles Dickens, James Joyce and even Jane Austen. In those quiet times together, away from Robert's hectic world, we were connected on an emotional level—the way I had always wanted to connect with someone. So what if some of my former friends had drifted away? I'd finally met my soul mate, and what was more important than that?

But the truth was, Robert was *not* my soul mate. Today I couldn't help wondering if there even was such a thing.

For some reason, I thought of the sexy stranger with the hazel eyes right at that moment. No, Robert was definitely not my soul mate. Maybe my subconscious had accepted that fact months ago, which was why I'd started having those hot sexual fantasies about a stranger. As I'd grown more and more concerned about the state of my marriage, fantasizing about the man with those alluring hazel eyes had brought me a sense of *something*.

Excitement? Relief?

Escape.

Yes, escape. An emotional escape from a marriage I had known was falling apart.

And right now, I needed him. Needed him to take me away from the pain that was overwhelming me.

I let my mind wander back to some of the fantasies I'd enjoyed recently. Remembering the one where I'd been on the love seat, my thighs spread wide with his face buried in my pussy, I felt a zap of electricity between my legs.

Suddenly, I needed a sexual release. I'm not sure why, at that moment of all moments. Something was changing inside of me. I was becoming more aware of my sexual side. Or perhaps not repressing it anymore.

In my fantasies, he had mostly pleased me. Now, I wanted to please him—if only in my mind.

I wanted to feel the kind of power that came when a woman tried to seduce a man and succeeded. The power that came when you knew the man you desired wanted you as badly as you wanted him.

I closed my eyes. Imagined my phantom lover in front of me with his pants loosened and his shirt off. I ran my hands over his torso, feeling the strong muscles there. And then I pressed my lips against his belly.

Slowly, I kissed a path downward, dragging his jeans over his hips. Then I ran my hand along the length of his cock, which was hidden by his briefs.

It was hard. Thick and long.

I wanted to taste him. I pulled his black briefs down

and his cock sprang free. And I took a moment to look at him.

He looked even more impressive than he felt. His cock was beautiful. With no foreskin, the head was exposed. It was perfectly rounded and wide.

I lowered myself to my haunches, then took his beautiful, hard penis in my hand. I pumped it with slow, steady strokes, looking up at him as I did.

His eyes had grown darker with lust. He was gazing at me with an expression of need that said I had total control of his pleasure.

I guided him to my mouth. Flicked my tongue over the engorged head. His cock throbbed, and he moaned.

I ran my tongue around the tip of his shaft in a slow, wet circle. Then I wrapped my lips around his head and sucked it like it was a giant lollipop.

My lover tangled his hands in my hair. I opened my mouth wider, drew him deeper inside. Took him to the back of my throat. Then I slid my mouth back, my lips still suctioned to his cock. When his head met my lips again, I sucked it, dipped my tongue into the groove there.

He groaned. So did I.

I took him deep into my mouth again, moving up and down his cock faster, using my hands to tease his testicles. Suddenly I was carnivorous, unable to get enough of him. I pumped his cock while I gave him head, using my teeth and tongue to drive him wild.

My pussy was throbbing. And wet. I needed him. But first, I needed to make him come in my mouth.

To know that I had the power to give him the ultimate pleasure that way.

As my mouth worked hungrily, taking him to the back of my throat, I felt his cock begin to pulse in steady, rapid movements. Then I felt warmth on the back of my tongue, tasted his essence. I gripped his thighs and sucked him, drinking every last bit of his seed while his cock convulsed in my mouth.

Then he was pulling me to him, kissing me desperately, sucking on my tongue and my lips. He squeezed my breasts with urgency. He needed me.

As much as I needed him.

"Spread your legs for me," he demanded, his voice a throaty growl.

I did, and he covered my pussy a moment later, sighing with pleasure as he trailed a finger along my opening and found me wet. He slipped a finger inside me. Then another. And another. He finger-fucked me until I was panting, devouring my lips and swallowing my sobs of pleasure.

"Fuck me," I begged him. "Fuck me!"

He lowered me onto the bed, spread my thighs and rammed his cock into me.

In my mind, he filled me with powerful, fast strokes. But it was my own hand that was playing with my pussy. I furiously massaged my clitoris, needing relief.

And then, with the image of my lover fucking me wildly, I came hard, my spine and neck arching, a crushing orgasm roaring through me. I bit back my cries of passion, wanting no one to overhear me—but almost not caring if they did.

As I lay there, my fingers between my legs, savoring every bit of my orgasm, I knew that my fantasies would not be enough.

I wanted to experience the real thing.

At some point I must have drifted off, because the sound of the bedroom door opening woke me with a start. I looked up to see Robert standing in the doorway.

"There's dinner downstairs," he announced.

"I'm not hungry."

"You need to eat."

I glanced at the digital clock beside the bed. It read 6:42 p.m. "I want to be left alone."

"Are you going to hide from me forever?"

Maybe I should have gone to my shop. At this hour, Spike, Tabitha and Maxine would have locked up for the night. I could leave now, get a head start on the work I normally did in the morning. Every day I made an assortment of arrangements that customers could walk in and buy, without having to order them in advance. Rose bouquets for anniversaries, arrangements that brightened a sick person's day. Something special for a man courting a woman.

Sighing, Robert stepped fully into the room and closed the door. Clearly, he wanted us to talk.

I stared at him, my heart pounding. I wasn't ready for the talk I wanted to have with him. I'd thought about it for hours after I'd fucked my phantom lover, could think of nothing else. It was pretty clear to me what I had to do, and I was dreading the reality of it.

I threw the covers off and sat up.

"I told Olga you weren't feeling well."

"At least that's true," I mumbled, sarcasm dripping from my voice.

"She was very concerned. She wanted to stay and take care of you tonight. I pretty much had to force her to leave, with the promise that I would call and have her come back if you wanted me to."

I said nothing.

"I'm hoping we can talk," Robert went on.

"There's really nothing to say."

"You're still angry. I understand."

I stood up, crossing my arms over my chest. "No, Robert, I don't think you do."

"I wasn't up front with you. I hurt you." He paused, stepped toward me. "I do understand. I'm sorry I didn't handle things differently."

Differently? What exactly did that mean? That he *wouldn't* have had the vasectomy? Or that he still would have had it, but been honest about it?

It didn't matter.

"I think we've said all there is to say about this." My head hurt, my pulse was racing. But I needed to go on. "If you truly realize the extent to which you hurt me, then you'll understand that you undermined our marriage. I thought we were partners, but your decision… You left me out of a decision that directly affected my life."

"A life I gave you," Robert said, with a pointed look. "Before I met you, you could never imagine living in a house like this. Traveling to the places we've traveled."

"I didn't marry you for this!" I gestured at the massive room.

"Giselle and Christine said the same thing. And yet when they left, they demanded that I pay them thousands a month."

I had heard Robert arguing often with his ex-wives, had heard him threaten to cut off support payments if he was upset with them. I had never asked him any questions about his personal affairs, feeling it wasn't my business. Now I was certain that he had tried to control them the way he had me.

"I'm not them."

Robert raised an eyebrow in challenge.

"You think all that matters to me are material things?" I asked. "I loved the Robert who courted me with gentleness and persistence. The one I would lie with in bed at night and read great literature. The one who would take time out of a business meeting to call and tell me he loved me. But you turned into someone else. You're not the man I fell in love with."

"I gave you a life better than any you could have ever imagined."

"So I have no right to be mad at you." It was a statement, not a question, because it was clear that's what Robert believed. "I have no right to want a baby." My God, I couldn't believe he could be so shallow. That he could believe since he had all the money, it meant he should have all the power in our relationship.

But more so than that, I couldn't believe *I* had

subscribed to that belief. Because I had, even if I hadn't meant to. I had lived my life as though I didn't deserve to be Robert's equal.

"I'm trying to keep things in perspective," he said, an edge to his voice.

"What perspective is that? That I have no right to expect anything in this marriage other than what *you* choose to give me?" I asked, unable to keep the anger from my voice now. I was glad Olga wasn't here to overhear what might turn into an ugly argument. "That's bullshit!"

"I didn't say that."

"But that's what you meant. And you know what's sad? In my heart I believed it, too. I always did what *you* wanted as I kept things in *perspective*. But no more, Robert. No more."

"Let's have this conversation when you're in a better mood. Perhaps in the morning."

And as Robert had done so many other times when he decided to end a discussion, he turned his back on me. He turned his back and walked out of the bedroom.

Appalled, I hustled after him and pushed in front, blocking his path. His eyes filled with surprise. "There's no other way to say this than to just say it. I'm leaving you. We have nothing left."

That got his attention. He raised an eyebrow, but then his expression turned skeptical. "You're leaving?"

"Yes." I didn't bother to give him another speech as to why. All that mattered was the bottom line. I was moving on with my life.

"Oh, Elsie." Robert actually chuckled softly. He was

being patronizing again. Treating me like a child who didn't know what she wanted.

"I'll probably go stay with a friend, but for now, I've moved into that spare bedroom."

"This is ridiculous."

"If you say so." He could think what he wanted. I wasn't going to argue with him.

"What's this really about?" Robert asked, his voice rising.

"We've discussed that."

"I don't accept it!"

I shrugged. "I don't know what you expect me to say."

"I never thought I'd see the day." Robert shook his head, his lips curling in a frown. "I never thought I'd see the day when..."

I stared up at him, waiting for him to continue, but he just kept shaking his head. He looked at me as though he couldn't have been more disappointed.

I had a pretty good idea what he was going to say, the one thing he'd thrown at me from time to time during our marriage, knowing how much it hurt. A way for him to control me, keep me in place.

"Why don't you say it? Finish your statement."

"I never thought I'd see the day when you became like your mother."

Every time I heard it, it stung. And this time was no different. But this was the first time I decided not to let the comment slide. "Thank you for giving me more reason to leave."

"Do you have a boyfriend, Elsie? Your slut mother always had someone else waiting in the wings."

"Don't you talk about my mother!" I was surprised at my words, surprised that I was in some way defending her. I'd stopped doing so after she'd taken me to Philadelphia. But I had not shared the pain of my past with Robert only for him to use it against me.

"So there is someone else."

"You're unbelievable. You actually think that your betrayal doesn't warrant me wanting to leave. That it has to be about another man."

"Do you have a boyfriend?" Robert repeated.

I didn't have a boyfriend. I had only the lover in my mind. A phantom lover who had filled a void in my life.

"No," I told my husband.

"You had to think about that one."

"I don't have a boyfriend."

"Then what's the rush? Why make the decision to end a marriage when you're angry? Take some time to think."

I had a feeling this was a fight I wouldn't win. Or at least one that Robert wouldn't give up on. And already, I was exhausted from the argument. So I told him what he wanted to hear.

"All right. I'll take some time. Evaluate my options. But I'm not going to sleep in our bedroom."

I had no intention of reevaluating my decision. My mind was already made up.

But I didn't have to go anywhere tonight, and the house was more than big enough for the both of us.

★ ★ ★

All night I tossed and turned, unable to sleep. How could I when my marriage was falling apart? I might as well get up and do something that would take my mind off my problems.

That meant heading to my shop earlier than normal.

I hadn't eaten any dinner last night, and my stomach rumbled in protest. But I'd be damned if I'd stop in the kitchen and have breakfast. The only place I wanted to be in this house was the spare bedroom, the one spot I could have any privacy.

I would pick up an egg sandwich and a coffee along the way to work. And probably by the end of the day I would call Sharon and ask if I could stay with her for the time being.

I went downstairs, hoping to make a clean getaway. But damn, no such luck.

As big as the house was, when I saw Robert sitting in the great room, it felt incredibly small.

"Shit," I muttered.

He lowered the paper he'd been reading and regarded me as I stepped onto the main level. To my surprise, he smiled.

"Good morning, darling."

Was he simply being cordial, or had he decided that our conversation last night had never happened?

"Good morning," I replied, pausing only briefly to greet him. Then I continued on to the door.

"Elsie, wait."

Cringing, I halted. Yes, Robert was still my husband,

but I wasn't up for any chitchat right now. Besides, I was fairly certain he wanted to continue to discuss the issue of our separation, and I wasn't in the mood to humor him as he tried to change my mind.

But I stopped nonetheless, waiting to hear what he had to say.

"Please, have a seat." He gestured to the spot beside him on the sofa.

"Where's Olga?" I asked.

"She's setting the table for us on the terrace. It's a beautiful morning. It'll be nice to have our breakfast out there. We don't do it often enough."

"I'm—"

"And don't say you're not hungry. You ate nothing last night."

"That's not what I was going to say. I was going to say that I plan on picking something up on the way to work."

"Please, Elsie. Won't you just sit?"

Olga appeared at the entrance to the great room then. "Good morning, ma'am," she said, acknowledging me. Her gaze went to Robert. "Sir, the table is prepared. I'm just about to bring the food out."

I gazed fondly at Olga. Leaving Robert meant I would be leaving her, too, and that reality made me sad.

She was a strong woman, and that's what I had to be now—strong. While in her thirties, Olga had suffered tragedy when she'd lost her American husband to brain cancer. A widow at that young age, she had become a housekeeper to take care of her two young daughters.

Those daughters were grown now, with one going to college. The other had just gotten married.

Olga was a sweet woman. I liked her a lot, and I hated that Robert required her to address us as "sir" and "ma'am" or "Mr." and "Mrs." I'd never liked it, and I saw it now for what it was—his way of controlling everything. Of making himself feel important.

Robert folded the front section of the paper back into place and stood. He was dressed in maroon silk pajamas and a black silk robe. "Thank you, Olga. My wife and I appreciate it. Is the coffee on the table already?"

"Yes, sir. The caramel-flavored one, just like Mrs. Kolstad prefers."

"Good, Olga." Robert looked at me. "Let's go outside now, darling."

I couldn't very well refuse, and insult Olga, as Robert was well aware. So I said, "Okay."

She slipped away quietly, and Robert and I made our way to the patio. The sun was shining, the sky clear. Our patio was situated so that it was almost completely beneath the master bedroom, so a good amount of the area was shaded by the roof above. If it was raining, we could sit out here without getting wet. If it was sunny, we could enjoy the comfortable shade. A portion of the patio extended beyond the upper level, so you could sit by the wrought-iron railing and get sun on your face.

We had a view to die for. Because our basement was actually on ground level, the patio was on the second level of our home. It overlooked our pool and a large body of water beyond—Lake Norman. The Peninsula—

the exclusive area where we lived—was highly sought after real estate because it was on the water.

"Sit," Robert instructed me.

I pulled out the plush chair and sat across the table from him. He reached for the silver coffeepot and began to pour the delicious smelling brew into my cup. He filled mine, then his own.

"It certainly is a lovely day," he commented.

I almost didn't reply. I didn't want to sit here and have a meaningless conversation.

"We should really do this more often. We have so much beauty here, and we don't take advantage of it often enough."

I reached for the sugar and cream to avoid responding to that one.

"People would kill for this home we have. We're very lucky."

Sipping my coffee, I gazed out at the view. Our house had a basketball court in addition to the pool, but what I loved most was our private stretch of beach. Beyond the trees that gave our property some privacy was a path leading to the sand. There were two chairs where we could sit and watch the sunset, and in the beginning of our marriage, we'd done that often. Just a short walk down the beach was our own dock, where Robert kept one of the toys he enjoyed—a speedboat.

The door opened and Olga approached with a large tray. There were fresh scones, cantaloupe and honeydew slices, and two large omelets.

My mouth watered and my starving stomach grumbled. Olga made the best omelets, stuffed with vegetables and cheese. They were fluffy and full and absolutely delicious.

"Thank you," I said as she placed the tray on the table. "This is wonderful."

"It looks like you've outdone yourself again," Robert added.

She set our plates on the table before us, then arranged the fruit platter and scones in the center.

"Enjoy." Olga gave a little nod and headed back into the house.

I took a fresh scone, broke it open and added butter, then popped a piece into my mouth. It was fantastic.

"I've been thinking about our discussion last night," Robert began. My eyes met his. "You say you want to have children."

"I think I've made it clear how important it is to me to have children," I quipped. My stomach lurched. My hunger turned to nausea.

Robert nodded while he ate a bite of his omelet. He moaned in pleasure. "Try yours. This might be the best one Olga has ever made."

I took a bite of the omelet, wondering why I was doing so. Robert said eat, so I obeyed. Robert said sit, so I sat. When was I going to stop letting him control everything I did?

I'm sure the omelet was fabulous, but my taste buds had gone dormant because of my anxiety. I ate a bite, but was unable to enjoy it. After I swallowed, I spoke. "I don't have much time, Robert. Why don't you make the point you want to make."

He finished chewing. "You want children. I understand that. But what if you leave me and you can't get pregnant? Won't you feel a little silly?" He raised his eyebrows as if to emphasize the reality: that I hadn't considered that possibility. "If you're set on leaving, I propose this first—let's set up an appointment with a specialist and have the required medical tests done to deem whether or not you're even fertile."

Whether or not you're even fertile... It almost sounded as if Robert hoped I wouldn't be.

"You're going on thirty-eight," he went on. "A woman of your age...it's not that easy to get pregnant."

I'd heard enough. "It's especially not easy to get pregnant when your husband has had a vasectomy." I no longer had an appetite. I pushed my chair back on the tile patio and stood. "This is about more than getting pregnant. It's about your deception."

"Sit down, Elsie."

"I have to go."

"Give it a few months. We've got Saul Bloomberg's daughter's wedding on Mother's Day."

"Which I already told you I'd be too busy to—"

"And another couple of weddings over the summer. I won't be going alone."

"Then find someone to accompany you," I snapped.

"Elsie."

I started to walk away, but as Robert called my name again, I stopped and faced him.

There was something I needed to know. Something else I was pretty sure had been deception. I walked back to the table, but didn't sit.

"Tell me something," I began. "That night I was in Charleston with Sharon—when you called me saying you were having chest pains?"

"Yes?"

"You never did go to the hospital, did you? For whatever reason, you felt threatened that I was out of town with Sharon. Maybe you thought my pregnant friend was really on the hunt for a new man—you mentioned something to that effect."

"I was kidding."

"And you were *kidding* about chest pains, weren't you? You wanted me home, so you lied."

Robert scoffed. He obviously felt I didn't deserve an answer.

"Is that a yes?"

"No, it's not a yes," Robert said indignantly. "I was having chest pains."

"And you went to the hospital and they told you it was gas pains."

"Yes."

"Just like before."

"Yes, just like before. People can suffer from gas pains more than once in a lifetime."

"How convenient," I mumbled.

"Pardon me?"

"I called every hospital in Cornelius and Charlotte. Every single one. Several times. You weren't at any of them."

"I can't control whether or not some idiot clerk couldn't find me in their system. But I was there, Elsie."

"Then why didn't you have any lactulose—that prescription medicine you got the first time? It was nowhere in the house."

"You know I hated that stuff. I refused the prescription."

He had an answer for everything. And what he'd said *could* be true. He was so smooth. He knew just how to make a person second-guess herself.

"You accuse me of being a liar? I think I'm owed an apology."

"I would apologize—if I believed you. But I don't."

Once again I turned and walked away.

"Elsie. Elsie!" Robert continued to call after me. I didn't answer.

Olga gave me a confused look as she saw me whiz through the kitchen.

"The breakfast was not good?" she asked.

"Everything was fine." I forced myself to sound cheery. "I'm running late is all."

I felt a sense of relief as I stepped out the front door. I'd made my decision and conveyed that decision to Robert twice without caving to his pressure.

I gazed up at the blue sky, let the sun's rays kiss my face.

This was a new day.

The beginning of my new life.

13

Just minutes out of my driveway, I found myself slipping on my Bluetooth earpiece and dialing a number.

"Elsie?" Sharon said.

Hearing my best friend's groggy voice on the other end of the line, I realized what I'd done. I'd called her without thinking...without considering the time.

"I'm sorry, Sharon," I said, my eyes darting to the digital clock on the dashboard. It was ten after eight. "I'll phone you back later."

"The hell you will," she said. "If you're calling me this early, something must be wrong. Besides, I can hardly sleep—the baby is doing acrobatics. I swear, I can't wait for the next few months to pass."

She was complaining like a typical pregnant woman, but I heard a smile in her voice. She would go through all the pain in the world while pregnant, if it meant she would carry this baby to term.

"So, tell me," she insisted. "What's going on?"

A beat passed as I considered exactly what to say. Then my eyes teared up and I replied, "Everything. Oh, God, Sharon—it's everything."

"Are you driving?"

"Yes. I was on my way to the shop, but I don't have to be there for another hour and a half."

"Then come here first. I'll make a pot of tea."

"Thank you, Sharon." My shoulders drooped, and I realized right then how much I needed someone to share my problems with. I couldn't do this all alone.

I needed someone to listen, to offer me tissues as I cried. Someone to pamper and coddle me. Sharon was excellent at that. A born nurturer, she'd be a fantastic mother, I knew. For her, being a good mom usurped everything else. And she was the same way when it came to being a good friend.

I didn't know where my own mother was. Perhaps still in Cleveland, Ohio. I'd heard that she'd moved back there once I'd left Philadelphia. Or maybe she was in Seattle, where she had some family. Hell, she could be in Timbuktu.

Wherever she was, she was probably still living the same life she always had. Filling the void in her life with a string of men. Still not interested in a relationship with the child she'd brought into the world.

I take some of the blame for that. When I moved to North Carolina with my friend Treasure, I'd put distance between me and my mom. I'd needed to for my sanity. I'd gotten therapy, tried to understand why she had never truly been there for me, and attempted to deal with the pain. Then I'd reached out to her—first by letter, then by phone when there was no reply to my letter.

She'd angrily told me that I'd made my choice and had nothing more to say to me. A week later she had called me, crying, telling me to go on with my life and forget her, that I was better off without her.

The next time I'd tried to reach her, her phone had been disconnected.

My therapist had said that my mother likely needed to deal with her own personal demons before she would be ready to reach out to me. Of course, I'd been devastated. As much as I'd resented her for hurting my father, she was still my mom.

A mother who was hurting me with her neglect.

But that was something she had always done, a fact I had to accept. Eventually, I also had to accept that I was probably better off without her in my life.

I had vowed to be a different kind of mother, one who would play at the park with her kids and color with them and read to them at bedtime. One who would be faithful to their father and never do anything to make her children feel neglected or unloved.

The kind of mother Sharon would be.

Sharon lived only five minutes from my house, also on the lake. Her place was large as well, but at approximately five thousand square feet, it was half the size of mine.

But still big enough for both of us.

As I was pulling into her driveway, I saw her peering out the living room window, awaiting my arrival. She moved the moment she saw my car, and by the time I reached her door, she was swinging it open.

As I looked at her beautiful face and the small bump growing beneath her robe, I thought again about the tragedy she'd endured. About how she had lost a husband, and yet was still strong. For the most part she compartmentalized her heartache, wanting to do everything in her power to keep from affecting the baby with her sadness.

I was about to lose a husband, and it was unlikely I'd ever get pregnant.

I burst into tears.

"Oh, Elsie." Sharon put her arms around me and hugged me. "Whatever it is, you're gonna be okay."

From her, those weren't just words. She was a testimony to triumph after adversity.

"I want to believe you, Sharon. But…"

She released me and closed the door. "Let's go to the kitchen. The tea's ready."

I followed her there, noting how she rested a hand on her belly. She would walk through fire to deliver that baby when he was due.

I would do the same—if I ever got the chance.

But because of Robert's lies, I might never know that joy. That kind of enduring, unconditional love.

It was something I'd never experienced from my own mother. Maybe that's why I was so desperate to have my own child—to in some way correct the wrongs I'd suffered in my youth.

In the kitchen, Sharon went to the marble counter and lifted the tray with the teapot and cups.

"I can get it, Sharon," I protested.

"I'm pregnant, Elsie. Not disabled. You sit."

She brought the tray to the table, then immediately poured me a cup. She added milk, no sugar, knowing exactly how I liked my tea. The moment she handed me the cup, I took a sip. And then I started to cry again.

Sharon sat down beside me. "I've never seen you this devastated. Is Robert ill?"

"Robert is a liar and my marriage is over." The words tumbled from my lips.

"What?" Her eyes widened. "What did he do?"

So I told her. Told her everything. Even how he'd likely lied about having chest pains the night we'd been in Charleston.

"Oh, my God. A vasectomy? I can't believe it." She shook her head.

"I feel so stupid."

"No. No, sweetie. Don't say that. You trusted your husband. That's exactly what you were supposed to do."

"But how could I have missed the signs that he was lying?"

"How were you supposed to know?" Sharon countered. "Short of hooking him up to a lie detector..."

That made me smile through my tears.

"If I've learned anything, it's that you think you know a person, but some people you never can know," she mused. "They put on a certain face to the world, present themselves one way, but in their hearts they're nothing like that."

"Are you talking about Felicity and Carmen?" I asked.

"Among other people, I suppose. Only a handful of individuals who used to associate with me even bother now."

"So, you still haven't seen or heard from Carmen or Felicity?"

Sharon shot me an ironic look.

"Not even a…a card in the mail?"

The look intensified. But there was no bitterness there, nothing at all.

"I don't understand," I said. "You knew them longer than I did. They're not the warmest people in the world, perhaps, but doesn't it bother you that in your darkest hour, they've dropped you?"

"It's in your darkest hour that you discover who your true friends are. You were there for me, and I'm here for you."

She gave me a look ripe with meaning, and I smiled in appreciation.

"Now, what are you going to do?"

"I'm done." I didn't hesitate before saying the words. Didn't have to ponder the question. "I'm leaving him. Maybe you'll say this is a knee-jerk reaction, but—"

"I'm not saying anything. I'm listening and supporting. That's what friends do."

"Thank you."

"And to be honest, I'm not surprised."

"What do you mean?" I asked.

"It wasn't something I could put my finger on in the beginning, but it always seemed...kind of like I was only seeing part of you when you and Robert were together. Whereas at the shop, you were a different person. When we were out together, you were different. Happier. Full of life. But with Robert, that wasn't the case. You exuded a different kind of energy when you were with him. Kind of like you were a meeker, weaker person. I don't know."

My eyes widened in shock as I regarded my friend. "You never said anything."

"Because it wasn't my place. Did I think you would thrive without him? I'll admit I did, yeah. But if you were going to leave Robert, it had to be because you came to that decision on your own, not because I encouraged you to get there."

I nodded. I understood. If Sharon had ever expressed any doubts about my marriage, it might have affected our friendship. And she was right—I needed to get to this point without help from anyone else.

"For now, I've moved into another bedroom," I explained. "But I think I need to move out. It will be too hard to stay there."

"Lucky for you, you can have your pick of spare bedrooms here," she said, smiling softly.

"Oh, Sharon." I knew she would offer, and I'd planned to ask, but I still didn't want to impose. "What if I'm such a downer I depress you?"

"Nonsense. We're here for each other, right? We're both going through...challenging times. I'm living in this big house all by myself. Trust me, it'll be nice to have the company."

I knew she was right. Rather than imposing, I would be company for her, and she for me.

"And I can help you when the baby comes," I said.

"See—it's perfect."

I was feeling better when I left Sharon's, but that happy feeling didn't last very long. The moment I pulled up in front of Distinct Creations, my stomach twisted into a knot. Seeing my floral shop reminded me that I just might lose what had been a dream come true, if Robert decided to take it from me in the divorce.

His money had allowed me to open the store, and I dreaded the idea of losing it. Especially to a man who would most likely sell it, possibly just to spite me.

I put that thought out of my mind as I entered, and instead concentrated on getting to work. The Mother's Day weekend was approaching, one of the busiest times of the year for a florist.

I'd arrived later than I'd planned, after spending a good hour talking with Sharon. So I was surprised that Spike wasn't there yet. At ten minutes to ten, he was clearly running late, too.

I quickly got to work, checking the logbook for orders that were due to be picked up, and making sure they were all in the fridge. When the door chimes sounded several minutes later, I expected it to be him.

"I'm back here, Spike. Will you turn the Open sign on?" I had a neon sign in the window that indicated to the world the shop was open. And it had to be ten already.

"Actually, I'm here to place an order."

The sound of the deep voice, so clearly not Spike's, had me whirling around and throwing a hand to my chest.

My heart nearly imploded when I saw that I was staring at the hazel eyes I had seen so many times in my fantasies.

Oh, shit.

"I'm sorry," the man said. He wasn't an apparition. "I didn't mean to startle you."

"Uh…" My breathing had gone from normal to heavy in an instant. "I'm sorry. I thought you were someone else."

"You *are* open, right?" He glanced at his watch. "It's ten. A minute after, actually."

"Yes. Yes, I'm open." I wiped my suddenly damp palms on my black slacks. "How may I help you?"

The stranger smiled. The kind of smile that was warm and sexy all in one. He wasn't the same man he'd been that day in February. The worry in his eyes was gone, the burden lifted from his shoulders.

And he was here. Today of all days.

It's fate, I thought, and believed it.

"It's Mother's Day on Sunday," the man said. "My mother just conquered breast cancer."

"Oh, that's wonderful."

"Yeah. Yeah, it is. Officially, she's in remission, but we're hoping for the best. I'd like to order her something spectacular. Something that shows how happy I am that she won the fight, and how proud I am that she's my mother."

His words touched me. Almost made me cry. I was thinking about my own mom, how she hadn't inspired that kind of pride.

"Aren't you the thoughtful son," I said.

"I've only got one mother. And she means the world to me."

"As she should." I smiled. He smiled.

Were we flirting?

The door chimes sang, and in rushed Spike. "Sorry," he mumbled. He carried a tray with two large coffees.

I hardly cared that he was late. My phantom lover was standing right in front of me, and he still made my pulse race.

The timing…this wasn't an accident.

"So," I said, and took a deep breath. "How spectacular is your budget?"

"My budget is limitless. Within reason," he added.

That smile again. And this time I knew. It wasn't a casual I'm-being-nice smile.

It was a smile just for me.

My stomach fluttered. And I found myself doing something that surprised me: easing my left hand behind my back so that I could hide my wedding bands. Wedding bands I had forgotten to take off.

Was I interested, or just interested in flirting?

Hell, yeah, I was interested. I wanted to experience the reality of what it was like to feel this man's hands and mouth on my breasts and my pussy. Would it be as amazing as in my fantasies?

"Miss?" he prompted.

I jerked my gaze to his, feeling my cheeks flush. "I'll come up with something special," I told him. "Do you want flowers only, or a foil balloon added to the arrangement? And I assume you want big."

"Whatever you think is best. Big, definitely. As to what kind of flowers and all that, I leave it in your hands."

I was already picturing something with pink roses. Pink was the color associated with the fight against breast cancer. A stunning arrangement full of pink roses, maybe with some pink Peruvian lilies, and some colorful mokara orchids. A crystal vase as opposed to a basket.

"Does she like chocolate?" I asked. "I could add a small box of Godiva chocolates. Nothing that would ruin any particular diet she might be on."

"My mother will love the chocolates. And she'd be the first to tell you to make it a big box."

"All right, then." I angled my head and smiled coyly. My left hand remained behind my back. "You won't be disappointed."

Goodness gracious. I *was* flirting.

Maybe it was just a way to keep my mind off my problems. Whatever it was, it felt good.

No, that wasn't it. I had already fucked this man in my mind. More than once. My body was tingling with desire—a reaction I didn't understand, because I'd never experienced it before. But I wanted to make my fantasies a reality.

I was driven, for the first time in my life, by carnal need.

I didn't think, *no, it's too soon to think about really fucking him.* I didn't think, *How could you even consider something like that?*

Because let's face it—I had had thought these thoughts for over three months now.

But he was here about business, and fantasies aside, I had to keep that in perspective. So I glanced away. Took a break from his hypnotic gaze.

After a moment, I faced him again. "I know you said money isn't an object, but give me a cap."

The man pursed his lips and looked upward as he thought about his answer. My own eyes went to the vee of his neck, and lower—to the section of his chest that was evident beneath his partially unbuttoned dress shirt.

I had a wicked image of me trailing my tongue across his skin….

"Can I get something spectacular for two hundred?"

I jerked my gaze to the left, hoping to hell he hadn't caught me checking him out. "Absolutely." My God, I felt flushed. "Two hundred will buy you way more than spectacular. Not that it'll cost that much, but at least I know what your budget is."

"When will it be ready?"

"When do you want to pick it up?"

"Sunday is fine. Oh, wait. Your sign said you're closed on Sundays."

"Because it's Mother's Day, I'm making an exception. I'll be here from ten until two."

"Is noon a good time to come by?"

"No problem."

Again he stared at me, and I at him—as though we both wanted to say something else. Something that had nothing to do with business.

He finally broke the silence. "I'm Dion."

He extended his right hand, and I grasped it. An electrical charge shot up my arm. "I'm Elsie."

"I came in before," Dion said. "A few months ago."

"I remember you," I told him—as if I hadn't imagined his mouth and hands all over my body since that meeting. I released his palm, which I'd held just a little too long.

"My mother was in the hospital then, and I...I didn't know how it was going to go. I was kind of a mess that day I came in here."

"That's understandable. I can only imagine how stressful that was."

"But those dark days are over."

I wondered if he would have come back before—if not for what his mother was going through. If he had felt the same inexplicable connection I had.

"So do you want me to pay now?"

"A deposit, yes. And let me take down your number. A way to reach you if by any chance you don't show up."

"Oh, I'll be back."

My heart pounded a little harder. Was I reading into it, or was there another meaning to his words than the obvious?

"Well." I cleared my throat. "If you'll come to the counter, I can take your deposit, and your information."

I noticed Spike was regarding me curiously. I ignored him as I opened the order book to write down Dion's name and phone number.

"If you want, I can add you to our mailing list," I said. "Send you news of specials and such."

Behind him, I saw Spike playfully roll his eyes.

"Why not?" Dion said.

"In that case, why don't you fill out this card." I handed him a blank address form and a pen. "Later, I'll add you to my mailing list."

"Sounds good."

While he filled out the card, I caught Spike making suggestive expressions in the background. I didn't know if he was simply checking Dion out, or teasing me for my flirtation.

When Dion passed me the completed address card, I handed him a business card. "So I'll see you Sunday at noon?"

He took the card and looked at it briefly before meeting my gaze again. "Thank you, Elsie. I'll see you Sunday at noon."

14

I didn't realize that I was standing motionless, watching Dion walk away, until Spike came up beside me.

"Mmm–mmm–mmm. That is one sexy man."

I turned to gaze at him, giving him a lopsided grin. "He's straight, Spike."

"Oh, I know that, honey. He was looking you up and down like you were a hot, buttered biscuit." Spike raised his eyebrows. Gave me that curious look again.

"What?" I asked, feeling as though he could see right through me.

"Other than the fact that there's something you're not telling me?"

Spike, like Sharon, was one of my best friends. The kind I could trust completely. I'd met him when he'd come into my shop looking for a job, shortly after I'd opened the new location in Cornelius. Despite having no experience in the field, he'd seen my Help Wanted sign in the window and had been willing to learn. And more importantly, he'd been desperate for a job. Marcus, his partner of two years, had kicked him out of *his* house, leaving Spike destitute. Knowing a thing or two about what it was like to need a break, I'd hired him on the spot.

Over the course of the last five years, he'd become one of my closest friends. The kind you couldn't keep anything from.

"You know me too well," I said in response to his comment.

"Well?" He planted his hands on his hips as he stared at me. "Are you gonna tell me?"

The buzz I'd felt at seeing Dion again faded as grim reality came to the forefront of my mind. Sighing, I said, "I'm leaving Robert."

I steeled myself, waited for Spike to say, "What took you so damn long?" But instead he put a hand on my back and asked, "How are you feeling, doll-face?"

My shoulders sagged, as if the weight of the world had just been lifted from them. "I...I don't know."

"You know I never felt Robert was right for you," Spike said gently. "But this can't have been an easy decision."

He had never made his feelings about my marriage a secret. He'd never expressed anything negative about Robert as a person, but he did feel that my husband was too old for me, and that someone my age didn't realistically have a future with a man who was nearly seventy. I'd respected his honesty. I knew other people in my circle held that same view, but would never dare express their true opinion.

But given Sharon's comment earlier, that she thought I was a different person when Robert was around, I wondered if there was more to Spike's opinion about my marriage other than the age factor.

He squeezed my hand. "It's for the best."

"Why do you say that?"

"You know I always thought Robert was too old for you. He's in the winter of his life, while you're still enjoying the summer. At least you should be." He gave me a pointed look. "And this whole talk about you wanting a baby... I just don't see you having a child with a man who's already raised his children and is now enjoying grandkids."

I opened my mouth, but Spike shot a finger up, silencing me before I could speak.

"But the real reason I knew this day would come has nothing to do with children. You wouldn't be the first person to have a baby with an old man. It might not be ideal, but it wouldn't be the end of the world."

"Let's hear your insight."

"Deep inside you, I know there's a vibrant and exciting person. But I think being with Robert has killed that individual."

"I'm not vibrant and exciting?" I said the words with a smile.

"You were vibrant while you were flirting with that hottie."

"You thought I was flirting?" I asked sheepishly.

"Girl, please. You know you were flirting. And guess what? I approve."

"He's very cute."

"That he is."

Again, I thought about the timing of Dion's return to my store. I didn't typically believe in fate, but in this case, I felt it was at play.

"You don't even know what Robert did," I said, getting back to the unpleasant topic of my husband. "He lied to me, Spike. All this time I've been trying to get pregnant and he…he had a vasectomy," I finished painfully.

"Oh. My. God."

"Yeah." I sniffled, feeling a wave of emotion.

"Oh, baby." Spike put his arms around me and gave me a warm hug. "I'm so sorry."

I pulled out of Spike's embrace and reached for some tissue. "I knew something was wrong. Something was off between us. But I never expected that."

"I've heard some devious things in my time, but that's just wrong. That's evil."

Dabbing at my eyes, I nodded. "So here I am. About to start over."

"But you'll be okay," Spike told me. "I already saw a different you when you were flirting. A spark I can't say I've seen before. That's what I meant when I said I know there's a vibrant and exciting person inside you waiting to come out. Someone you can't be with Robert."

"Meaning?"

"All I ever hear you say when you're with him is 'Yes, dear. No, dear. Sure, Robert.' When you're with him, *you* are lost." He gestured to my face and upper body, talking with his hands, as he often did. "It's like you're this beautiful butterfly who doesn't know how to fly. Or a bird that's had her wings clipped."

I clasped my fingers together and held them in front of my face.

"Was that harsh, doll-face? I'm sorry."

"No." I shook my head. "Sharon pretty much said the same thing. Almost verbatim."

Spike shrugged, as if to say he wasn't surprised.

"Then I'll ask you what I asked Sharon. Why did you never mention this before?"

"Girl, part of being smart is knowing when to bite your tongue. You think I wanted you going home to Robert, sharing my thoughts with him? Or throwing out my observations when you two were having a dis-agreement? Whatever decision you were going to come to, you needed to come to on your own."

Exactly what Sharon had said.

Spike started toward the fridges. "Besides, Robert isn't a man you want on your bad side."

"Wait a minute." I followed him. "Why would you say that?"

Spike opened a fridge door. "He's rich. He's powerful. He ran a successful Fortune 500 company. He was used to telling people what to do. Used to getting his own way. Probably had to be a little ruthless in the board-room. You think I wanted him hearing I was saying he wasn't the man for you? He'd probably force you to get rid of me. And you know this job means the world to me."

"As if I'd ever get rid of you. Robert has no say over the running of this store. Sure, he bought it for me, but he stays out of the day-to-day operations."

"That's gonna change." Spike turned back to the fridge.

I placed a hand on his arm, and he once again met my gaze. "What do you mean?"

"Because Robert's used to being ruthless, used to being in control," he said, echoing his earlier comments. "He's not going to be happy that you're leaving him."

"He's been through two divorces already."

"And he hates his exes. You've told me that."

It was true. Robert had nothing good to say about his ex-wives. He maintained some civility with them because of the children they shared, but if he never had to see them again, it would be too soon.

"He can hate me if he wants," I said. "I hate him for what he did to me."

"In all seriousness, talk to a lawyer right away. You married into his fortune. I wouldn't put it past him to take it all away from you."

"I don't want it."

"You say that now. But you're going to need to live. And you're entitled to something."

"All I want is this store." Spike made a face. "And I suppose that some support would be in order. But I'm not going to go crazy and ask for thousands a month, or a multimillion-dollar settlement."

"I'm going to pretend you didn't just say that. Robert's going to be looking out for number one, and you need to do that, too. Take it from me. I know how vindictive a person can get when a relationship ends. What Marcus did to me…the way he threw me out of his place and left me without a penny… And I had no legal recourse."

He'd had no legal recourse because he'd been in a same-sex relationship in a highly conservative state.

"I know Robert will be hurt, possibly angry, that I'm leaving him. But I was his wife for nearly a decade. Even if he did try to completely screw me over the way Marcus did you, the law wouldn't allow it."

Spike's expression said he knew better. "Talk to a lawyer, doll-face. And get ready for a battle. Because when two people split, it's often war."

15

Shortly after two o'clock, I left Spike, Tabitha and Maxine at the store and went out for lunch. I wanted some time alone and wasn't interested in any chitchat. I drove to a pita shop about ten minutes away, picked up a chicken pita and ate it in my SUV at the back of the parking lot.

My thoughts were on Dion. I wanted to get to know him. Whether that would land us in bed or in a relationship, time would tell. All I knew right now was that I wanted to experience with him in real life all that I had experienced with him in my dreams.

I thought of the electrical charge I'd felt this morning when he'd shaken my hand. Of the way his eyes had heated my body.

And suddenly I was aroused. What was it about this

man that had me thinking about hot sex every time he entered my mind?

I wasn't this woman. This woman I was becoming who was driven by sexual needs.

At least I hadn't been.

But I was enjoying the feelings this man was bringing out in me—and I barely knew him.

Right there at the back of the parking lot, out of view of anyone, I eased my skirt up and slipped my hand into my panties. I stroked my clit. Up and down. Up and down. And imagined Dion's tongue flicking over my nipple. Imagined his teeth grazing my breast. Imagined him pushing his fingers deep into my pussy.

Heat enveloped my body. I was wet, my breathing shallow. I wanted to come. Needed to come. I thought about my legs spread wide, exposing my pussy to Dion. I thought of him suckling my clit so damn sweetly. Thought of him spreading my folds and thrusting his tongue deep inside me.

He ate me like a man starved, groaning lustfully as he drank my nectar. His fingers and his tongue stroked me, heated me, fulfilled me in a way that made me absolutely crazy.

The pressure built inside me, a rising crescendo. And as I thought of those hazel eyes staring deeply into mine from between my legs, I came.

For several seconds I sat still in my car, my hand between my legs as I rode the wave of my orgasm. Panting, I glanced around, saw that no one was around me. Even if there was someone, they wouldn't be able to see what I'd been doing behind tinted windows.

But *I* knew what I'd been doing—something I had never done before. Something I never would have imagined doing, in my wildest dreams.

Was I losing my mind?

I should have been embarrassed, felt some level of shame. But I didn't. Because I was discovering a part of myself I had repressed for far too long.

And I was liking it.

I went back home after work to get some clothes. Robert wasn't there, which was a huge relief. I didn't want to run into him. If I could move on with my life and never see him again, I would be only too happy.

I threw myself into work for the rest of the week, putting particular attention into the arrangement for Dion's mother. Thinking about seeing him on Sunday gave me something positive to look forward to. When the reality of my life crept into my brain in the middle of the night, I thought about Dion.

Nights were quiet time. And in quiet times, I couldn't block out my reality with work.

The same was true on Saturday night.

I lay awake in Sharon's spare bedroom, thinking again about the nights I'd slept in Robert's bed. So often, he would sleep with his back to me. There was something symbolic about that. Something I should have realized at the time, but didn't.

Did Robert ever love me? Or was I simply a young, beautiful wife he could be proud to have on his arm? One he had recognized was broken enough that he would be able to control her?

I didn't want to think about the answer to that question. I didn't want to believe that my whole life with him had been a lie.

Dion wouldn't be the kind of guy to lie in bed with his wife and sleep with his back to her, I thought.

What was it about Dion that so intrigued me? He was a stranger, and yet there was something about him that spoke to me, though I wasn't sure what. A primal need? Something else?

I slipped my hand beneath the waist of my pajamas. Pushed it lower, to my center. Let my fingers gently rest on my pussy. Almost every time I thought of Dion, I felt a rise of desire.

I swirled my middle finger lazily around my clitoris from outside the lace, stoking the embers of my desire. Making myself wet.

But this time after I came, there was a sense of emptiness. As much as I enjoyed fantasizing about Dion, my fantasies were no longer enough.

I wanted the real thing.

Eleven fifty-three.

I glanced at the clock for the gazillionth time that morning. Even though Dion had said he'd be coming at noon, each time the door chimes sang, I looked up in anticipation.

But now the time was getting close, and my heart was on overdrive as I waited for him to appear.

The door chimes sang again. Butterflies danced in my stomach as I hurried from the fridge area toward the front of the store. Tabitha was walking toward me, no doubt about to pick up an arrangement from the fridge for another customer.

"Maxine's not back yet?" I asked.

"No. She has been gone awhile, hasn't she?"

Since the shop was normally closed on Sundays, except for special occasions like Mother's Day, my deliveryman had the day off. Maxine was playing the role of driver with the company van today, for the one delivery I had scheduled, for a Jewish wedding.

"She's probably helping the family set up the flowers in the synagogue," I commented, certain that was the case.

I went to the door, hoping to see Dion. Disappointment hit me like a punch in the chest when I saw one of my other customers there.

"Good morning, Brad," I said warmly. He was a real estate agent who gave me a lot of business. Whenever his clients purchased a home, he had a floral arrangement delivered to the house as a personal touch.

He was also gay, and I always thought he'd be a good match for Spike. If Spike would ever dare give his heart to another man.

"Morning, Elsie."

"I'll get your flowers."

I went to the fridge and withdrew the festive bouquet Spike had made. The yellow daisies, red carnations and pink asters were radiant in a gold-colored basket. I'd had Spike make one for Sharon, too, which I would surprise her with later.

She was almost a mother, and I wanted to celebrate that.

"Lovely," Brad said as I carried the bouquet to the front of the store. "My mother will be very happy."

"I'm sure she will be." The bouquet was wrapped in cellophane. It made it easier to carry to the car, and minimized any damage during transport. "And you've already paid for your order in full, so you're good to go." I handed Brad the bouquet.

"Thank you, Elsie. You outdid yourself."

I was tempted to tell him that Spike was behind the magnificent creation, but refrained. There was no point trying to play matchmaker until Spike was ready to let his guard down.

So I simply said, "You're welcome." And then, "I'll get the door for you."

I stepped ahead of Brad to the door. It opened before I could get there.

And in he walked.

Dion.

My heart slammed against my rib cage. I stood, pretty much dumbfounded, my eyes drinking in the sexy sight of him.

Dion held the door open, and Brad exited. "Thanks again, Elsie," he called over his shoulder.

Dion let the door swing shut. And then he faced me, his striking hazel eyes locking on mine.

You are entirely too sexy, I couldn't help thinking. *So damn delicious...*

"Hello, Elsie."

"Afternoon." I hoped my thoughts weren't evident on my face. Then again, maybe that was exactly what

I wanted. I wanted Dion to know how much I desired him.

"How are you?" I asked.

"I'm good, thanks. You?"

"Good," I replied, nodding. A few moments of silence ensued, and I tucked a strand of hair behind my ear.

"I suppose the bouquet for my mother is ready?" he asked at last.

"It is." Goodness, why couldn't I think of anything intelligent to say? "Let me go back and get it."

I went to the fridge and held the door open with my hip. "It's rather large," I called out as I gingerly lifted the vase. "I hope you like it."

The bouquet was large and blocked my view, so I had to angle my head to the side as I carried it to the front of the store.

"Wow." Dion's face lit up as he saw it. "That's huge."

"It's one of the best I've ever made," I said proudly as I gently set it on the front counter. And it was. I'd placed each blossom with care. "I figured it was fitting to create an arrangement with pink roses and lilies, adding a splash of color with mokara orchids. They're the ones shaped like starfish. Yellow and orange and bright, warm tones that signify the bright days to come."

"That's nice. You put a lot of thought into it. I appreciate that."

"The story you told me about your mother was inspiring. I wanted to create a bouquet that celebrated that story."

"Thank you."

"I decided against the balloons, at least as part of the arrangement. It wouldn't look right. But I have an array right here." I indicated the various helium balloons that were prearranged for Mother's Day.

"This is nice." Dion pointed to a large metallic one with Happy Mother's Day written on it in a cursive font. Pink and gold latex balloons filled out the tall arrangement. "I'll take this as well."

"Everything's wrapped in cellophane to keep it in place, but you can see the Godiva chocolates in front." I pointed to the box, which I'd wrapped in gold foil and tied with an elegant cream-colored ribbon.

"I can't thank you enough," Dion said. "How much do I owe you?"

I added the balloon cluster to the tally, and gave Dion the total price. He passed me two one-hundred-dollar bills.

"Keep the change," he told me.

"But that's over a thirty-dollar tip."

"No other florist would have gone to the lengths you did to make this bouquet so personal and meaningful."

I was humbled, and touched. "I'm glad you like it."

"Let me take the flowers to the car," Dion said. "Then I'll come back for the balloons."

"I'll get the door for you." I hustled past him.

As Dion went outside, I headed back to the counter. It wasn't a windy day, but I wrapped the balloons in a bag nonetheless to protect them.

He came back inside just as I finished securing the arrangement. "And here you go," I told him.

"I can't thank you enough, Elsie."

"It was my pleasure."

A few beats passed, and I grinned at him for lack of anything better to do. I wanted to tell him that I would love to see him again, but I couldn't find the courage. It was one thing to be bold with him in my mind, but being bold in real life was another thing altogether.

Dion went to the door, and I watched him leave. He made his way to a white Buick Enclave, opened the back door and put the balloon bouquet inside.

I watched. Waited for him to look back.

But he didn't. He opened the front door and got into the car.

My happiness dissolved, just like that. My stomach twisted, and I felt sick with disappointment.

What had I been expecting? For him to sweep me into his arms and kiss me?

I returned to the counter, sighing as I did. I'd been so looking forward to seeing him again. He'd represented hope for me, I guess. Hope that was now deflated.

Trying to hide my emotions from Tabitha, I looked down at my order book and put check marks beside Brad's and Dion's names.

The door chimes sounded. I whipped my head up as Maxine rushed in.

"God, talk about a nightmare." She ran her hands through her layered blond hair. "The traffic to Charlotte was brutal, even on a Sunday."

"Charlotte?" I said, certain Maxine had misspoken.

"Why didn't you tell me that the location for the delivery had changed? I was a good five minutes in the wrong direction when I got the call from the bride's father."

"Bride's father?" Now I was alarmed. "No one told me there was a change in location." I frowned. "Mr. Bloomberg signed for the delivery?"

"Actually…"

"Actually what?"

"Mr. Bloomberg said the family was going to be late getting to the synagogue, but to leave the flowers."

"Someone had to have signed for the delivery," I said. "That's company policy."

"Someone did sign, but…but now that I think of it, he seemed a bit confused."

"What does that mean?" Sensing a major problem now, I was getting anxious.

"He was…a janitor, I think. I told him about the wedding, and he seemed not to know what I was talking about. But he signed for the delivery, anyway."

"Oh, fuck," I muttered. *Robert.*

"Elsie?" Maxine said, but I was already heading to the phone.

I called Mr. Bloomberg, who said he was just about to phone me. He wondered why the delivery hadn't yet arrived.

I hung up, cursing. "There was no change in location," I said to Maxine.

"What? But the father called! I was driving, and he phoned the company cell. He said he was sorry for the mix-up and last minute change, and gave me the new address and everything!"

"Well, the Bloombergs are at the synagogue in

Cornelius, wondering where the flowers are. You need to head back to Charlotte immediately and pick up the arrangements. You've got about an hour and a half before the wedding starts. Damn it!"

Maxine jumped.

"Now," I snapped, though I wasn't angry with her.

I was pissed with Robert. *He* was behind this.

He knew Judge Bloomberg. Was going to his daughter's wedding. He'd left me a message last night pleading with me to go with him. I hadn't responded.

Robert would know to call and screw with this order.

A big order.

He did it to get back at me. To punish me for not going to the wedding with him.

The bastard must have been waiting outside the shop until he saw us loading up the van. Then he'd called Maxine, shortly after she'd set off.

She hustled out the door now, nearly bumping into a customer.

In my frustrated state, I didn't immediately see who it was. But a moment later, the fact that it was Dion registered.

And just like that, despite my stress over the botched flower delivery, my hope was restored.

"Everything okay with the bouquet?"

"I've been trying to talk myself out of doing this," Dion said as he walked toward me. "I guess because I figure you're probably involved with someone. But even as I drove away, I knew I had to come back and ask you." He paused. Drew in an audible breath. "I'm wondering if you'd like to have—"

"Yes," I interjected.

He chuckled. "I didn't finish my question."

"It's still yes." Now I giggled. And I could feel that vibrancy Spike was talking about. I could feel myself morphing into a different person.

I wasn't going to let Robert get to me with his childish antics. I wasn't going back to him no matter what he did.

"So you'll have dinner with me?"

"I'm free tomorrow night."

Dion smiled, seeming pleasantly surprised by my boldness. "Tomorrow night works for me. Any particular time?"

"Seven's fine. Is that good for you?"

"That's good for me."

God, I wanted to kiss him. I really did. I wanted to feel those thick lips of his molded to mine. I wanted to feel his muscular arms wrapped about my body.

His cock in my pussy…

"Shall I pick you up?" Dion asked. "Or do you want to meet me somewhere?"

I had to swallow away the sinful image before I could speak. "Why don't you meet me right here?" I suggested.

"All right, Elsie. It's a date."

I liked the way he said my name. How it sounded in his deep baritone.

This time, as Dion walked away, he glanced back. Glanced back and waved.

I followed him with my eyes as he passed the front window. When he was almost out of sight, he looked inside, caught my gaze and smiled.

Giggling, I waved.

I couldn't wait for tomorrow.

16

I was bubbling with giddiness for the rest of the day. Sharon noticed the change in me, even though I tried to keep my mood under control.

"What is going on with you?" she asked. "You haven't stopped smiling since you got here."

"I'm happy for you. This time next year, you're going to have a beautiful baby in your arms."

"I know." Sharon rubbed a hand over her belly. "But that's not why you're wearing a permanent smile."

"Okay, I'll tell you. I have a date."

"A what?"

"A date. And I can't say I've ever felt like this. Totally bubbly and excited and hopeful."

"Who is he?"

"A definite hottie. Muscular and strong. I'd guess mid to late thirties."

"My God, you're smitten," Sharon said in a singsong voice.

"To tell the truth, I've been thinking about him for a few months."

Her eyebrows shot up. "Huh?"

I explained what I meant. That I'd first seen Dion in February and hadn't been able to stop thinking about him since. How I'd even fantasized about him.

"I'm shocked," Sharon admitted.

"In a good way or a bad way?"

"I'm happy for you. If he ends up as just a friend, fine. If he's a fling, you deserve it. If it ends up being more…"

"One day at a time."

My cell phone rang. I knew before looking at the screen that it would be Robert. I made a face.

"Robert?" Sharon asked.

"He's called a few times today."

"That's to be expected. Maybe he's ready to apologize."

I guffawed. "Apologize? Let me tell you the stunt he pulled."

"What stunt?"

"He messed with my business. No doubt trying to ruin my reputation." Thank God Maxine had been able to make it to the appropriate location in the nick of time. I'd apologized profusely to the Bloombergs and even offered to refund ten percent of their purchase. "Girl, it's a doozy of a story."

"Tell me, already."

So I did.

★ ★ ★

At six forty-five the next evening, I was in my bathroom at the shop, getting ready. I closed at six-thirty,
and Spike was taking care of end-of-day business while
I was taking care of prettying myself.

I had no clue where Dion was taking me, but I was
dressed to kill. Deciding to go for sexy and seductive, I
was wearing the black dress with the plunging neckline
that Robert hadn't approved of, this time minus the
shawl. I was betting that Dion would like it.

I'd also flat-ironed my hair, just as I had that disas-
trous evening at The Melting Pot. Maybe I was subcon-
sciously replaying that evening, knowing I was about
to rewrite the ending with one far more favorable.

"Oh, my Lord." Spike's eyes widened and his mouth
fell open when he saw me. "Okay, what did you do with
Elsie Kolstad?"

"Elsie Kolstad is gone," I announced. "I'm Elsie
Campbell."

"Already using your maiden name. Doll-face, you are
a different person."

"I am," I agreed. "I'm leaving the person I was with
Robert behind."

Spike's eyes roamed my body from head to toe. "Love
the hair. It's nice to see you with it down and straight, as
opposed to tied back or curled like a little grandma."

"Ouch."

"It's a compliment. Take it."

"All right."

"Do a twirl," Spike told me. I did, and he whistled.
"You are sex on a stick."

"Too much?"

"Hell, no." He grinned devilishly.

I returned his smile. I wasn't trying for demure. I knew where I wanted this night to lead, and if this dress helped me get there, so much the better.

A couple minutes after seven, I saw Dion's car pull up. Dressed in a sharp black blazer and white shirt that was open at the collar, he looked like a model.

I let out a shuddery breath. So did Spike.

I faced my friend. "Isn't it time for you to leave?"

"Not before I say hello."

Dion's face broke into a dazzling smile as he stepped into the shop. His lips parted, his eyes lighting up with approval. "Wow."

I smiled coyly.

Spike stepped forward, extending his hand. "I'm Spike. I work with Elsie."

Dion pumped his hand. "Hello, Spike."

"You take good care of her now," Spike added.

"Spike," I admonished.

"What?" he said innocently.

"It's okay," Dion said. "I plan on taking good care of her."

I looked up at Dion, wondering if his words held more meaning.

I sure as hell hoped so.

Minutes later, we were outside the store, slowly strolling toward Dion's car. I'd left Spike to close up shop.

"You look amazing," Dion said. "Too amazing to go to dinner around here."

Most of the establishments in the Lake Norman area were fairly casual, with the exception of the private clubs. When people got dressed up, they typically went into Charlotte.

"You look pretty good yourself," I told him.

"I figured we'd go to Charlotte, find someplace there to eat."

"That's a great idea." I didn't want to be in the Cornelius area. Though I'd left Robert, it was still too close to home for my liking.

"Do you want to ride with me? Or do you want to take your own car?"

"It makes more sense to go together," I told him. Maybe I was throwing caution to the wind, but I got a good feeling about him. And if by chance I mysteriously went missing, Spike had all of Dion's information on the shop computer.

"I think so, too."

Dion electronically unlocked the doors to the Buick, and made his way to the passenger side. He opened the door for me, and I slid in.

Moments later, he got in the other side of the vehicle. My stomach fluttered as I met his gaze. Here I was, for the first time in nine years getting into a vehicle to go on a date with a man other than Robert.

It felt a little weird.

And a lot exciting.

"Is there a particular place you'd like to go?" Dion asked. "I should have asked yesterday and made reservations."

"It's Monday, so I'm sure we'll be fine."

He started the car, and turned on the stereo. The sounds of soft jazz filled the airwaves. "Is there a station you like to listen to?" he asked, his finger poised over the console.

How different he was from Robert. One of the things that really irked me about my husband was that whenever he drove my car, he changed all of my preset radio stations. Yes, he was the official owner of the car, but I drove it most of the time. Why did he have to change the radio stations to *his* preference?

"That sounds lovely," I told Dion. "I'm happy to listen to that."

"Back to restaurants. Do you have a favorite spot?"

I thought about it for a minute, then said, "Have you ever been to The Melting Pot?"

"I love it there."

"I've been dying to try their food."

"The Melting Pot it is."

As Dion began to drive, I laid my head back and softly smiled.

Yes, I was rewriting my story. There was no denying that.

I was giving myself a chance to have a happy ending this time around.

17

All through dinner, I couldn't stop mentally comparing Dion to Robert. Robert was arrogant. Dion was thoughtful. Robert was often curt with people. Dion was respectful. As the CEO of a successful company, Robert was used to controlling people—and that had extended to me. Dion was a college football coach who spent his downtime and the off-season mentoring students.

Their personalities were as different as night and day. I didn't have to be on pins and needles with Dion, worried that I would do or say something wrong. And unlike Robert, who expected to make the final decision when it came to our menu choice, Dion let me choose the signature platter for two.

I saw Alexander, but he wasn't our server. When he

spotted me, he did a double take. But his face visibly relaxed when he saw that I wasn't with Robert.

I gave him a little wave and a smile, though I'd been tempted to apologize to him again.

After a meal that could only be described as delectable, I was nowhere near ready for the night to end.

I wanted to slip my arm through Dion's as we strolled out of the restaurant, but I didn't. Instead, I watched him head to the valet stand. *Tell him you don't want the evening to be over,* a voice in my brain screamed. *Tell him you really like him.*

He came to stand by my side while we waited for the car to be driven around. "Thank you for a fabulous dinner," I told him.

He snaked his hand around mine, the move tentative. I curled my fingers around his, reciprocating the gesture.

"Thank you for agreeing to be my date," he said.

"I had a really, really good time."

"Do you have anywhere you need to be?"

"You mean right now?"

"I mean, I know you have to work in the morning."

"What did you have in mind?" I asked.

He paused briefly. "I don't want to overstep anything, but I really enjoyed getting to know you, and if you were up for a nightcap…"

"At your place?" I asked.

The Buick pulled up in front of us then, and Dion didn't answer. The valet attendant opened the door for him, then came around the car and opened my door for me.

Inside the privacy of the car, Dion spoke. "I don't want you to think I'm being forward. I just...don't really want our night to end."

I fastened my seat belt. "I don't think you're being forward. I was kind of hoping you'd ask."

"Really?"

I reached for his hand. "Mmm-hmm."

A smile lit up his face. It made me feel good. Made me feel hopeful.

Inexplicably, Dion and I had connected. And our connection was real and intense and exciting.

We were on the same page.

We held hands almost the entire drive to his place in Cornelius. When he had to turn or maneuver the car in a way that required both hands, he released mine briefly before taking it in his once more.

Again, I thought of how different he was from Robert. Yes, there was the age difference. But what I thought of now, as he pulled into the driveway of a modest house, was the simmering desire I had for Dion compared to what I'd felt for Robert when I'd started dating him.

Sex with my husband had been nice, and sometimes even hot, but not drive-me-wild crazy. And that hadn't mattered, because the emotional connection had been the most important thing for me.

But it mattered now. The tingle I felt just holding Dion's hand told me how much I needed passion in my life.

I was ready for it.

I wanted the whole package—hot sex combined with an emotional connection.

"I should have asked if you wanted to come to my place," Dion said as he put the car in Park. "Or if you wanted to go to yours."

"Your place is fine," I whispered. "Just fine."

And then, acting on instinct, I leaned forward and kissed him.

As my mouth pressed against his, I sighed, intense sensation exploding inside me. God, I'd wanted this. Wanted it so badly.

The kiss started slowly, our lips playing over each other's tentatively. We took our time exploring. There was no need to rush, and I wanted to savor every delicious moment with this man.

I parted my lips, and Dion groaned. He brought both hands to my face, framing it gently. He sucked softly on my bottom lip. Nibbled on it with his teeth.

And then his tongue was in my mouth, and we were all-out necking, our lips fused together, our tongues tangling in deep, hot kisses. I wrapped my arms around his neck, pressed my body to his.

Dion lowered his hands to my back, smoothing his palms over my dress. I had been fantasizing about this moment for so long that if he wanted to get me naked in the car, I wouldn't have stopped him.

Dion was the one who paused. He eased his head back and stared down at me. Smiled that incredibly sexy smile.

"I say we head inside—before we give the neighbors something to talk about."

He gave me a quick peck and pulled back. But I moaned softly in protest. So Dion leaned forward again and kissed me deeply, until I was moaning in pleasure.

As my body grew hotter than a Louisiana summer, I was the one to pull away this time. "You're right. We should go inside."

He stroked my face and regarded me with a mix of admiration and desire. It was a way of telling me that what would come next wasn't about a random fuck, but about two people who liked each other acting on mutual desire.

I turned my face into his palm and softly kissed his hand.

"Come on," Dion whispered. "Let's go inside."

18

We didn't get past the entranceway before we picked up where we'd left off in the car. Dion pulled me into his arms and kissed me.

It was a hot and urgent kiss, all tongue. His hands roamed up and down my arms, over my back. I pressed my palms to his chest. Dug my fingertips into his flesh through his shirt.

His warmth consumed me. His kiss electrified me. I wanted to get naked and fuck.

Dion broke the kiss, only to take my hand and lead me to the nearby living room. There, he took his blazer off and set it on the leather sofa before once again drawing me into his arms.

As we necked, he pulled me down onto the sofa with him. This time, his hands ventured lower than my back, to my ass. He gently squeezed my flesh, groaning as he did. The sound was like an aphrodisiac, making me dizzy with desire.

My body was on sensory overload. Every touch of his fingers against my skin sent a new rush of excitement through me. I hardly knew Dion, and yet I felt that I already knew him intimately. I wanted him to rip my clothes off and fuck me. Fuck me in a way that I hadn't been fucked in years.

I thought of Robert then, and that put an immediate damper on my desire. I didn't care that I'd only just left my husband. I was entitled to get laid. But I needed to be honest. To lay my cards on the table before we went any further.

I eased backward, breaking the smoldering kiss. Dion's lips didn't stop, however. They moved to my cheek, the underside of my jaw.

"Dion," I said, breathless. "Dion, wait."

He stopped then, cupped my cheek and stared into my eyes. There was a slight look of confusion on his face, as though he wondered if he'd been moving too fast for my liking.

"I just…I need to tell you something," I said huskily.

"Okay." His voice had a note of concern.

I didn't know how to say it, but had to do so. "Dion, I'm married."

His lips parted, forming an O. He lowered his hands from my face.

"I shouldn't have blurted it out like that. But I wanted to—"

"Look, if you're married, that changes everything."

"I'm separated," I clarified.

Dion's look of confusion deepened.

I blew out a deep breath. "I just left my husband. It's over. Absolutely. No going back. But I wanted you to know my circumstances. Before…" I left my statement unfinished. My body knew what I wanted, but verbalizing it was another matter.

"You say you just left him. When?"

"Last week."

Dion's eyes widened, registering his surprise. "And how long were you married?"

"Eight and a half years."

His face grew serious. "That's a long time. If you're newly separated, it might not be over."

"It was a long time coming," I told him. "Even though I didn't know it. My husband has always been controlling, but recently I discovered a lie. A big one. It's one I can't forgive."

"Infidelity?"

"No. Something worse."

Dion gave me a curious look. "What's worse than infidelity?"

I chuckled mirthlessly. "How much time do you have?"

Two hours later, we were sitting side by side on the sofa, a second bottle of wine half-finished. I had recited a novel to Dion—retelling practically all the events that had taken place in my life since the moment I'd met Robert.

"And now here I am," I concluded. And for the first

time since I'd started talking, I glanced at my watch. My eyes bulged. "Oh, my God. Is it actually twelve forty-five in the morning? Have I just talked for two hours straight?"

"Has it been two hours?"

"Yes, because it was almost eleven when you went to get that first bottle of wine."

I had dominated the conversation for all that time, as if the floodgates had been opened and I'd had to get my story off my chest. I should have been surprised that I could share all that information with a man I barely knew. And yet I wasn't. I felt a connection with Dion that was inexplicable.

I'd snuggled against him as I'd told my story, and he'd held my hand much of the time. He was quietly offering me the support I needed, and not judging me in the least.

"So if it's two hours since you started talking," Dion began, "that means it's two hours since we last kissed."

A frisson of heat coursed through my body. "Are you saying you want to kiss me again?"

He trailed his fingers along my neck. "I want to do more than kiss you."

The heat went straight to my pussy this time, making me instantly wet.

You could call me reckless, or on the rebound, or whatever. But I wanted this.

I wanted Dion.

He lowered his lips to my neck. I arched my head

backward to allow him more access. Closed my eyes. But his lips didn't touch my skin.

Instead, I felt the warmth of his breath on my neck. The brush of his fingertips.

"I have only one question for you," he said softly.

I opened my eyes and met his gaze. "Okay."

"From all you said, your marriage wasn't exactly ideal. Your husband is significantly older. Many women in your situation would probably have a boy toy on call. You never mentioned one, so I'm wondering."

"If I have a boy toy on speed dial?" I echoed, smiling coyly. "Or are you wondering if I've had many lovers since I've been married?"

He paused. "Have you?"

"Would it matter?"

Dion shrugged.

"I've only just left my husband. When I was with him, I was faithful to him. So yes, you're the first. But you're not a boy toy."

Dion arched an eyebrow. "I'm not?"

"Well," I murmured, eyeing him flirtatiously, "not unless you want to be."

"Oh, I want to be."

He eased his body over mine, and I moaned. I think we both did. He caressed my face as if I were an exquisite piece of art. I loved that. Loved how he liked stroking my face and neck.

"I have my own admission," he said softly.

"Please don't let this be the moment you tell me *you're* married."

Dion chortled. "No. But I was involved with someone when I first met you."

"Oh?" I felt an irrational spurt of jealousy.

"Yeah. I thought I was going to marry her." He paused, and I didn't breathe as I waited for him to continue. "But for some reason, I couldn't get you out of my mind."

"Are you serious?" I asked.

"You'll probably think I'm crazy, but the first time I saw you...I don't know why, but I couldn't forget you. My relationship with my girlfriend just wasn't the same."

"How long were you together?"

"Three years."

"Three years!" I hadn't expected that answer.

"Yeah." Dion nodded. "It was a comfortable relationship. Nice. But not...I don't know. And then I saw you."

It felt as if something bigger was happening between us, even if I didn't understand why. For Dion to echo the same things I'd been feeling since I'd first met him... it was overwhelming.

"There were many, many days I wanted to go back to your store and talk to you. A couple times, I walked by. That's when I knew I needed to end my relationship. How could I continue to be with her when I couldn't get another woman out of my mind?"

"Oh, my God." I pressed a hand to my forehead.

"That bothers you?" Dion said.

I lowered my arm. "No. Not at all. In a way, it makes

a weird sort of sense. I couldn't stop thinking about you, either."

"Really?"

"Really."

For a moment we stared at each other, and I saw my own amazement reflected in his eyes.

And then Dion kissed my lips, and when he did, it was as if our mutual need exploded, and I was grabbing at his clothes, he was pulling at mine. I heard a rip and knew I'd torn his shirt. But the ripping sound didn't alarm me—it turned me on.

The shirt had torn near his shoulder, exposing his flesh there. As Dion buried his face in my neck and pressed his palms against my belly, I sank my teeth into his skin.

"Ooh, so you want it rough," he rasped.

"Any way you want to give it to me…I just want it."

Dion eased back and tried, unsuccessfully, to tug my dress down my arms. "How do you get this off?"

"You have to unzip me." I lifted my left arm and dragged the zipper down. The fabric loosened. Dion pulled the top of my dress to my waist.

As his eyes feasted on my naked breasts, he made the kind of low, growling sound a lion makes. "You're beautiful," he breathed. He brought a hand to one nipple and fingered it gently. Instantly, the tip grew hard. "Absolutely beautiful."

Already, this was so much better than my dreams. My entire body was thrumming, desire flowing through my veins like molten lava. I stared at him, watched him taking in my nakedness. My clit was pulsing, a reaction not just to the touch of his fingers, but to way the he was regarding my breasts with such awe.

I couldn't wait for him to put his wet, hot mouth on me.

He ran the tip of his finger over my other nipple, and I shuddered.

"You like that?"

"Yes." My voice was barely a whisper.

"How much?" he asked, taking both of my breasts into his hands and running the pads of his thumbs over both nipples.

"*Very* much…"

"If I were to do this—" he guided one nipple into his mouth, suckled it a couple seconds, then grazed his teeth over it "—could you come? Could you come before I even touch your pussy?"

"I don't know…."

He closed his mouth around my other nipple, and pleasure rippled through me. He suckled, and I watched, my pussy pulsing harder.

"I'm already wet, and my clit is throbbing." A jolt of heat went through me at the sight of him circling his tongue around my nipple—before it disappeared into his closed mouth. "Oh, God, I think I could. I think…" I arched my back. My eyelids fluttered shut as he moved his warm mouth to my other breast and suckled there.

I was panting, my need fiery and all-consuming. But when Dion moved his mouth from my breast to my torso, I moaned in protest.

"It's all right, baby. I'm not going to disappoint you."

I said nothing, only whimpered.

"How long has it been?" Dion ran a hand up my thigh and cupped my pussy.

"How long since I had sex?" I asked, dazed from the pleasure. Confused by the question.

"Since you've come," he clarified.

A beat passed. "I don't understand."

"If it's been a while, then I want to extend your pleasure. Draw it out as much as possible."

When was the last time I had come? If only he knew how many times I'd brought myself to orgasm thinking of him eating my pussy.

"Maybe I shouldn't admit this, but I've been fantasizing about you for weeks. I've made myself come plenty of times…imagining you exactly where you are now. On your knees between my legs…"

"Is that so?" Dion asked, his voice perking up as he stroked my pussy through my panties.

"Yes."

He pushed the bottom part of my dress up over my hips, so it was bunched around my waist. His eyes went to my center, and the sheer lace fabric covering my vagina. "Then I say it's time you get to experience the real thing."

The thought of him finally eating me in real life was such a turn-on, I couldn't speak. I could only moan again.

He stroked my pussy through my thong, then used a hand to pull the fabric aside, exposing me. And he stared. Drank in the sight of me. Once more, the expression in his eyes said he was regarding something exquisite. Priceless.

It was a look suggesting that just by gazing at me, he was enjoying immeasurable pleasure.

I drew in a sharp breath when he slowly ran a finger over my opening. And when he stroked my clitoris, I flinched.

"You've got a pretty pussy, baby."

No one had ever told me that before.

"And you're wet. Ohhh."

He dipped a finger into my wet folds, then used that same finger to circle my clit. He was being gentle, treating me like fine china.

And then he brought his mouth down on my pussy, covering my clitoris with his hot tongue. He suckled me hungrily, buried his face in my pussy and ate me. He dipped his tongue into my folds, circled it around and around my clit. Suckled it again before grazing the sensitive flesh with his teeth. He was all over me, lapping up my essence, driving me delirious.

He paused to blow on my pussy, and oh, what a sensation. And when he drew my clit into his mouth yet again and suckled me gently, that's when I let go. My body jerked as I came forcefully. I was whimpering, nearly crying, unable to contain myself as wave after dizzying wave of pleasure rocked through my body.

I heard the tearing of a condom wrapper as I lay breathing heavily, my body spent. With his tongue, he'd made me feel amazing, but when his hard cock filled me the delicious sensation was far more intense.

I wrapped my arms and legs around him and held on tight as his thick shaft moved inside me in a way I'd never experienced.

On my back. On my side. On my knees. On my back again. It went on and on, his erection never failing. The sensations were overwhelming, and though I tried to hold on, I came again, moaning wantonly. I gripped Dion's legs, tightened my calves around his ass.

Moments later, he was coming, his body jerking, a pleasurable groan escaping his lips. I clung to his sweat-slicked body, never wanting to let him go.

His lips found mine, and as he ravaged my mouth the way he'd ravaged my pussy, I knew I would never tire of him.

Dion had fucked me the way I'd longed to be fucked. The way I had dreamed of him fucking me so many times.

Finally.

19

Dion and I made love half the night, and when morning rolled around, I knew I wouldn't be able to make it into the shop bright and early.

At eight, I got up and called Spike.

"Good morning, doll-face," he said, clearly having seen my number on the caller ID.

"Hey, Spike. I don't have long. I just wanted to let you know that I'll be late getting into the shop today."

"So the night went well," he said smugly.

"Very," I admitted. "And I'm going to need another couple hours of sleep, at least."

"You'd better tell me all the details later!"

I giggled. "I will."

I put my phone back into my purse and crept to the bedroom. Dion was sleeping peacefully, his arm still outstretched where I'd been nestled.

As softly as I could, I got back into the bed. Snuggled against him. Closed my eyes, content.

We didn't get up until ten-thirty. Dion planted slow, hot kisses along my jaw—the kind meant to arouse me again.

"That's not fair, Dion," I told him, sighing. "You're off for the summer—you don't have to go to work. But I do."

"You own the store. Who'll fire you if you don't show up?"

I considered his words. Surely I could spend a couple more hours with him. Tabitha was also on the schedule, so Spike wouldn't be alone. And it was a Tuesday, hardly the busiest day of the week.

Lord knew I wanted more of him.

"I guess I can spare another hour or so."

"Mmmm." Dion wrapped his arms around my naked body. "That's what I'm talking about."

"And I'm free tonight—if you want to see me again."

"*If* I want to see you again?" Dion slipped his hands between my legs and began to massage my clitoris. "What do you think?"

"I think you put some sort of spell on me that first day I met you." He slipped a finger into my vagina. "Because I can't…get…enough… Oh, God."

Dion slipped another finger inside me and drew my nipple into his mouth.

He suckled my breast as he fingered my pussy, tugged

at my nipple with his teeth. He was titillating every erotic zone in my body.

I had never felt more alive.

I came, squeezing my legs around his hand and crying his name. He didn't move his hands or his mouth until he'd coaxed every last bit of my orgasm out of my body.

He kissed me then, and I stretched my naked form against his. I reached for his cock, still amazed at just how beautiful it was.

How powerful.

"Not yet," Dion said.

"Not yet?"

"I was thinking we could have a shower," he whispered in my ear, his hot breath stimulating me again. "Have a little fun while we get cleaned up. Kill two birds with one stone...."

We got into Dion's shower, which was comfortably big enough for two. As we both stood under the stream of warm water, Dion kissed me.

God, this man was incredible. Our instant connection was about more than the physical. He was the complete package—total sex appeal combined with that emotional bond I'd always craved.

Dion broke the kiss, eased back and grinned at me. Then he reached for the shower rack and took the shampoo bottle. He squirted shampoo into his hands and began to rub it into my hair. As he washed my hair, he kissed my forehead, my nose, my cheek. And then finally my lips again.

"Turn around," he whispered.

I did, and he worked his hands through my hair to rinse the strands free of suds. I closed my eyes as water streamed down my face, and the next thing I felt were Dion's soapy hands working over my back and my shoulders. It was all very functional, even as he lathered my behind—until a hand slipped into the crack of my ass.

He trailed his fingers lower until they met the back of my pussy. Then they moved forward and stroked my clitoris. I braced my hands on the shower wall and spread my legs, giving him more access.

With the water beating down on my back, Dion played with my pussy until I could barely stand it. Turning, I threw my arms around his neck and planted my mouth on his. Then I pushed him backward against the wall.

And I stared at him. Let my eyes feast on every inch of his gorgeous body.

His cock was even more beautiful than it had been in my dreams. Just like in my fantasies, it had no foreskin. It was large, the girth impressive, and it curved slightly to the right. I loved it.

Dion began to reach for me, but I said, "No, stay right there." Then I took the soap, lathered it in my hands and spread it over Dion's chest, his six-pack abs and his thighs. I got more soap and worked it over his cock. My body responded immediately. We had spent the night fucking and coming, and still I hadn't had enough of him.

I lowered myself in front of his beautiful penis. I ran my thumb over the head, which the water had rinsed clean of soap. Then I curled my fingers around his cock and guided it to my mouth. I suckled the tip, and was rewarded by Dion's groan as he tangled his hands in my hair. Opening my mouth wider, I took him deep inside, sucking him hard. I ran my palms up and down his strong thighs as I worked my mouth over his amazing cock. When I used my teeth, he groaned harder.

Gripping my hair, Dion guided me back up to his mouth, then kissed me ferociously. I felt his penis throbbing against my pelvis. And I wanted him desperately, as if we were about to fuck for the first time.

Wrapping his arms around my waist, he lifted me and carried me out of the shower. We were both soaking wet when he placed me on the bed, but neither of us was concerned with the bedding. I played with my nipples as I watched him put on a condom. Then he lay down beside me and pulled me on top of him. I straddled his thighs as he held his cock and guided it into my warm, wet opening.

I rode him hard, the sensations beyond thrilling. He held my hips as he thrust his shaft upward, hitting my G-spot with every delicious stroke. I squeezed my vaginal walls around him, hoping to heighten his pleasure.

We came together, both of us swallowed whole by a giant wave of pleasure. I fell forward, my body quivering against his, Dion growling long and loud.

And it struck me anew that this was real. My fantasy lover in the flesh.

And it was better than anything I could have ever imagined.

★ ★ ★

Afterward, Dion slathered my body with lotion. I was totally at ease standing naked in front of him, letting his palms work over every inch of my body in the light of day. His hands stoked the embers of my desire, but we both knew we weren't going to end up fucking again.

It was amazing how comfortable we were with each other. I wasn't experienced in terms of having many lovers, but the ease with which we'd fucked, then fallen asleep together, not to mention being able to shower together the morning after, surely wasn't the norm. Spike wasn't a woman, and maybe his flings weren't typical, but he said that most of the time he didn't feel comfortable staying the night with a new lover.

I didn't feel any shame over the way I'd shared my body with Dion. In fact, if I didn't have to go to work, I would happily have spent the day with him, walking around stark naked the entire time.

Why put clothes on only to have to take them off again and again?

"There," he said, rubbing the unscented lotion over my belly until it dissipated.

I took the bottle from him and squirted some into my palm. "My turn."

I smoothed lotion over his hard chest, his broad shoulders, then moved lower, to his abdomen. My fingers traveled the length of a jagged scar, then my eyes followed. It was a scar I'd seen the night before in the heat of passion, but the timing hadn't been right to ask him about it.

"What happened here?" I asked. It was about three

inches long, and thick where it had formed a keloid. The location of it—on his abdomen as opposed to an arm or a leg—was an odd place for such a scar.

Dion looked down at my hand on his body, taking a moment before answering. "I…I was stabbed," he said.

"What?" I shrieked. "How? Who?"

"It was a long time ago. I'm thirty-six now, so… nineteen years? I can't believe it's been that long."

I could see it now—the anger in the scar. It wasn't neat, the way it might be after a surgical procedure. I slipped my arms around Dion's waist, offering comfort for whatever he'd gone through. "You were seventeen."

"Yeah."

Whatever had happened, it was difficult for him to talk about. "Do you want to tell me about it?"

"One of my mother's boyfriends," he said, putting his hands on my shoulders. "He used to knock her around. I got between them, trying to protect my mom, and… and I paid for it."

"Oh, my God."

"The knife punctured my small intestine, and I had to spend a week in hospital."

"Dion!"

He tightened his arms around me. "But I was fine. And my mother's boyfriend went to jail. He never hurt her again."

"I'm so sorry. What an awful thing for you to have to go through."

"I'd do it again," Dion said with resolve. "Anything to protect my mother."

So far, he hadn't mentioned his father. I sensed there was a story there, that perhaps we had some common ground.

But I didn't have time to ask him about it. I had to get to work.

My dress was wrinkled from the night before, but I had nothing else to put on. I couldn't very well show up at my store dressed in one of Dion's T-shirts and a pair of his shorts, which would be too large for me. Especially not wearing my heels from the night before.

My hair was a mess. I didn't have my flat iron or any other accessory. I would have to pull it back into a ponytail.

"Can I get you some breakfast?" Dion asked.

"I wish I had the time, but I'd better get to the shop. I have a feeling that if I stay any longer, I won't make it to work at all."

"Are you sure? You haven't eaten Cheerios until you've tried them Dion-style."

"What do you do—something special with the milk?"

"I never reveal my culinary secrets."

I chuckled. "I guess I'll have to see for myself. But another time. I'll get some coffee at work."

We left his house, and a short while later, Dion was pulling up to the curb in front of my store. Given that I was wearing my dress from last night, I wished I didn't have to exit his vehicle to get my car, but what choice did I have? Hopefully, I could slip into my vehicle un-noticed and head back to Sharon's place to change.

I put my hand on the door handle to open it, but Dion's fingers went to my chin. He turned me to face him.

"Tonight, right?"

"I'll call you before I come by."

A few seconds passed as we stared at each other. Dion was the first to break the silence. "I had a great time last night. And this morning," he added with a grin.

"So did I."

Leaning forward, he kissed me, and warmth spread through my body. Groaning, I pulled away.

"Tonight," I told him as I got out of the vehicle.

I hoped to make it to my Mercedes without Spike seeing me, but no such luck. By the time I was opening my car door, I heard his voice on the street.

"Oh, no, doll-face. You're not going anywhere." He scurried toward me. "What on earth did you do in that dress? Wait, don't answer that."

"I know," I whispered. "That's why I'm trying to get home to change."

"And girl, you need to fix that hair."

"Shut up!"

"I'm just bugging you. Though you do have a very nice 'just been fucked' look."

I quickly got into my car. "Spike, you know I love you, but I'll talk to you when I get back to the store."

"Okay, okay. But I thought you should know a pack-age arrived for you today. From Robert. Chocolates. I think they came from—"

"Paris," I finished for him, and felt my stomach sinking. My favorite chocolates in the world were from La Maison du Chocolat. I'd tried them the first time I'd gone to Paris with Robert, and he had them delivered for me on various special occasions. Normally, a box of the exquisite assorted chocolates would brighten my day.

Not now.

"Spike, will you get the package for me?" I didn't want to walk into my store in a wrinkled designer dress.

Spike disappeared there and returned less than a minute later.

I took the card from the package and opened it, though I didn't want to.

My dearest Elsie,
I know I hurt you and I'm sorry. One week is too long to be without you. How about a trip to Paris for a second honeymoon? In the meantime, enjoy your favorite chocolates from the most romantic city in the world.
I love you,
Robert

As I read the card, my stomach lurched. In the past, when I'd longed for Robert's attention, when business caused him to neglect me, he could buy me delectable chocolates, or a beautiful dress, and it would make me feel better. Make me believe that my husband was one hundred percent committed to our marriage.

How could he equate the magnitude of his lie to the

nights I'd had to spend at home alone without him? How could he think that an apology and a box of chocolates from Paris would make what he'd done okay?

"You can have the chocolates," I said to Spike, tossing him the box. "I'll see you later."

Before he could say a word, I closed the door and started the engine. He stood on the sidewalk, watching as I drove away.

Robert's gift shouldn't have upset me. I should have known something like that would come. But still, it brought me back to the place I was trying to escape. A place I wished I didn't have to go back to in order to move on.

But I did. I had to deal with the reality of ending my marriage.

When I was a few blocks from the store, I pulled into a parking lot and turned off my car. Except for when I'd called Spike this morning, my phone had been off the entire time I'd been with Dion. I hadn't wanted any calls from Robert. I'd also avoided checking my voice mail over the past few days, not wanting to hear his voice. But the chocolates had made it clear I couldn't avoid him forever.

All the messages were the same. "Elsie, I'm sorry." "Elsie, I miss you. Please call me." "Elsie, everyone missed you in church yesterday." "Elsie, I love you. Will you call me, please?"

Something about them got to me. A sense of regret, I guess. Robert truly sounded sorry in his messages—but what he'd done was inexcusable. There was no going back now.

But I didn't look forward to dealing with ending our marriage. I honestly wished I could move on without having to look back.

The truth was, I couldn't avoid my husband forever. For several seconds I summoned my courage, then called our house.

"Kolstad residence," Olga answered.

"Hello, Olga."

"Mrs. Kolstad!" She sounded relieved. "Robert has been so worried."

Worried? What had he told her?

Before I could say anything else, he was on the phone. "Where are you?" he demanded.

The sweet, charming Robert of the voice mails had morphed into angry Robert now that he had me on the line.

"I got your messages," I said, not answering his question. "And I got the chocolates."

"When are you coming home?"

"I called because I felt I owed you a response. But, Robert, I meant what I said to you before I left. I'm not coming home." I paused. Sighed. "It's time we talk about how we'll go about ending our marriage. It doesn't have to be—"

"You have a boyfriend, don't you?" Robert snapped.

"What?" The question stunned me.

"Where were you last night?" he went on. "I called you at Sharon's, but you were nowhere to be found. So I drove by the store. Didn't I get a shock when I saw your car was parked there? And again this morning?"

Robert had driven by the store? He was keeping tabs on me?

"I slept in the store," I lied. "I wanted…some time by myself."

"Bullshit."

His harsh tone reached through the phone line, causing me to reel backward.

"You're screwing someone else, aren't you? Spreading your legs for another man like a common whore. Like your mother."

I hung up on him. And then sat motionless, not even breathing.

Why, oh why, had I called him?

Because I'd wanted to show some semblance of respect. Because he'd sounded so damn contrite in his messages.

I'd wanted to call and be civil and see how he sounded. To gauge for myself whether or not we could end our marriage on good terms.

Obviously not.

I should have known that Robert would try to clamp down on me with an iron fist. And why not? That's what he used to do in the past. Get angry if I didn't agree with him. If I didn't bend to his way of thinking.

Once he got angry, I always became the spineless wife, acquiescing to his will.

Not anymore.

20

I was in a foul mood when I got to Sharon's. "Hey, you," she said as I stepped into her house. When she saw my wrinkled dress, her eyebrows shot up. *"Ooohh."*

"What did Robert say to you last night?" I began without preamble.

Sharon frowned. "He wanted to know where you were."

"So you just told him I was on a date?" I quipped.

She held up both hands. "Whoa."

"Sorry." I dragged my palms over my face. "God, I'm sorry."

"I didn't tell him anything. But he called a few times. I told him you weren't around. I think he thought I was lying, because he came by."

"He came here?"

"Yeah. Around ten last night. It was pretty obvious

then that you weren't here, and I told him I had no clue where you were, that you hadn't come home from work."

"Damn."

"Why? What happened?"

"He decided to drive by the store last night. He saw my car there. And I guess he figured I was out with someone."

"You're separated," Sharon said gently.

"Tell Robert that. He thinks he can woo me back with a box of chocolates."

"Okay, I'm confused. Why don't we sit down and you tell me what's going on?"

Sharon put a hand on my back and led me to the sofa in her great room. "I didn't mean to snap at you," I said as I sank onto her plush sofa. "I'm...I'm stressed out."

"Did you talk to Robert?"

"Yeah." I told her about the chocolates he had sent me, and about our phone call and what he'd said. "And it just hit me, you know? I want my life with Robert to be over, but it's not that easy. I can't simply leave and that's it. He sends me my favorite chocolates and I think, maybe he's gonna be nice. Then I call, and he's an asshole. And I wonder, is he going to be decent about this divorce, or is he going to be a jerk? He's so used to having his own way. He doesn't like to lose."

There it was. The crux of my concern. It wasn't even Robert's anger when I spoke to him that made me believe our divorce had to be ugly. It was knowing his personality.

He hadn't built a successful company by accepting

loss. I'd overheard many of his conversations when it came to business, and when he wanted to get his way, he'd bully people and push them until they broke. I worried that he would do the same to me.

"He can't force you to stay with him."

"I know." I sighed. "But what if he tries to punish me for leaving? What if he takes my shop away?"

"Have you talked to a lawyer yet?"

"No."

We were quiet for several moments. I stared at the floor, my thoughts a whir in my brain. Sharon rubbed my upper back. She was simply being there, waiting for me to get them out.

"Robert called me a whore. Accused me of being like...like my..."

"What an absolute jerk," Sharon said firmly. "And to think I ever liked him! He's abusing you with words and bullying you in an attempt to knock down your self-esteem. Don't let him get to you. You're a beautiful person. Inside and out. You're moving on to bigger and better things. Don't let him drag you back down."

"I slept with Dion last night," I blurted out.

"And?"

"And it was amazing." Despite my mood, I smiled.

"Good for you!" Sharon exclaimed, and she meant it.

"It was absolutely incredible. Not just the sex," I said in a whisper, giggling. "But we have a connection. I know I haven't dated in ages, and maybe I'm out to lunch, but I really believe it."

"I'm happy for you. Lord knows you deserved a booty call."

"If it was just a one-night thing, maybe I wouldn't be so stressed out. But I like him a lot and I want to see where this leads. It would be so nice to move on with someone else and not have to look back."

"Wow."

"I know. It sounds crazy."

"It doesn't sound crazy."

"And it's mutual," I went on. "He likes me, too." I told Sharon what Dion had told me about his girlfriend, and how he hadn't been able to stop thinking about me. "It's almost as if fate put us together. I just want Robert to let me go without a fight."

"You're going to get through this, Elsie. I realize you're scared and stressed right now and don't know what to expect, but you'll get through it." She patted my hand. "Hang in there, okay?"

I thought of Dion, the silver lining on my dark cloud. I suppose a part of me was worried about losing him before we had a chance to explore how deep our connection might be, but another part of me felt there was no reason to be concerned.

I smiled as I faced my friend. "Okay."

I looked up divorce lawyers at work later that day and called several. The first three told me they would love to take my case but couldn't. They'd worked with Robert in the past and it could be a conflict of interest. Some I didn't get a good feel for. But a woman by the name of Diane Delko sounded like a fighter. I made an appointment with her for Friday afternoon.

And then I resolved to put Robert out of my mind. I wanted to concentrate on Dion alone when I got to his place.

This time, I wasn't dressed like a sexpot. I was wearing a denim skirt and a pink cotton, scoop-neck shirt. Simple and cute.

But when I got to Dion's door, he gave me a smoldering look as if I were wearing a hot negligee.

"Hey," I said.

"Hey, you." He drew me into his arms and rocked me while he hugged me, before planting a kiss on my temple. "How was your day?"

A loaded question. But I wasn't about to tell him about my interaction with Robert. So I looked up at him and said, "Good. I had a good day. Did you see your mother?"

"Yeah. She's planning a trip to Hawaii."

"Hawaii? Alone?"

"No, with a girlfriend of hers. Someone she met during breast cancer treatment. Another survivor. They promised they'd reward themselves with a trip once they were in remission."

"Nice. What a great reward."

Dion nodded. "It's a place my mother always wanted to go, but never got around to. Now…"

"And now she's not waiting for tomorrow," I finished for him. "She's going to take advantage of everything life has to offer today."

"Exactly."

My words had meaning for me as well, not just Dion's mother. I had wasted most of my adult life being afraid to love, and then opting for what I thought was an emotionally safe marriage.

Now, I didn't want to waste another minute.

Dion lowered his lips to my neck, brushed them across my skin and whispered, "I missed you."

Just like that, a sensual heat warmed me. We hadn't even made it past his doorway.

I looked up. Dion's eyes were fogged with desire.

All it took was being in each other's presence to get us in the mood. It was a raw physical reaction to another person that I'd never experienced before. I didn't understand it.

But I knew I didn't want to fight it.

Lifting his hand, I brought it to my mouth and kissed each finger. I kept my eyes on his as I took his thumb in my mouth and sucked gently.

"Oh, baby."

I flicked my tongue over it. Up and down the sides. Around the tip.

Groaning, Dion pulled his thumb out of my mouth, framed my face and planted his mouth on mine. His tongue played over mine, stoking my desire with each delicious, hot, hungry flick.

Breaking the kiss, he spun me around in his arms, positioning my back to his chest. My heart pounding wildly, I pressed my arms against the wall and braced them against it for support.

His fingers skimmed my neck as he swept my hair to the side. And then his hot lips were on the back of my neck, his fingers slipping beneath my shirt and tickling my skin.

"Every time you touch me…" I eased my head back against his shoulder as his hands moved to my breasts. He pushed my bra up. Tweaked my nipples. I dug my fingers into his thighs, reveling in the exquisite pleasure.

I wanted more of him. Needed more of him.

I turned in his arms and threw my arms around his neck. As we kissed, he gripped my ass. Held me against his rock–hard erection.

I would never tire of him. I knew that. Moaning, I curled one leg around his calf. And then Dion was lifting me, and I was wrapping both my legs around his waist.

He kissed me as he carried me through the house to the bedroom. The mattress bounced as we landed on it, me on my back, our lips still connected. We pulled apart only to tear at each other's clothes, and when we were naked, we started to kiss again, my hands moving over his body with urgency, and his over mine, heating every part of me.

I maneuvered myself on top of him and kissed his hard pecs. Trailing my lips higher, I moved them to a nipple and flicked my tongue over the small, tight bud, hoping that it would be even half as pleasurable to him as it was when he did it to me.

I bit it gently. Kissed it. Dion groaned and slipped his fingers into my hair.

His reaction empowered me, and I ran a wet path down his abdomen with my tongue.

"Ooh, Elsie."

I lifted my head and met his gaze. Smiled. And then I looked at his cock. Marveled at the sight of it.

"Do you know how much I love looking at you?" I asked. "How much it turns me on?"

"Not as much as I enjoy looking at you."

My eyes drank in every inch of his penis. The exquisite thickness. The impressive length. The way it curved slightly to the right in its erect state.

I touched the base of his cock, my fingertips gently playing over his pubic hair. He didn't have a lot of it. I wondered if he trimmed it, or if it was naturally that way.

I trailed my fingers up the length of Dion's shaft, and watched it throb. I grinned, satisfied. Touched the tip. There was a bead of moisture there.

"You're wet," I said.

Dion didn't reply. But the intense look on his face spoke volumes.

I kissed his cock, and again it throbbed. Meeting his gaze, I parted my lips. Slowly. Deliberately. Wondering if watching me was as much a thrill for him as it was when I watched his face settle between my thighs.

"My God, baby. You're killing me."

I circled my tongue around the tip of his cock, tasting a hint of salt. His scent was musky and alluring. But his reaction—a deep shudder and groan—turned me on more than anything else.

As Dion twisted his hands in my hair, I took him deep in my mouth. I moved my lips up and down his cock, moaning with delight. He was so hard. So wonderfully hard and strong.

I pumped his length as I pleased him. Teased his testicles with my fingertips. Each of Dion's uninhibited grunts said he was in heaven.

But soon he was urging me up, by grasping my shoulders. And then he was kissing me deeply. My legs were straddled over him, my pussy grazing his cock. I was desperate to slide onto him, but I managed to tear my lips from his and whisper, "Condom."

Dion kissed my chin. "Right. Condom."

He kissed my lips again, and all reason fled my mind. If he thrust inside me at that moment, I wouldn't stop him. I wouldn't want to. If I got pregnant because of my carelessness, so be it.

But with a groan, Dion pulled away, sliding me off his body. He rolled to the side of the bed and opened the night table drawer. I ran my palm over the corded muscles of his arm as he got a condom and put it on.

Then I climbed on top of him, straddling him again. Gazing into his magnificent hazel eyes, I wrapped my fingers around his penis and guided it to my pussy.

Our eyes remained locked as his body completed mine. My mouth fell open, and I gasped from the luscious feelings washing over me. As I rode his cock and fucked him until I was throwing my head back and screaming his name, the pleasure deeper than just the physical level.

As we connected—body and soul.

21

I was alive again.

No longer was I a ghost of a person, walking on eggshells to keep my husband happy. No longer was I trying to keep my sexuality repressed. I was a fully fledged woman, enjoying her sensual side as much as every other part of her.

Enjoying it not just for the sake of getting pregnant. Being with Dion had liberated me.

I couldn't get enough of him. Every day for the rest of the week, I went to see him after work. All he had to do was touch me, and I was aroused. We were like teenagers who had discovered the amazing world of sex, and I didn't think I'd ever tire of messing around with him.

But it was more than merely fucking. I knew that in my heart, even if the thought seemed irrational. At the very least, I knew we had a mutual admiration and were both interested in seeing what would develop as the future unfolded.

All week, I was able to put Robert out of my mind and concentrate on Dion, but by the time Friday rolled around I had to get back to reality. At least in terms of dealing with ending my marriage.

I was nervous as I drove out to meet divorce lawyer Diane Delko. But she put me at ease after a few minutes of talking.

"I understand your concerns," she said, once I'd explained my situation. "But rest assured, divorces are so common these days, there's a playbook that's pretty much standard. So no, you don't have to prove mental cruelty or anything like that. It doesn't even matter if someone's had an affair. North Carolina is a no-fault state. You can file for divorce for any reason—something I see all too often in my position."

"What about the financial aspect?" I asked. "My husband is very wealthy. Much of his fortune he earned before he ever met me. But I suppose that doesn't matter, because I signed a prenuptial. I agreed to a million dollars if we split before the ten year mark."

"I'd like to see that agreement," Diane said. "It might not be legally enforceable. I know of your husband, Elsie, and I believe you could be entitled to a lot more than that."

I held up a hand. "I'm not interested in milking my husband for half his fortune. All I really want is to be able to keep my store. The money promised to me in the prenup will allow me to buy a small place, and have some security."

"All things considered, I'll still need to see that agreement." Diane paused. "Do you know who your husband has retained?"

"No, but I suspect it will likely be Clayton Gunter. He handled Robert's two previous divorces." The famed divorce attorney not only had a reputation for being the best in the greater Charlotte area, he was also a personal friend of Robert's.

"When you find out, let me know. The next step will be setting up a joint meeting to finalize a separation agreement, where we'll come to terms with issues like interim support. Are you both in the matrimonial home?"

"Uh, no. I'm living with a friend."

"That'll be something else we discuss. What will happen to the matrimonial home and—"

"He won't want to sell it. And I don't expect him to."

Diane nodded. She seemed to be eyeing me curiously. "Is there any chance of a reconciliation?"

"No," I replied instantly. "No chance."

"Is there someone else involved?"

"I just want to move on," I said, evading her question. "As you know, there's a substantial age difference between me and Robert and...you know."

"As I said, it doesn't matter, but I typically like to know if there's something else going on. For example, one partner might want to slow the process down in hopes of reconciliation, while the other is ready to move on because someone else is involved."

"Robert knows there will be no kissing and making up. He lied to me about something very significant and…" My voice trailed off. Though Diane was a lawyer, and I had every intention of retaining her, I wasn't comfortable telling her everything—at least not yet. I wasn't the type to open up about my life unless I was close to a person. As nice as Diane seemed, I didn't want to tell her about Dion. First of all, he wasn't the reason for the breakup of my marriage. And secondly, I didn't want any information about him to inadvertently slip out during meetings with my husband and his lawyer.

She spent the next few minutes discussing her fees and her retainer. I hired her and wrote her a check. Then I took a few of her cards—one to give to Robert.

I would either have to call Robert and give him Diane's information, or I would hand him her card when I saw him.

But I didn't have to do either this weekend. Monday would come soon enough. Until then, I would enjoy Dion.

Robert continued to call my cell phone. Most of the time, he didn't leave a message, but I knew he'd phoned because I saw his number on my caller ID. A couple times he left amicable messages asking me to call him. But over the weekend, his messages became curt and snarky. "How long are you going to play this little game of yours? You've made a fool of me for long enough,

Elsie. I think it's fair to say we're even. Come home. Come home now."

We're even? As if my leaving had been about punishing him for his lie.

I called him from work on Monday, when Spike had left for his lunch break. Robert answered his cell before it could ring a second time. "Elsie." A beat passed. "Oh, my love. Thank you for calling."

"I've seen a lawyer," I said without preamble, before I lost my courage. "Her name is Diane Delko—"

"A lawyer?"

I drew in an anxious breath. "Yes."

"You want to talk about divorcing me, you come and talk to me. I won't have this conversation over the phone."

Maybe he was right. Maybe this was something I needed to do in person. "Will you be home later?"

"I was going to have dinner at the club, but if you're coming home, I'll be here."

"Then I'll see you after work."

"So, depending on how things go and the mood I'm in, I might not see you later," I told Dion a couple hours later when I gave him a call. "I might just stay at Sharon's place."

"You know you can come here, no matter how late it is."

"I know. But seeing Robert might not be pleasant, and I don't want to be bad company."

"I'm here for you regardless. No matter your mood.

I'm capable of holding you all night and not taking advantage of that beautiful body of yours."

"That remains to be seen," I joked.

"Hey—it's not like you make it easy," Dion countered. "Seriously, though, if you want to come here and chill and put your head on my shoulder, I'm a good listener. Ask any of my boys. They'll tell you Coach Barry's got a good ear on him."

"I don't have to ask anyone," I said softly. "I know that already. And thank you for the offer. I might take you up on it."

"Even if you don't come by tonight, give me a call after you see your husband. Let me know you're okay."

"I will." I heard the door chimes from where I was in the rear of the store, and knew I needed to get off the line. I had to go back to work. "I'll call you later."

By the time I closed up shop, I was feeling anxious. Nothing about the idea of seeing Robert was appealing. I could only hope that after this first meeting to discuss our divorce, subsequent meetings would be more comfortable.

Though I'd spent nearly nine years living with Robert, as I approached his home, I felt like a stranger.

I parked the car in the driveway and killed the engine, then sat behind the wheel for a couple of minutes. *This is silly,* I told myself. *Get out of the car and get on with it.*

So I did.

Robert's face lit up when he saw me, as if there was no tension at all between us. As if I'd been away on holiday, rather than living with a friend until we could sort out our divorce.

"Hello, Elsie," he said warmly.

"Hello." My tone was frank, businesslike. I kept my arms crossed over my chest as I slowly stepped into the house. It was amazing how quickly a place where you'd once felt comfortable could become foreign. Being here was like going back to an old neighborhood you'd moved away from months earlier—familiar, yet oddly different.

"Thank you for coming back, Elsie. Thank you for coming home."

I ignored the comment as I strolled to the sofa in the great room and took a seat. Robert knew I was here to discuss our divorce face-to-face. Now he was acting as though I'd come home to reconcile.

"Olga's gone home," Robert said as he moved to stand in front of me. "But she prepared dinner for us."

"I'm not really hungry."

"Okay." He nodded, then sank onto the sofa beside me, leaving a comfortable distance between us. "It's good to see you here, Elsie. This place hasn't been the same without you."

Why was he doing this? Acting as though we hadn't spoken about divorce just this afternoon? "Robert…"

"I called our travel agent," he went on. "First-class tickets are reserved for Paris, leaving on Saturday. At the Ritz—in the same suite we had the last time. I know we've hit a rough patch, but two weeks in Paris, walking along the Seine, eating breakfast at that beautiful spot near the Tuilleries… What could be a better way to get us back on track?"

"Robert, please." I closed my eyes, as if that would block out his attempt to persuade me to change my mind. "Please…"

"Two romantic weeks recapturing our love. You know that's what you want. Why are you fighting it? To prove to me how strong you are? Okay, you made your point. I was wrong. Let's move on."

"Just stop." I buried my face in my hands, surprised to find they were trembling. I drew in a deep breath to calm my nerves, then I continued. "When we spoke this afternoon, you said to come by so we could discuss our divorce in person. That's why I'm here. Not to talk about Paris or to hear you act as though I'm a child who can't make up her mind."

"If you want a divorce, why can't you look at me?"

I turned my head to meet Robert's gaze. I didn't flinch. I held his eyes, not blinking, letting him know I was serious.

"You think you've been perfect?" he asked, irritation creeping into his voice.

I wasn't here to argue. "My lawyer is Diane Delko," I said as I reached into my purse. "We need to know who you've retained so we can get everything started." I produced Diane's business card and handed it to Robert. "Here's her card."

He took it from me and flung it onto the floor.

I sighed. "Do you have a lawyer yet?"

"Do you have a boyfriend?"

"This isn't about anyone else but us, Robert. Your lie."

"But if you weren't fucking someone else, you would come back to me."

"Why do you have to make this difficult?" I asked him.

"Do you think I'm going to give you millions of dollars so you can spend it on some worthless guy who doesn't deserve it? Some man who'll use you and won't respect you?"

"I don't want your millions. Is that what you're worried about? All I want is my store. And in the prenup, we agreed on one million—"

"After ten years of marriage."

"If we split *before* ten years," I corrected him.

"That wasn't the agreement."

"Whatever you think I deserve then," I said, already exasperated. "All I want is for you to be fair, and we can get this over with."

"Get it over with. Like a root canal, perhaps? Or a colonoscopy?" Robert asked, his voice rising. "Our marriage is on the same level as some unpleasant procedure you want to get over and done with?"

"You're twisting my words."

"What's the rush, Elsie?"

I opened my mouth, but didn't say anything. I didn't have an answer to that question—at least not one Robert would want to hear.

And I wasn't about to tell him about Dion. He would make it seem like my wanting to leave was about another man, and that wasn't the case. My dissatisfaction in my marriage had been building for a long time, and I was ready to embrace my new life. Something Robert clearly didn't understand.

"If you agree to stay until the ten year mark and decide at that point that you still want the divorce, I'll give you five million. I'll call my lawyer and have him amend our prenuptial agreement."

"This isn't about the money! I just want my freedom."

Robert stood. "Then you get nothing. Not the store, and certainly not a million dollars."

"What?"

"You'll be penniless. Just like you were when I married you."

"You can't do that."

"Oh, but I can. Especially if you're screwing around on me. Because our prenuptial agreement specifically said that if you cheated, you'd get nothing. Which is exactly what a whore deserves."

"There was no stipulation like that." As I said the words, I tried to recall. Tried to remember if there was some language like that that I might have forgotten. I shook my head. "No. There was the ten year issue, but that was all."

"You're mistaken."

"No, I'm not."

Robert walked to the nearby wall console and lifted an envelope from the top shelf. He made his way back to me, holding it like a trump card.

"Refresh your memory," he said. "You signed this."

He tossed me the envelope and I opened it. My eyes scanned the legalese quickly.

Then I saw it. At the bottom. A paragraph I could have sworn wasn't there before. It stated that if I got involved with another man during the course of our marriage, I would forfeit any financial benefits, including support, in the event of our divorce.

"I never signed this," I said adamantly.

"You most certainly did."

"I never signed *this*." The agreement was a photocopy, so perhaps Robert had done some cutting and pasting to make it look as if my signature was on that page. "The real document—the original one—is what's going to stand up in court."

"Your signature is on the original."

I was about to reiterate my point when something made me stop. Just like that, I *knew*.

"You wrote a new agreement and forged my signature?" I couldn't hide my outrage.

"That's quite the accusation."

"You did, didn't you? My God. When?"

"For someone who's not seeing someone else, you're quite concerned about the language of the prenup. According to you, you should have no cause for concern."

"You've done some shitty things," I said as I rose to my feet, "but you can't do this. You can't take my store from me."

"I've given you an option. The choice is yours."

"Go to Paris with you, stay in a marriage for another year and a half, just so you can hand me another forged agreement?" I shook my head in disbelief. "God, I should have figured you out a long time ago. I should have known."

I hurried out of the great room, despair making my head throb.

I didn't care about Robert's fortune. I could easily try to go after my rightful share of it, but that wasn't what mattered to me. Not even as a way to spite him.

And yet that's what he was doing—trying to take everything from me just to spite *me*. After he'd been the one to lie to me, deceive me. Crush my hopes and dreams.

What kind of man had I married?

22

I got a clearer idea of just how spiteful Robert was the next day.

I was driving to Dion's place after work when I saw the flashing lights of a cruiser behind me. I wasn't speeding. Hadn't run a stop sign.

But there were no other cars on the quiet street, so I knew the cop was intending to stop me.

I slowed down and pulled over to the curb, then reached into the glove box and withdrew my insurance information. I was digging in my purse for my driver's license when the officer reached the car.

He motioned for me to roll the window down. I did, saying, "Sorry. I was getting my information together."

"License and registration, please."

I handed both to him. "What's the problem, Officer?"

He peered into my car as though he thought I had a kidnapped baby inside, then took a step backward. "Step out of the vehicle, ma'am."

"What did I do?"

"Step out of the vehicle," he repeated, sternly this time.

I wasn't stupid. I got out of the car.

"Will you tell me now what the problem is?"

"This vehicle's been reported as stolen."

"What? Th-that's impossible."

"I assure you it's very possible."

"This is my car. It has been for three years."

The officer examined my driver's license and the registration form. "The vehicle is registered to Robert Evan Kolstad."

"My husband. You see my name. Kolstad. The same as his."

"I guess there must be some misunderstanding," the officer conceded.

"Obviously." I chuckled to relieve the tension.

He gave me back my information. "Your husband called the department to report the car as stolen."

"I…I'll phone him," I stated. What else could I say?

"Sorry for the intrusion." The officer turned and started back to his car.

I got back into my SUV and immediately dialed Robert's cell. He answered after the first ring.

I spoke before he could. "You reported my car stolen?"

"Elsie?"

"You know damn well it's me. Why on earth would you report my car as stolen?"

"The lease is up at the end of the week. It needs to be returned."

"So you report it as *stolen?*"

"The officer I spoke to was mistaken. I only called requesting they contact you, since you don't like returning my calls."

"I saw you *yesterday.* You could have reminded me then."

"Now you know."

I wanted to scream. To tell Robert that he was the world's biggest asshole. Instead I said, "I'll drop it off at the dealership."

"If you meet me, perhaps we can arrange for a new vehicle."

"I'll get my own car, thank you." *One I like,* I thought, and clicked the button to end the call.

I immediately punched in Dion's number, but hesitated before completing the call. I didn't want to phone and bitch about my husband. So I called Spike instead. Someone I knew I could bitch to without remorse.

"Hey, doll-face," he greeted me. "You know I'm about to meet Marcus, so I hope this is good."

Out of the blue, Marcus had phoned Spike over the weekend, apologizing for how he'd treated him, claiming that he missed him and wanted another chance.

For all Spike's talk about being over Marcus, after five years it was clear he still carried a torch for him. Personally, I didn't think, after how Marcus had kicked

Spike out and left him penniless, that he deserved the time of day. But whatever happened was Spike's decision, not mine.

I had enough to deal with.

"Right," I said. "I'm sorry. Look, I won't keep you then."

"No, no. Tell me what's up."

"It's Robert. I just got pulled over by a cop. He reported the car stolen. *Stolen*."

"Oh, fuck."

"He's going to do anything—anything!—to make me pay for leaving him."

"Oh, doll, I'm sorry you're dealing with this. But I'm not surprised." He paused. "Kind of makes me wonder why I'm going to meet Marcus."

"Because you're hoping that after five years, he's contacted you because he really does love you." But for a person to do what Marcus had done to him, then expect a second chance… It was exactly the kind of thing I wouldn't put past my own husband. He actually expected to be able to force me back into submission.

"We'll see how it goes," Spike said. "I need to do this—even if it's to close the book on us, once and for all."

"You go meet Marcus. Hopefully, it all goes well."

"Maybe Robert just needs time. Time to accept what's happening and let you go."

"Yeah. Maybe." A beat passed. "I'll see you tomorrow."

I ended the call and started the car, the reality of my situation playing out in my mind. No doubt Robert wanted to see me, to give him the car, or perhaps meet him at the Mercedes dealership. That wasn't an option for me. The less I saw of him right now, the better.

My cell phone trilled. I feared seeing Robert's name as I glanced at the display, but instead the name Treasure flashed on the screen.

Treasure was an old friend whom I'd moved to North Carolina with, straight out of high school. She had since married and moved about an hour north, to Winston-Salem. We weren't in touch often these days, but I still considered her a friend.

"Hey, Treasure," I said when I put the phone to my ear. "What's up, girl?"

"Oh, I'm just touching base. It's Shane's birthday in a couple weeks, and I was hoping you and Robert could come up for a party. Not this Saturday, but the next. Nothing fancy—just some friends over for a barbecue."

I laughed uneasily. "I can come, but I won't be with Robert."

"Yeah," Treasure said softly. "I heard."

"What? How could you have heard anything?"

"I called the house first. I spoke to Robert."

"Ah."

"What's going on?"

"It's a long story, and I can tell you all about it on the weekend. But the bottom line is it's over."

"Robert said you moved out. Who are you staying with?"

"A friend."

"I don't know what's going on," Treasure began

cautiously, "but don't you think this is premature? Before you leave your marriage, you should do everything in your power to save it. Go to counseling. Talk to your pastor. When Shane and I had problems, our pastor really helped."

"Treasure, please. I really don't want to talk about this right now."

"I understand. I'm just saying a marriage is worth fighting for."

"I will explain everything when I see you. What time?"

"Around two."

"I'll be there."

I ended the call and went straight to Dion's. During the drive, I came up with a plan. I had first considered dropping the SUV off at the dealership, but instead I would return it to Robert's house. I still had a closetful of clothes to clear out, as well as some other personal items.

On Wednesdays, Robert always had lunch at the club with a group of men with whom he'd formed a board to help support emerging entrepreneurs. Typically, they played golf before lunch and after, and Robert was often gone all day.

I knew that he would be out of the house for sure between twelve and two, discussing whatever business the board had to deal with. And that's when I would return to Robert's house, collect my belongings and leave the car in his driveway.

I could ask Sharon to help me, but I didn't want her

going up and down the stairs, lifting things. I could ask Spike, but someone had to man the store.

But Dion would be home. He would take me.

Olga's face lit up as soon as she saw me. Then it fell in surprise when she noticed I wasn't alone.

"Hello, Olga."

"Mrs. Kolstad." Her eyes flitted from me to Dion. "What's going on?"

"These are the keys to my car," I told her, handing her them. "Please give them to Robert."

"Oh, Mrs. Kolstad." Pain streaked across her face. "You're not coming home?"

"No, Olga." I squeezed her hand. "I'm not. I just came to get some of my things."

Tears filled Olga's eyes—a sight that surprised me. I wasn't used to her showing this kind of emotion.

I pulled her into an embrace. "I'm sorry. Maybe we can get together sometimes, have dinner or something."

But as I said the words, I doubted they would come to pass. Olga would continue to work for Robert, and I would go on with my life. Our paths might never cross again.

We filled Dion's car with most of my clothes and toiletries, my computer, most of my DVD collection, and a couple crates of my books. I couldn't fit everything, but took what was most important to me for the time being.

That included the framed photo of my father when he was a teenager. A wave of regret washed over me when I remembered how Robert had robbed me of the chance to be there for him in the end.

I left the wedding photos. I didn't care about those. But there were other framed photos of me and friends. Memories that meant the world to me.

Olga looked shell-shocked as I gave her one last hug. I knew she wanted to ask about Dion, but didn't, knowing it was a question that would be inappropriate.

"So that's your house," Dion said as he began to drive away. "It's quite amazing."

"But it wasn't a home," I pointed out. My heart was racing. I only now realized that though I hadn't expected Robert to return home, part of me had been terrified that he would walk through the door.

"My friend Sharon doesn't live too far from here. I've already called her. We can drop my stuff off there."

"Or—" Dion faced me "—we can take it to my place."

I'd been staying over at Dion's a lot since our first date, but his suggestion shocked me nonetheless. "What are you saying?"

"My place is big enough for both of us. And…" He took my hand in his. "I like having you around."

"You want me to move in with you?"

"We've hardly been apart since we started seeing each other." When I didn't respond, Dion continued, "You think it's too soon?"

I didn't know what to think. I only knew that I loved being with him.

That perhaps what I was feeling—

"I love you, Elsie," Dion said softly.

My mouth fell open in surprise as I met his gaze.

"It's true," he said. "I didn't want the first time I told you that to be while we were making love, because you might not believe it. And I know it probably seems impossible even now. It's too early. That's what everyone would say. And I can't explain it—"

"You don't have to," I said, my pulse accelerating. "I know exactly what you're saying."

My eyes locked on his, and now he was the one to look surprised. "I love you, too." I leaned toward him and kissed his cheek. He turned his face and met my lips. The kiss lingered a moment too long for someone who was driving, so he soon turned back to the road.

"I think...maybe I loved you right from the start," Dion said to me as he reached to link his fingers with mine. "That very first day. That's why I had to end things with Tisha. That's why I had to go back and see you." He brought my hand to his lip and kissed it. "That's why I want you to move in with me."

Happiness spread through my body like an injection of warm liquid. "I honestly feel the exact same way, Dion. The connection right from the start. Everything."

"So—are we going to Sharon's place or mine?" he asked me.

"Yours," I told him. "Let's go to yours."

"Good," Dion said. "Because I have a surprise."

23

I was nervous and giddy the entire drive to Dion's place, wondering what his surprise might be. When we reached his house, we released hands to get out of the car, but as I joined him on the driveway, he took my hand again.

Inside, he led me to the dining room, where the table was already set for two, complete with candles. The delectable aroma of seasoned chicken filled the air.

"I know I probably scared you about my culinary abilities when I mentioned Cheerios," Dion began as he lit the first candle. "But I'm actually quite good in the kitchen."

"You cooked!"

"A late lunch for us. Southern fried chicken. I got most of it done this morning. All I have to do is prepare the collard greens and rice."

"Sounds lovely. I'm starving."

"I've even got cherry cheesecake in the fridge."

"You made cheesecake?"

"My mother taught me how. It's the best cheesecake you'll ever taste."

"I can't wait."

Dion didn't want my help in the kitchen, so I made use of my time by hanging some of my clothes in the spare room's closet and putting others in a dresser drawer. Things were moving fast between us, but it felt right. I was embracing the next phase in my life and not holding back.

We ate around three-thirty, and it was scrumptious. The chicken was so delicious that I had to have a second piece. "You're in trouble," I said as I licked my fingers.

"Why's that?"

"Because now that I know you can cook like this, I'll never move out."

"In that case, I'll do all the cooking." Dion eased up from his seat next to me, leaned across the space between us and kissed me. A deep, smoldering kiss that put me in the mood.

"I hope you saved room for some dessert," he said as we pulled apart.

"I don't know I if I can eat another bite."

"You have to try the pineapple."

"Pineapple? I thought you said you made cheesecake."

Dion didn't answer, just took my hand and led me

to the kitchen. He lifted a bottle from the counter and showed it to me.

As I read the label, I smiled. "Chocolate fondue sauce from The Melting Pot."

"I picked it up today." With his free hand, he cupped my breast. "I thought we might have some fun. Pineapple slices. Chocolate sauce." He kissed me briefly. "Each other."

"*Ohh.* I see. Gosh, suddenly I'm famished for something sweet."

Dion's lips curled in a smile before they landed on mine, kissing me deeply and hotly. My body came alive, sending heat and wetness to my pussy.

My lips molded to his as he pulled me to the floor. He broke the kiss and tugged my cotton shirt over my head. Then his lips met mine again, his tongue delving into my mouth, twisting with my own.

I slipped my hands beneath his shirt feeling his scar with a fingertip before running my palms over his chest. I squeezed the strong pecs, the act of touching him turning me on even more. Dion pulled my bra straps down from my shoulders and dragged the garment lower, freeing my breasts.

"Stay right there," he whispered.

As I watched him go to the fridge, I unfastened my bra and tossed it aside. Dion produced a plastic tray of sliced pineapple, which he put on the floor beside us. He gave me another kiss before lifting the Saran Wrap.

"Close your eyes," he whispered.

I did. A moment later, I felt something cold and wet

passing over my lips. I opened my mouth. Flicked my tongue out. Tasted the sweetness of pineapple.

Dion played the morsel over my tongue and my lips before dropping it into my mouth.

"Keep your eyes closed," he whispered against my ear.

I waited for him to run another piece of pineapple across my lips, then I flinched when I felt cool wetness brush my nipple.

He circled my areola with the pineapple, causing the skin to tighten and my nipple to harden. Then I felt it on the other breast, teasing the hard bud of my nipple.

"Mmm," I moaned.

"You like that?" Dion asked.

"Mmm-hmm."

He kissed me, sucking gently on the tip of my tongue. Then his mouth was gone and I felt his finger on my lips, followed by the piece of luscious fruit.

Dion's hands traveled down my neck to my breasts. As he touched me, he groaned with delight. My eyes remained closed, so when his tongue circled one of my nipples, I didn't expect it. My body jolted with pleasure.

As he suckled me, he urged me backward, and soon I was lying flat on the cool tile floor.

"Keep your eyes closed. I want you to feel."

My body was alive with anticipation. Dion traced the edge of my jeans with his fingertips before undoing the button, and I sucked in a quick breath. The light touch of his fingers on my skin caused heat to flood through me. And when I was naked on the floor, knowing that his eyes were feasting on me, I was so ripe with excitement that I knew a few strokes of his tongue on my clit would make me come.

But Dion had other ideas. I gasped, unprepared, when I felt something warm and gooey hit my stomach—the chocolate sauce.

Dion's finger rubbed it around my belly. "How does that feel?"

"Mmm. Good. Really good."

He licked the chocolate off my skin, nibbling at times, suckling at others. I flattened my palms against the floor and arched my spine.

"God, you're so beautiful," Dion rasped.

A dollop of chocolate sauce landed on my nipple, and I mewled softly. And then I felt his lips brush across the taut peak before he opened his mouth and took my nipple deep within his mouth. My clit flinched. I was nearly ready to explode.

Dion tweaked one nipple into a solid peak, all the while teasing my other nipple with his mouth, as if he couldn't get enough of me. He sucked, then licked, then sucked again, driving me mad with lust.

My breathing was ragged when he pulled away from me, soft moans escaping my throat. I waited, eyes closed.

The sensation of warm chocolate hitting my clitoris made it pulse like my rapid heartbeat. This was so fucking erotic…

Dion massaged the folds of my sex, spreading the chocolate around. "You're driving me crazy," I rasped. "I've never felt so—"

My words died in my throat when his mouth covered my pussy. He sucked me hungrily.

"You're so sweet, baby," he murmured. He flicked his tongue over my clit. "So damn sweet."

He suckled me slowly, sweetly, the sound and feel of his tongue and mouth bringing me closer to the edge. And then I came, my orgasm erupting from my clit with enough force to make my back arch and my hands ball into tight fists.

I heard the rustling of Dion's clothes as I whimpered. "I need you inside me," I said between ragged breaths. I reached for his upper body and urged him to settle on top of me. "I love you, baby." I opened my eyes now, saw his face over mine. "I love you, Dion. I do. Please—make love to me."

Dion made a soft sound, a deep and meaningful expression passing over his face. An expression that spoke volumes about what we meant to one another. Sex between us was so amazing not just because of our undeniable chemistry, but because of what we felt for each other.

I'd heard people talk about love at first sight, but I hadn't known it was possible. But now, after meeting and falling for Dion, I believed it.

I wrapped one leg around him, letting him know I didn't want him to go anywhere but my soft, wet pussy. "It's okay, baby."

"Are you sure?"

I pressed my lips to his ear and pleaded, "Yes. Make love to me. *Right now.*"

Dion needed no further encouragement. Without a condom on, he entered me. And it was glorious.

Though the floor was hard, I was too consumed with passion to be concerned with any discomfort. We made love with tenderness, each deep, pleasurable thrust so much more than the physical act of fucking. My second climax was even more forceful than the first, making my body convulse uncontrollably for several wonderful moments. Dion succumbed to his own orgasm while I was still quivering, my body weak with dizzying sensations. My soul brimming with love.

Slowly, I opened my eyes and smiled up at him. His cock was still inside of me, and I tightened my legs around him.

"I love you, Dion," I whispered.

His grin was like a ray of sunshine. "Ah, baby. I love you, too."

And then he kissed me. A soft and sweet and significant kiss. And we stayed like that for a long while, with his penis still inside me.

We'd made love without protection, and I knew I might get pregnant.

Dion had to know it, too.

But the thought didn't frighten me. It warmed my heart.

24

Dion and I were inseparable.

Unlike some people you get bored with when you're together all the time, the more time he and I spent with one another, the more our feelings deepened.

I got my period, so Dion and I hadn't made a baby that night on the kitchen floor. But I wasn't worried. It was probably better that I got through my divorce before trying to take that step.

I leased myself a Pontiac G6 Coupe, which was sporty and sexy at the same time. It felt good to lease a car on my own. Like I was establishing my independence.

I hoped Spike was right, that some time and distance would give Robert a chance to accept our separation. He hadn't called me in nearly two weeks, and I hadn't called him. I advised my lawyer that Robert had her information and would get in touch with her when he'd retained counsel.

And then I went on with my life.

"Are you sure you don't want to invite Robert to the barbecue tomorrow?" Treasure asked when I spoke with her the day before Shane's party.

"No, Treasure. We're definitely over. But if you don't mind, I'd like to bring a friend."

"What kind of friend?" she asked.

"You'll see," I told her.

"Elsie, are you sure?"

"Yes, I'm sure. I've never been more certain."

"I'll see you tomorrow, then," Treasure told me, but she sounded more wary than curious.

Treasure was my oldest friend, and I knew she was worried about me. No doubt she was concerned about the breakup of my marriage. I would explain everything to her when I saw her, and introduce her to Dion. He was a part of my life now. A big part.

I hoped that Treasure would be receptive to meeting the new man who'd captured my heart, but her smile was guarded the next day when she shook his hand.

"So you're Elsie's friend," she said.

"Yes," Dion answered, and he slipped an arm around my waist. But the way he touched me said we were much more than friends.

The backyard was full of people. Husbands and wives and a number of children. Women sat around the table, smiling and chatting, while Shane and the other men were around the barbecue, drinking beer.

I put the gift I'd brought for Shane on the deck with

other presents, then went to greet him and introduce him to Dion. Shane greeted him with a broad smile and handshake, showing none of the reservation his wife had.

"Can I talk to you for a moment?"

I turned to face Treasure. "Sure."

"Privately."

I nodded and followed her to the side of the house. Treasure's hair was pulled back from her face in a tight, short ponytail. Her dark skin was flawless and she hardly looked as though she'd aged in the past twenty years. But there was something different about her. From her hair to her clothes to her makeup, she was more conservative.

"That's your boyfriend?" she asked.

"Yes," I told her. I hadn't brought Dion here to pretend he was just a friend.

"And it's serious?"

"Yeah." I nodded. "It is."

Treasure sighed. "I'm surprised."

"I'm sure you are. I haven't been able to tell you everything about what happened with Robert, but things went sour real fast." I quickly filled her in on the lie that had changed everything. "But the truth is, there were signs from before that things weren't right. I ignored them, because I wanted a baby, but when I found out that he'd had a vasectomy…"

"And you can't forgive him?" she asked.

The question surprised me, I guess because all my other friends who knew the truth had supported my leaving Robert. "Even if I can forgive him, it still changes our relationship."

"I've only known Robert to be sweet and giving."

"I'm not saying he's a bad guy. He's just not the right guy for me."

"And you've decided this after nearly nine years of marriage?" Her expression said she didn't believe it. "Marriage is sacred, Elsie. Don't rush into a divorce. And committing adultery—"

"Adultery?" I narrowed my eyes as I stared at her. "I'm separated."

"In the eyes of the Lord, you're still a married woman."

"Mommy, mommy!" Treasure's four-year-old son, Javan, appeared at the side of the house. "Mommy, come see my new trick!"

He tugged on Treasure's hand, giving her no choice but to follow him. She gave me a "what can you do?" look and trotted off with him.

And just in time. I didn't like where our conversation was headed. She'd become a Christian several years ago, but it wasn't her right to judge me. She was a friend, and I wanted her support—not any lectures on morality.

Maybe you're overreacting, I told myself as I wandered back to the table where the women were sitting. The news of my separation was a shock to Treasure, that was all. Seeing me with Dion was a bigger shock. Wasn't it natural for her to have questions?

Dion seemed content with the men, and I watched them across the yard laughing at something someone had said.

An hour passed with happy chatter among the women, the children screaming with delight as they played in a kiddie pool. There were barbecued ribs and chicken and salad and broiled corn. The last time we'd been at Treasure's place for such a gathering, Robert had been miserable—I think because of all the young couples and children. Though Treasure's friends had gone out of their way to make conversation with him, Robert had been stiff and unfriendly. And when someone asked if he was my father, Robert looked as if he'd wished the young man an instant death.

Dion, on the other hand, fit in at this gathering right away, establishing an easy rapport with everyone.

Though I was sitting among the women, I was only half paying attention to what they were saying. Every part of me was involved in watching my man, who was now tossing a football with the guys. I didn't know much about the game, but it was clear he had a good arm. The ball went right to whatever man he threw it to.

I was fiddling with the fruit on my plate, waiting for Dion to make eye contact with me.

Shane caught the ball Dion had thrown, and he ran with it, but was tackled by one of the other men. The two fell onto the grass, laughing as they did.

And then, as if Dion sensed my eyes on him, he turned and looked straight at me. I spiked a piece of the pineapple off my plate and lifted it to my mouth. I parted my lips slowly, then popped the fruit in. Lust darkened Dion's eyes, and I knew what he was thinking.

"Elsie?"

Treasure's voice brought me back to the present. I swallowed the fruit before speaking. "Hmm?"

She turned to look at Dion and then back at me. Realization dawned in her eyes. She knew that despite the distance between us, he and I had just been sharing an illicit moment.

She didn't look pleased.

"Well?" she asked.

"Well what?" I countered.

She forced a smile onto her face. "What would you prefer?"

Treasure wasn't giving me any more than that, almost as if she wanted to embarrass me for my inattention in front of her friends.

Kathy, the woman to her right, came to my aid. "Treasure said you'd tell us about Paris, since you've been there a few times. I'm dying to go—if I can get Bill to take me."

"Paris." Why had Treasure mentioned Paris? Her way of reminding me that I was married? "Paris is an incredibly beautiful city, rich with history. It's very romantic. And of course, the cuisine is exquisite."

"What about the shopping?" Deanna, the woman to my left, asked.

"It's a woman's dream, of course. Christian Dior, Yves Saint Laurent... Bring an empty suitcase if you can—you'll need it."

"Her husband has taken her so many wonderful places all over the world," Treasure said, her eyes lighting up. "And you should see Elsie's house. The Peninsula. On the water. It's like a European villa for a countess."

The women all looked at me with interest. There was a chorus of "oohs."

"It is quite the house," I said good-naturedly, wondering again what Treasure was trying to do. "But it's my ex-husband's house. Not mine."

"Oh, you're divorced?" A woman named Sydney asked.

"Not yet," Treasure said. "It's more like they're taking a break from each other."

Now I knew something was up with her. I eyed my friend with disapproval.

Deanna looked confused. "So Dion is—"

"My boyfriend," I said. "I'm separated." I smiled sweetly, hoping to hide my annoyance. "Hopefully, the divorce will be final soon."

"Oh," Kathy said knowingly. "My cousin's going through a divorce, too. It's been taking a while, but she said she had to move on with her life, so she found herself a new man. One who treats her real well, too."

I pushed my chair back. I wasn't interested in talking about divorces and new boyfriends. Truth be told, I was pissed off with Treasure.

But I couldn't confront her without looking like a bitch. I stood. "If you'll excuse me, I need to use the bathroom."

I exhaled sharply as I turned to the house. I wanted to throttle Treasure for bringing up Robert. Clearly, she couldn't accept the fact that I'd brought Dion with me to this party, and wanted to punish me for that decision.

I didn't need to use the bathroom, but walked toward

the house nonetheless. I entered through the patio doors and went to the powder room off the kitchen.

Inside, I braced my hands on the edge of the pedestal sink and closed my eyes. *Treasure just needs time,* I told myself. *She likes Robert, and I can't expect her to stop liking him just because we're getting a divorce.*

I flushed the toilet to make it look good, waited a beat, then opened the washroom door. Seeing a form in the doorway, I started.

Dion stared down at me, and the look in his eyes set my body on fire.

"Hey," I said.

"Hey."

He shot a quick look over his shoulder, then snaked his arm around my waist and urged me back into the bathroom. He closed the door, and his lips went immediately to my neck.

I giggled. "What are you doing?"

"I saw you with that pineapple. I know what you want."

"You do, huh?" I giggled again.

"Yeah." He kissed me. All tongue and heat.

And despite where we were, I was turned on. I wanted to fuck my man.

Dion's hands slipped beneath my shirt, skimmed my rib cage and went up to cup my breasts. "Oh, baby."

He pushed my bra out of the way and ran the pad of his thumbs over my nipples, hardening them. As I moaned, he lowered his mouth to one breast. He flicked his tongue over it, up and down, down and up, bringing my desire to a fever pitch. Then he gently bit it, grazed his teeth over it.

"I want to make you come," Dion said, then closed his lips around my other nipple.

And I wanted to come. I wanted this moment of pleasure with the man who excited me more than anyone ever had.

He eased me backward with his body, pressing me against the wall. All the while, his tongue never left my nipple. He suckled it, vibrated it with his tongue. Drew it completely into his mouth as though he wanted to swallow it.

"Oh, God, Dion." I lifted my skirt up, slipped my hand into my panties. Felt the wetness covering my clitoris.

Dion's hand covered mine there. Twining our fingers together, he guided both my middle finger and his into my pussy.

"Shit, you're so wet...." He suckled me harder, thrust both of our fingers deeper into my vagina. I cried out, then bit my bottom lip to silence my moans.

He moved our fingers faster and deeper, worked his tongue harder. The pad of his thumb moved around my clit in hot, delicious circles.

I felt my pleasure building, and I knew it wouldn't take long for me to come.

Dion sank to the floor, pulled my panties down my thighs, then brought his hot tongue to my clitoris. I looked down at him, watching his tongue flicking up and down.

Then he began to suckle me. I gripped his head as I started to come.

And then the bathroom door opened—and my orgasm promptly died.

"Oh, my God—"

Dion reacted quickly, jerking backward and thrusting out a hand to slam the door shut.

"Shit," he uttered.

Alarm and embarrassment shot through me. Turning back toward me, Dion kissed my clit as though he would continue to pleasure me if I wanted him to. He looked up at me, and I saw my own shock reflected on his face.

And then he smiled—a wickedly satisfied smile that made me feel better.

Well, a little better. Because my body ached to reach climax, and it wouldn't—at least not right now.

Dion stood, kissed me quickly and helped me right my clothes. "We should have locked the door," he whispered.

I giggled into his shoulder. But as he turned the doorknob, I felt mortified. I hoped that whoever had been there a moment ago would have had the sense to leave.

No such luck.

Treasure stood there, her arms crossed over her chest, a scowl on her face. "I can't *believe* you," she began without preamble. "This is a barbecue, not a sex party—or whatever the two of you are used to!"

"I apologize," Dion said. "We just…got carried away."

Treasure glared at him, which pissed me off. She'd been waiting for this moment—the moment she could look at him with open disdain.

"Dion, I'll see you in the backyard," I said. I gently caressed his arm. "I need to speak to my friend."

He looked at me, then at her. "I take full responsibility for this, Treasure," he said. "And I apologize. We didn't mean any disrespect."

She didn't reply.

"I'll see you in a few minutes," I told him.

He walked away, turning back as he reached the patio door. I nodded, indicating that it was okay for him to leave us alone.

I was about to speak, but one of the husbands entered the kitchen. "Someone in the bathroom?" he asked as he approached us.

"No. It's free now." To Treasure I said, "I'd love to see that dress you bought."

Turning sharply, she stalked off toward the master bedroom. I followed her and closed the door behind me.

As Treasure faced me, it was clear she was livid. Far too livid, as far as I was concerned.

"If you think that you can excuse what you did…" Her voice trailed off as her chest heaved.

"Why are you so mad?"

"There are kids here!"

"And I'm sorry. But it's not like we were on a table in the backyard for all to see."

"So that makes it right?"

"We got carried away."

"Carried away," Treasure echoed, then scoffed. "You're acting like you've lost your damn mind."

"I'm thirty-seven, Treasure. I don't need a lecture."

"So you think it's completely appropriate to be making out in someone else's bathroom when there are guests around?"

"I didn't say that."

"You've lost all sense of boundaries," Treasure continued.

"Yeah—Dion and I fuck everywhere. Gas stations, public parks."

"You watch your language in my house."

"I'm sorry." I inhaled slowly, blew the breath out in a rush. "I know you don't like profanity."

"Or adultery." She gave me a pointed look.

"That's the thing, Treasure. I'm not having an affair. And I don't appreciate you bringing up Robert to your friends. You're painting me out to be a harlot."

"If you're still married, it's called an affair."

"And that's why I know you were looking for an excuse to hate Dion. Unfortunately, I gave that to you on a silver platter."

"I don't hate him. But you don't have to flaunt your affair in my house." Treasure exhaled loudly. "Look, Robert told me everything. Why you left. All of it."

"Robert told you what?" I asked, bowled over. "I already told you everything."

"Actually, he called me a few days ago."

Anger began to brew inside of me. Robert hardly even liked Treasure. What was he doing calling her?

"Did you expect him to want to have a child with you when you were seeing someone else?"

"Wow. So that's what he said." I shouldn't have been surprised. He was trying to make me look bad—most likely hoping he could turn my friend against me.

"I know he's getting older—"

"I was not seeing anyone while I was married to Robert."

"You're still married," Treasure pointed out.

"Before we *separated*," I snapped. "You know what I mean."

"You weren't seeing Dion before you left Robert?" Treasure asked, eyeing me doubtfully.

"No. Absolutely not."

"Robert thinks you were."

"Well, I wasn't."

Treasure shrugged. "When Robert spoke to me, he said that he's willing to have the vasectomy reversed."

So Robert had called Treasure not only to make me look like the guilty party, but to get her to do his bidding. "That's not what he said to me," I told her. "Not even since I've left him. He very clearly said that he was too old to have any more children."

"He said he told you that because you refused to leave your boyfriend."

"He's lying." And if he expected me to take him back after filling Treasure's head with lies, he was delusional.

"I know you might think it's too late to save your marriage," Treasure began gently. "But it doesn't have to be. Forgiveness can lead to a new start."

Something occurred to me then. That this wasn't about me. It was about Treasure. A couple years ago, she'd confided that Shane had left her for another woman—his secretary. Treasure had prayed about it, and ultimately Shane had come home, but I had a feeling she wasn't truly happy. However, her religious convictions made her determined to save her marriage because she believed her vows had been sacred.

The entire afternoon, I hadn't witnessed any affection between her and her husband. It seemed that she poured all her love onto her four-year-old son.

"And what do you really know about Dion?" Treasure asked me. "It seems to me you're moving too fast."

"You know, Treasure. I love you like the sister I never had, but I think I'm going to leave."

Treasure nodded grimly. "Maybe that's for best."

I turned to the bedroom door, then hesitated. Sighing, I faced my friend once more. "You know, I just wish you weren't so rigid. I understand your religious convictions, and I also understand that my relationship with Dion probably seems a bit sudden to you. But I wish you would treat me like the adult I am. Accept me and my decisions—even if you don't agree with them. I wish we could have sat down and talked about what I'm going through. Yes, my marriage is over—but I've met a man I'm crazy about. It's too bad you can't be happy for me."

Treasure said nothing. I left the bedroom and hurried through the house to the patio doors. I put on a brave face as I stepped outside, not wanting anyone to realize that anything was amiss.

Some of the husbands were now sitting at the table beside their wives, some were standing around it. Dion was chatting with Shane. He had a beer in hand, and looked comfortable.

Why couldn't Treasure try to understand what I was going through? I didn't expect her to jump up and down about my news, but at least she didn't have to be judgmental.

Seeing me, Dion winked. I strolled across the stone patio and slipped my arm through his. "You know what, sweetheart? I'm not feeling that well."

"You're not?"

"No." I pouted a little, putting on a show. "Would you mind if we left early?"

"Of course not," Dion said.

That was another difference between him and my ex. Robert would most likely have told me to stick it out, put on a brave face until he was ready to leave. At least if we were at a function he was enjoying. I didn't know if Dion realized I was telling a white lie or not, but clearly, my feelings mattered to him, in a way they hadn't to Robert.

"Thanks," I murmured. Turning to our host, I said, "Happy birthday, Shane. Hope to see you another time soon."

"Sure thing. Bring Dion by anytime."

I smiled in appreciation at his offer, but knew I wouldn't be taking him up on it, not until Treasure came around.

We said our goodbyes, then I went to Javan across the yard and gave him a big hug.

"Goodbye, Javan. Aunt Elsie loves you."

As I released him and stood, I saw that Treasure was standing a few feet away from me. She no longer looked angry. In fact, she looked solemn. Perhaps a little regretful.

"I'll talk to you later, Treasure," I told her. Then I slipped my hand into Dion's and led the way out of the backyard.

25

The car radio was playing a hip R & B tune I hadn't heard before. I could hear the song, but wasn't truly listening. Instead, I gazed out the window, lost in my thoughts, as we drove along the interstate.

The confrontation with Treasure weighed heavily on my mind. I hadn't expected leaving Robert to be easy. But I hadn't expected to lose my oldest friend over my decision to get a divorce.

Dion was holding my hand as he navigated traffic. Now, he gave it a supportive squeeze.

I turned to face him.

"You okay?" he asked.

I nodded. "Yeah, babe. I'm fine."

A moment passed. "I'm sorry I followed you into the bathroom."

"No, Dion. Don't apologize. What happened…it's not your fault."

"If I hadn't gone into the bathroom when I did—"

"You didn't force me to make out with you," I interjected. "I was a willing participant." For the first time since we'd left my friend's place, I smiled, remembering our hot and heavy session. Even if the location wasn't appropriate, it was nice to be able to be spontaneous with someone who, with just one look, set your body on fire.

"It was you and that pineapple," Dion said, clearly reading the direction of my thoughts. "I got hard watching you, I swear. And when I saw you head inside…" He bit down on his bottom lip. "Damn, I better stop this. I'm getting another hard-on now. I'm tempted to pull over."

"Which would be a bad idea, no matter how tempting." The last thing I needed was a police officer pulling up while I was giving Dion head.

"I know. Just like it was a bad idea to take you into the bathroom."

"Please, Dion, don't feel bad about that."

"I wanted your friend to like me. I don't think she does."

"I don't think Treasure's issue is with you. And I'm starting to think it has nothing to do with me, either."

"What do you mean?"

I shook my head. "It's just…she has her own issues in her marriage. But I wish she'd accept that I'm entitled to make decisions for myself and not be judged."

"She'll get there." Dion squeezed my hand. "It takes time."

"Yeah, I guess you're right. My marriage falling apart, the news that I'm already involved with someone else—it was all a shock to her."

"I'm sorry I caused conflict between you."

"The conflict with Treasure will work itself out. And I can't live my life for her. I'm not about to live my life for anyone else ever again. That said, I think it's probably a good idea if I don't tell her that I've moved in with you. Until some time has passed, I'll be more cautious about what I share with her."

"You're not regretting moving in with me, are you?"

"No!" I replied instantly. "Absolutely not."

Dion kissed my hand. "Good."

"This isn't ideal—me still being married. But I'm crazy about you. Am I supposed to put my life on hold for the next year until my divorce is final? To make everyone else happy?"

"You won't get an argument from me."

"And I'm thirty-seven, for God's sake. I don't need anyone's permission to live with you. Except yours, of course."

"You have that and then some," Dion said. He winked at me before turning his attention back to the road.

I gazed at him with affection. Maybe I shouldn't expect Treasure to understand what I was feeling for Dion. I hardly understood it myself. I only knew that from the time I'd met him, he had changed my life.

What do you really know about him? Treasure had asked me. *It seems to me you're moving too fast.*

Certainly words of caution I couldn't dispute, and yet… And yet, what had I known about Robert when I'd met and married him? Only that he was a gentleman, a romantic and caring and successful man. Our relationship had lasted a lot longer than many other couples who got married these days.

I'd given my marriage my best shot. I had nothing to feel guilty about.

I'd realized on the drive to Treasure's that I didn't have my cell phone with me. When we got home, I went straight to the kitchen, hoping to find it there. I had a vague memory of putting it on the countertop.

"Thank God," I exclaimed when I saw it, and quickly scooped it up. But a moment later, as I flipped through my missed calls, I grew wary.

There had been a dozen calls from the shop. And about five more from Spike's cell phone.

Dion must have seen the expression on my face. "What is it?"

"There were several calls from the shop. And Spike was trying to reach me."

I didn't bother checking my messages, just called his cell.

"Why haven't you been answering your phone?" Spike asked without preamble when he picked up.

"I forgot my cell," I explained. "What's wrong? Everything okay with Marcus?"

"Marcus isn't the problem. I've been trying to reach you about the shop."

"The shop?"

"Major problems. I called to place those orders today like you asked. But the vases, gift baskets, wet and dry foam—all those supplies you needed—well, the order wouldn't go through. The supplier said your credit was declined."

"Declined?"

"At first I thought there had to be a mistake, some computer glitch, so I went ahead and called the supplier for Godiva. And they told me the same thing. That your credit was declined."

"That's imp—" The word died on my lips. Instantly, I knew what was going on. "Robert," I said. "It has to be him."

"That's what I figured."

"Damn him!"

Before me, Dion mouthed the word *"What?"*

"Of course, it could be something else, doll-face."

"Oh, I doubt that." I drew in a deep breath. "Thanks for letting me know. I can't do anything about it until Monday morning. I'll go to the bank first thing and settle this situation."

But by the time Monday morning rolled around, I'd learned that the problem was bigger than I had anticipated.

All my credit cards had been declined when I tried to pay for gas on Sunday. I'd had to leave my driver's license with the gas station attendant as collateral so I kayla perrin

could drive to the bank and withdraw cash. Only when I got to the ATM, I discovered I had no access to any cash. The screen kept flashing the words *TRANSAC-TION UNAUTHORIZED.*

Crying, I had to call Dion, who had been out playing basketball with a teenager he was mentoring, and ask him to meet me so I could pay my bill.

By Monday morning, I was pissed. I marched into my branch and asked to speak to the manager.

The manager, a man I knew was a personal friend of Robert's, ushered me into his office ten minutes later.

"Mrs. Kolstad." He smiled warmly. "What brings you in today?"

I lowered myself onto the plush leather seat, my back ramrod straight. I counted to five before speaking, making a concerted effort to keep my anger under control.

Kenny Lyle wasn't my problem. Robert was.

"I seem to be having a problem with my accounts," I explained. "My personal account, my business account. I can't access any money."

Kenny gave me an odd look. "We froze the assets when your husband reported the identity fraud Friday afternoon."

"Identity fraud?"

"Yes. Robert came in, told me his concern that all your accounts had been breached. Sure enough, I found charges totaling nearly twenty thousand dollars that he said were bogus. I froze all the accounts immediately."

"What kind of charges?"

"Thousands of dollars worth of computer equipment and some other electronics." Kenny frowned. "Surely Robert advised you of this?"

"Mr. Lyle, I'm not sure if he told you the state of our marriage," I began gently. "We've separated."

"Oh, I'm so sorry to hear that."

"I'm not sure what's going on, but I need access to my accounts."

"I'm sorry, Mrs. Kolstad. They've been frozen. We'll have to set up new accounts for you, including personal and business credit—"

"And how long will that take?"

"I'll need both you and Robert to sign some paperwork."

"How can I set up my own account?" Why hadn't I considered doing that before? All my accounts had Robert's name on them, which I could see now had been a huge mistake.

"You can set up an account at any time. But in order to access the frozen assets, we need your husb—"

I pushed my chair back and stood. "I can't believe this. I have a business to run. I need access to credit to place orders."

"Your business account, your personal account— everything was joint with Robert. He'll need to authorize—"

I spun around and stormed out of the office. I'd been on the verge of grabbing something off Kenny's desk and throwing it.

Or bursting into tears.

I hurried onto the street, tears finally filling my eyes. What was I going to do?

26

I didn't call Dion to tell him what was happening. Instead I went to the shop and leaving Tabitha and Spike to work the front, locked myself in the back office and began calling my suppliers. I'd done business with them for several years and asked if they were willing to extend me credit on good faith, until my snafu was resolved.

With the economic climate as dismal as it was, all my suppliers said no—with regret. They needed to protect their bottom line.

I understood that.

But I also understood that without flowers and other supplies coming in, I would have to shut down the shop within a week.

I was certain that Robert wanted me to call him—and even Spike said I should—but I was hell-bent on finding another way to resolve my problem.

★ ★ ★

I couldn't have been more surprised when Robert appeared outside my shop two hours later. He smiled at me through the window, the kind of smile that didn't reach his eyes. The kind that made my back go rigid with alarm.

I realized I was scared of him. I truly didn't know how far he would go to make me come back to him.

Turning my gaze back to the customer I was serving, I tried to act as though Robert's unexpected appearance hadn't put me on edge. "So, Wednesday morning?"

"Yes," the middle-aged woman replied. There was sadness in her eyes. "Can you have it delivered to the funeral home?"

"Yes, of course," I told her gently.

"Good. Because there is so much to take care of. And I want…I just want…"

"To make sure everything's perfect," I finished gently.

The woman nodded, her eyes filling with tears.

My own eyes shot to the window. I watched as Robert spoke to a woman who looked as if she'd been about to enter my shop. Was I paranoid, or did the woman's expression register surprise at whatever Robert had told her? I saw him nod, and then the woman shrugged and walked on.

What the hell?

"She lived a good life," the woman in front of me was saying now. "And she went peacefully. But it's never easy to lose your mother."

"No. No, never. Don't worry. You write down all the

details here of where you want the flowers delivered, itemize the selections you want, and I'll take care of the rest." I paused. "And...I hate to ask this, but there's a problem with my computer system right now. Would it be possible for you to pay in cash?"

"That'd be fine."

Thank God. If I could collect cash from most of my customers, I might have enough to wire a payment to one of my suppliers. Because I had orders to fill for weddings and other occasions. I stood to lose a ton of business if I couldn't get what I needed.

Robert continued to stand outside, staring in at me. Obviously, he was trying to intimidate me. I hated the fact that he was succeeding. "If you'll excuse me for just a minute..." I said to the customer.

I started for the door. I had the awful feeling that Robert had just sent a potential customer away. What the hell was he doing?

Seeing me approach, he grinned.

But it wasn't any warmer this time around. Or any more sincere.

I opened the door and stepped outside. "What are you doing here?"

"Hello to you, too, Elsie."

"Cut the crap. Did you come here to gloat? To see if I had to close down the shop?"

"I don't know what you mean."

Bastard! I wanted to yell. Instead I said, "My accounts have been frozen, Robert. Because *you* alerted the bank manager to an *identity theft* issue. Do you honestly think that by intimidating me you'll make me want to forgive you? Not to mention the crap you told Treasure about me." I gritted my teeth, took a breath, then continued. "Fix this, Robert. Call the bank and fix this."

"Let's have dinner this evening and talk things through," Robert said. "If you can be reasonable, so can I."

He sounded so levelheaded, as if he was offering to be fair—but I knew better.

I didn't want the unpleasantness. And as far as I was concerned, I was being more than reasonable. I wasn't trying to fight Robert for his money. My lawyer believed I was entitled to more than a million dollars, given Robert's vast fortune. But all I wanted was to come out of the marriage with my business.

"Do the right thing," I reiterated, then turned and went back into the store.

My accounts were still frozen the next day, and the stress was getting to me.

Spike and Maxine were working with me, and I sat them down at the beginning of their shifts and explained to them that I was having a cash flow problem. Unfortunately, until the problem was resolved, I couldn't issue their paychecks. But I assured them I would have the matter settled by the end of the week.

Spike took the news in stride, as I knew he would. But late that afternoon, Maxine asked if she could speak privately with me.

"What's on your mind, Maxine?" I asked when we were both in my office.

She bit her cheek for a moment, not saying anything. She looked conflicted. "It's just…"

"Just what?"

"I know you and your husband are having problems, and I'm really sorry about that because I love working here. I was hoping to work as many hours as possible this summer to make enough money for my next semester of school. But it doesn't sound like that's going to happen now."

"It's a temporary setback, Maxine."

"My parents got divorced, and it was awful. Their assets were tied up in court for years as they battled over who would get what."

"I promise I'll have this mess sorted out by next week." One way or another, I would have to.

"Even if you do, I—" Maxine's voice broke off "I—"

"What, Maxine?"

She fidgeted with her hands, not meeting my eyes. "It doesn't matter. I—I have to. I'm really sorry, but I have to quit."

"Maxine, no."

"I'm sorry," she said, and fled from the office in tears.

By the next morning, I'd been able to meet with my lawyer, but the news wasn't good.

We would have to go to court and petition the judge to intervene. But it might be weeks before we could get a court date, even one considered an emergency.

"I'm going to appeal to your husband's lawyer that we

all sit down as soon as possible and iron out a separation agreement," Diane explained. Robert had, as I assumed he would, retained Clayton Gunter. "You shouldn't have to close your business temporarily to deal with this. Unfortunately, based on my conversations with Gunter, it's clear he's going to play hardball. Did you find your copy of the prenuptial agreement?"

I shook my head. "No. I'd had it in my home office with my files. I searched every box I took from the house and it's not there."

Diane frowned. "I'm sure the attorney who drafted it will have a copy—"

"But he's one of Robert's friends. I don't trust anything anymore."

"Don't you worry," Diane said. "You won't be left penniless."

I wasn't so sure about that, and as I left Diane's office and went back to work, I was torn. Should I see Robert, even though I hated the idea of caving? Or should I stand my ground, even if it meant I would possibly have to close the shop for weeks?

With no new supplies, and my accounts frozen, I couldn't stay open much longer. Dion had offered to lend me some money, but I declined. This was a problem I needed to deal with on my own.

But how to deal with it?

Unfortunately, I couldn't get around the fact that I might have to give Robert what he wanted in order for him to agree to solve the problem. As much as I didn't want to see him, maybe I had to.

Beg. That's what he likely wanted me to do.

I might just have to.

Or…perhaps there was another way. I had a good deal of jewelry. Maybe I could sell it.

I glanced at my left hand on the steering wheel. The indentation from my wedding bands was still evident. The engagement ring and diamond wedding band had cost thousands. I had stunning necklaces, earrings and bracelets. Surely I could sell those for a decent amount of cash.

The very idea made my chest tighten. I loved the jewelry Robert had bought for me, and there were happy memories attached to the pieces. I didn't want to hate Robert when we divorced. I wanted someday to be able to think of him with fondness. I wanted to wear my diamond and tanzanite necklace, for example, and remember with warmth the wonderful vacation we'd had in Aruba when he'd bought it for me. Just because we wouldn't be married anymore didn't mean there had to be bitterness and resentment.

But the sad truth was there would be no amicable parting from Robert. There was bitterness and resentment with his two ex-wives. I was bitter and resentful. It was becoming increasingly clear that our relationship would end up exactly the same way.

As I neared my shop, I felt better about the idea of selling my jewelry. I couldn't take it to a pawnshop. I would have to see if I could find some kind of broker who could sell the pieces for the best possible price.

But how long will that take?

My predicament was all I could think about as I pulled up in front of my store. I was out of the car and heading to the door when I noticed that the store's neon Closed sign was displayed.

Where was Spike? It was almost eleven, and the store should have been open. With Maxine gone, and Tabitha not scheduled until the afternoon, Spike should have been inside hustling to get the orders made with the flowers we had. I also wanted to create some bouquets to put on racks in front of the store, hoping to sell them quickly. The inventory I had wouldn't last forever.

As I unlocked the door, concern shot through me. Had Spike been in an accident? If he'd been unable to make it to work, certainly he would have called. So something serious had to be wrong.

I hurried into the shop and rushed right to the phone, ready to call his number. I was already trying to think who I could call to find out what might have happened to him if I couldn't reach him.

And that's when I noticed the small bouquet of flowers on the front counter, one that wasn't normally there.

Beneath the blue vase was a folded slip of paper.

With a bad feeling washing over me, I snatched it up and quickly opened it.

Elsie, I know you will be surprised that I'm not in today, working hard on the orders we need to fill. Rest assured, I haven't left you in the lurch. The bouquets being picked up today are complete—and if I say so myself, they look fabulous. Lou left at ten-thirty to deliver the funeral wreath.

Ten-thirty. If Spike had been here at ten-thirty, then

I had missed him by about twenty-five minutes. I continued reading.

> Doll-face, I tell you this with a heavy heart. I will not be returning. I hate to quit on you like this, especially after Maxine left. Please don't ask me why. Send my final check to my address once Robert stops being an ass and straightens this mess out. Or, if you're too mad, you don't have to pay me. I'd understand.
>
> This isn't about the financial troubles. You know I'd never leave your side if I didn't have to. I'm going through something, and I need you to understand that this couldn't be helped.
>
> I love you, and I'm sorry.
> Spike

I read the note again, not understanding it any better the second time around.

In the five years that Spike had worked for me, he had never called in sick—even when he should have. That's how responsible he was about his job, and how he showed his gratitude for me giving him a chance. And he had always shared with me whatever drama he was dealing with in his life, from his mother trying to bring about a reconciliation between him and his father, to the bad dating choices he made. I'd gone to the clinic with him when he'd had an HIV scare. As far as I was concerned, it didn't get any more personal than that.

I didn't doubt that he would still come in even if he thought he wouldn't get paid. He was that kind of friend. Which was why his writing me a note and telling me not to ask him any questions...well, it simply didn't make any sense.

I punched in the digits of Spike's home number. Either he wasn't home or he didn't pick up. I called his BlackBerry. Same deal.

Feeling slightly better because at least I knew he was okay, I sent him a text message.

What's going on? Please call me.

I didn't bother adding that I wasn't about to let him quit on me. When I spoke to him, I would tell him that in person—and find out exactly what was going on.

But that would have to wait, because it was shortly after eleven, and I had work to do.

My calls and texts to Spike went unanswered for the rest of the day, and I was very concerned. What if he'd been in a car crash, after all, or had done something crazy like overdose on pills? I didn't truly believe that scenario had happened, but what if Marcus had broken Spike's heart again and he was feeling depressed? A second breakup with the only man he'd loved could have him acting irrationally.

People always expressed complete surprise when they learned that someone close to them had committed suicide, believing the person incapable of anything so drastic. Unfortunately, I knew that Spike *was* capable. He'd confided in me that when Marcus broke his heart five years ago, he had been so despondent that he'd taken a bottle of Tylenol. A friend had found him passed out, seen the empty bottle and called 911, and he'd been rushed to emergency, where his stomach had been pumped.

In my heart, I expected to find Spike at home and depressed, most likely nursing another broken heart. But I'd be lying if I said the reality that he'd attempted suicide before wasn't playing on my mind.

I dialed Dion's cell. He picked up almost immediately. "Hey, babe."

"Hi, sweetie. I'm calling to let you know I won't be home for a bit. Spike didn't show up today—and I'm concerned. I'm heading to his place to check on him."

Dion's voice was laced with concern. "Of course. Want me to go with you?"

"No, I'm already on the road. Besides, if Spike's there, I have the feeling that I'll have to have a heart-to-heart with him. For him not to show up is totally out of character, and I'm betting his boyfriend broke his heart again."

"Will you call me when you get there? Let me know he's okay?"

"Of course." *I love you,* I added silently. This was another element about Dion that was as different as night and day compared to Robert. He genuinely cared about my friends.

Traffic was unusually heavy for a Wednesday, and it took me almost thirty minutes to arrive at Spike's town house in the north end of Charlotte. His car was in the driveway—both good and bad news. Good, because it meant he was home. Bad because of what I might find inside.

I walked up the steps to the door. I pressed the doorbell incessantly, indicating the urgency of my visit.

A couple seconds later, I tried the knob. It was locked. I began to ring the doorbell again.

And then I heard a shuffling sound on the other side of the door.

"Spike?" I called. "Spike, is that you?"

"Damn it, doll-face, you shouldn't be here."

Relief flooded me. "Let me in," I told him. "No matter what's going on, we're friends, right?"

A few seconds passed. Spike said nothing, and I wondered fleetingly if he was going to leave me standing on his doorstep. But then I heard the lock turn, and then the door was opening.

He looked okay. As if he had the weight of the world on his shoulders, but otherwise, okay. He didn't seem high or out of it.

I swept into his small foyer. "Spike, you gave me the scare of my life!"

"I'm sorry, doll-face."

"Tell me what's going on. Right after I call Dion to let him know you're alive."

"Oh, my word. You didn't think—"

"I didn't know what to think," I pointed out. I dialed Dion's cell.

"Is he all right?" Dion asked when he answered the call.

"Yeah, he's fine. At least physically."

"Good. That's good."

"I'll call you when I'm on my way."

Hanging up, I faced Spike again.

"I can't believe you thought I'd done something to hurt myself," he said.

"When you didn't show up, I feared the worst. I figured Marcus probably broke your heart again."

"He did," Spike admitted.

"Oh, Spike." I hugged him. "When?"

"Yesterday," he answered, as we pulled apart.

"I knew it," I said. "I knew he would hurt you again."

"It's fine."

"No, it's not." I rubbed both Spike's arms. "I figured as much, and I knew you would be hurting. And when people are hurting, sometimes..." I ended my statement with a shrug, knowing he could fill in the blank.

"They take a bottle of Tylenol?" he suggested. "I'm not the same person I was five years ago. Thanks in large part to you."

I grasped his elbow and led him into the living room. "That's good to hear. But I am worried. Your note...that wasn't like you." I stopped in front of the sofa. "Sit," I instructed him. "Talk to me."

Sighing, Spike sat. I sat beside him and took his hand in mine.

"You shouldn't be here," he said.

"Yeah, right. Like that was possible."

"I just want the best for you," Spike told me. "I never want to stand in your way."

"You could never stand in my way. I know my business wouldn't be what it is without you. You and me—we're a team. In fact—and this is something I was already thinking about, so don't think it's about pity—I was figuring I could make you a partner if you want. If I can disentangle myself from Robert with the separation agreement and get control of the store, we can go into business together."

"I meant it when I said I'm not coming back."

I crossed my arms over my chest. "You're not quitting. I won't let you."

"I've made my decision," Spike replied. "Effective immediately. Please, don't ask me to change my mind."

"Maxine bailed on me. You expect me to believe you'd leave me having to hire two new people at a time like this? I know you. You'd walk through fire for me. So whatever's going on, I know it's serious. Please tell me."

He looked away.

"If you're in some kind of trouble, you know you can trust me. I'll help you in any way I can."

"Exactly—I'm trying to help you," Spike muttered, so softly I wasn't sure I'd heard him correctly.

"What? What do you mean, you're trying to help me?"

He gave me a resigned look, knowing I wasn't going to drop the matter. "Doll-face, you have to promise not to say a word."

"I won't."

"Because the only reason I was reluctant to tell you the truth is that I know you'll want to confront Robert about it, and I—"

"Robert?" I asked, perplexed. "This has to do with Robert?"

"Yes, it has to do with Robert. But you can't say a word to him. Don't tell him we spoke. Promise me."

"I promise. *He's* the reason you didn't show up today?"

Meeting my eyes, Spike nodded. "You know I'd never desert you. No matter how depressed I might be. Work is therapy for me. Just like it is for you."

Of course Spike wouldn't abandon me. I knew that. Which was why his letter had caused me so much concern. It was completely out of character. And now I knew why.

"What did he say?" I asked urgently. "What did he do?"

Spike's eyes dropped downward. He was embarrassed.

No, I realized—he was afraid.

"You're afraid." My voice came out in a whisper.

Spike immediately met my eyes. "Not for me. This isn't about me. I'm afraid for you."

Spike's tone made the hairs on the nape of my neck stand on end. "Tell me."

"Robert showed up at my door last night, scared the shit out of me, I tell you. He said he needed to talk, that it was urgent. So I let him in."

"And what did he say?"

"He knew about my nervous breakdown. He knew that I'd tried to kill myself." Spike held my gaze for a moment.

310 kayla perrin

"I never said a word. I swear…I wouldn't betray your confidence."

"I believe you. I know Robert is a powerful man. He has a lot of resources available to him."

"Okay, so he found out about your past. How—"

"He wanted me gone. He made that *very* clear. I don't know why. But he stressed it would be in your best interests—and mine—if I quit. That if I didn't, he'd make it known to the hospice about my past."

"That's insane," I said. "You've volunteered there for years, helped so many people. They wouldn't judge you for a moment of weakness in your past."

"Which is what I told Robert. I dared him to go ahead and tell them this *shocking* news about me. It wouldn't matter one lick."

"Good." I was glad that Spike had stood up to him. But the next moment, I was back to being confused. "I don't understand. You stood up to Robert. You told him it wouldn't matter if he tried to badmouth you. So why didn't you come in to work today?"

"Because," he began, then sighed. "I got a really nasty vibe from Robert. And, Elsie, I mean *really* nasty. He didn't like it when he realized he couldn't threaten me. The look he gave me…it was pure evil. And then he said that if I cared about you, I would quit. That things would be easier for you if I did."

"Meaning?"

"I don't know, doll-face. He wouldn't say. For him, it was all about the power of suggestion. But I got the feeling…" Spike's voice trailed off.

"Feeling that what?"

Spike held my gaze a long moment before speaking. "I got the feeling that he would hurt you. And I mean physically."

A chill slithered down my spine. *Would* Robert hurt me? Once he realized he could no longer control me, that I wouldn't go back to him, would he do me physical harm?

No...I couldn't see that. He would hate me, try to make my life hell as a way to punish me. But hurt me? That would be going too far.

"That's the reason I can't go back to work for you. If he sees that I haven't quit and gets enraged and does something to physically harm you... Doll-face, I could never live with myself if that happened. *Never*."

I was silent for several seconds, considering Spike's words. "He must be pissed that I've managed to keep the store open," I concluded. I rose slowly, and as I did, an idea came to me. I suddenly had to wonder about Maxine. I was certain there had been something she wanted to say the day she quit. Had Robert gotten to her? Perhaps cornered her while she was out at lunch, and threatened her? Lured her away with the promise of a better job? Maxine's parting had been so sudden that now I had to wonder if she'd been influenced to quit.

"I think he expected that I would have run back to him by now so that he'd resolve my financial crisis," I went on, thinking out loud, trying to determine Robert's motives. I began to pace the floor. "I haven't run back to him, so now he's strong-arming my employees, knowing that without decent help I'll be forced to shut down. Maxine's parting was inconvenient, but I can find temporary staff fairly easily. But you—he knows that you've been my most loyal employee for years. He knows that you know the business inside and out. Losing you would be a major blow to my store."

Yes, that made sense. Robert was hoping to force my staff to quit, leaving me to run the store alone, something that would be an overwhelming task. It was yet another way he was trying to break me down—all in an effort to coerce me back into his life.

"Elsie, I just have this bad feeling. The feeling that this is the tip of the iceberg with Robert. The man is clearly unstable and determined to make your life miserable."

"I have to stand up to him," I insisted. "Sure, he gave me a great life, took me to fabulous places—but he micromanaged everything I did. Controlled me like I was his company. I can't let him control me now, which is what he's trying to do. Even if it means losing my store," I added with determination.

"Don't say that. Your lawyer is tough. She'll help you get what you deserve. You did your time. You deserve not to be broke and homeless. But maybe you ought to close the shop temporarily until this all plays out in court."

"If I let him bully me now, he wins," I said, defiantly. "If I close the shop, it's one more thing he was able to control. If you quit, it's one more thing he was able to manipulate." Spike's eyes widened in protest, but I continued before he could speak. "But I don't want you in the middle of the conflict with me and Robert. And I certainly don't want you blaming yourself for anything else he might do to make my life hell. And who knows how he might lash out at you if you come back to work despite his threat? Maybe it's best to let him think he's won this round."

I sat beside Spike again and placed a hand on his arm. "So why don't we do this—you take a leave of absence for now. When I've resolved things with Robert and we're divorced and the shop is mine, you'll come back. And I'll make you a partner then, if you want."

Spike gave me a warm smile. "I love you, doll-face."

"Is that a deal?" I extended my hand.

He reached out and shook it. "Deal."

27

I called Dion when I was back in my car.

"Hi, babe," he answered. "Everything okay with Spike?"

"Yeah, he's...he's fine."

"Then why don't you sound okay?"

"It was Robert," I said. "Robert forced Spike to quit. He threatened him."

"Physically?" Dion asked doubtfully.

"No, not physically. Even if he were young enough, that's not his style. He's all about intimidation." I gritted my teeth. "And I think he did the same with Maxine. Look, I'll talk to you when I get home, okay?"

"See you soon."

The moment I stepped in the door, Dion greeted me with a warm hug. I sagged against him, leaned into his strength.

"I poured you a glass of wine," Dion said.

I drew back, stretched up on my toes and planted a kiss on his nose. "Thank you, baby."

Releasing me, he took my hand. "Come on."

It was the simple things I was savoring with Dion now. Simple things like holding his hand and feeling alive. Alive in a way I never had with Robert.

Dion excited me. One look at his strong arms, his naked back…one stroke of my fingers along his skin. These things sent a rush of heady excitement tingling through my body.

I knew now that the love I'd felt for Robert had been a comfortable kind. The kind of love you feel for a family member, or someone you admire greatly. I'd been in awe of him when I'd met him, and he'd romanced me as no one ever had. I fell in love with the idea of being in love with someone like Robert.

But Dion's love was the kind that completed a person. Made you feel whole.

He released my hand to pick up the glass he'd already filled with red wine. I sank into the soft leather sofa, then accepted the wine he extended to me.

I took a long sip as he filled his own glass. He sat beside me and I leaned my head on his shoulder.

"So what did Spike say?" Dion asked.

"It's crazy, Dion. Totally nuts." I spent the next few minutes filling him in on what Robert had done. "He's trying to make everything in my life difficult."

"Because of me."

It was a statement, not a question. I reached for Dion's hand. "No. This is because I've left him."

"You haven't just left him—you've moved on with someone else."

"What does it matter who I'm seeing?" I asked. "Robert wants to punish me, make me think I can't survive on my own. Maybe I can't...but I'm not going back."

I watched Dion, knowing from the expression on his face that there was something else he wanted to say.

"What is it? What are you thinking?" I asked.

"I'm thinking that this whole thing with Robert is going to get worse before it gets better."

"I know. But it will pass."

"I hate this."

"I can deal with it," I assured him. I didn't know how it would play out, but I *had* to deal with it. There was no going back now.

"You know I would never do anything to hurt you."

That was an odd comment. "Yes, I do believe that."

Dion nodded. "Good. Because I was thinking... maybe until this whole thing is over...maybe we should cool things down."

Alarm shot through me, and my heart thundered painfully. "You're breaking up with me?"

"No. No, that's not what I'm doing."

"Then explain what 'cool things down' means."

"It means that if Robert is going to be a son of a bitch, use his power and lawyers to deny you a decent settlement—"

"I don't care about that."

"You say that now. But if you lose everything you're entitled to because of me—"

"Dion, stop." Leaning forward, I planted my finger on his lips. "I'm so sick of people telling me I should care about the money. I know firsthand that money is not what makes a person happy."

"I'm just saying that with me in the picture, it's obvious Robert is going to make this experience brutal. And you don't deserve that."

Myriad emotions were swirling inside of me. "So, what—you expect that for the next six months or a year I'm supposed to forget about you, not see you, just go on as if I'd never met you?"

"We can see each other—I'm not saying that. But I think it's best if we don't live together."

"Oh, my God." I shot to my feet and drank down the rest of the wine in my glass.

"Hey."

I didn't turn. "So now I'm supposed to lose you. Lose you when I've fallen in love with you?"

I felt Dion's hands on my arms. "Hey."

I swiveled to face him. And suddenly, I recalled Treasure's words. *What do you really know about Dion? It seems to me you're moving too fast.*

Was Dion not who I thought he was?

"Are you coming up with an easy excuse to dump me?" I asked him.

"Jesus, no."

"Maybe you said you loved me when you really didn't," I went on. "It's easy to get a woman like me to believe anything—I'm so damn gullible."

He put his hands on my shoulders, but I shrugged away. "Elsie—"

"Because if this has been a fun time but nothing more—"

"That's bullshit."

"—I won't fall apart."

"Gee, that's nice. Way to make a guy feel special."

"I'm not the one who wants to break up!" I exclaimed, moving away from him.

I stared at Dion, and he at me. I'd gone off. Lost it. That's how much I cared about this man. I didn't want to imagine being without him, not even temporarily.

Dion was the first one to speak. "I love you," he said softly. "Like I told you, I think I fell in love with you the first time I saw you."

"Then how can you suggest we slow things down?"

"It was just a suggestion. I thought maybe it would help."

"It wouldn't. It would make Robert win. And I'll be damned if I let him control my life any more than he has."

Dion took a step toward me. "Okay."

"Is this just about fun?" I asked. "Fun while it lasts?"

"You're not serious?"

I didn't answer, just lifted my chin and held his gaze.

"If I wanted fun, there are a lot of women without rich, vindictive husbands I would get involved with instead."

I looked down. Swallowed.

"You don't believe I love you?" Dion asked.

"Maybe you just think you do." I was experiencing a moment of insecurity—my past rearing its ugly head—but I couldn't stop myself.

"Hey." Dion wrapped his arms around me. "You know that's not true. You know it in your heart."

Warmth began to flow through my veins again.

"Why are we arguing?" he asked.

Why, indeed? The stress was getting to me. Robert's games were getting to me. But the thought that I might lose Dion had gotten to me most of all.

"Because I don't want to lose you. Not because of Robert."

"You're not going to lose me." Dion kissed my lips softly, reassuringly.

I moaned, the sound carrying with it the weight of my fragile emotions. "Promise me," I pleaded, snaking my arms around his neck. "Promise me that Robert won't make me lose you."

"I promise."

Dion kissed me again, another soft kiss, but I pressed my fingertips into his shoulder blades, urging him closer, and opened my mouth beneath his. I kissed him hungrily, with unbridled passion. I sucked on the tip of his tongue, felt dizzying sensations begin to take control.

I broke the kiss briefly and whispered, "This isn't about fun for me, Dion. I want a life with you. A family with you."

I moved my lips over his again, but he pulled away from me. Disappointed, I opened my eyes and looked up at him. I continued to dig my fingers into his flesh, a silent plea for us to keep going.

"What did you say?" he asked.

I inhaled a shuddery breath. "I'm in love with you."

"No, what you said after that."

"I want a life with you."

"After that."

"I want a family with you."

I can't explain the look that spread over his face. A smile of pure joy curved his lips. The kind of smile I'd seen on Javan's face on his last birthday, when he'd gotten the remote control car he had been asking for.

"Say it again."

Now I smiled. "I want a family with you."

"Music to my ears, sweetheart."

"It's true. I want to make babies with you. Lots of them."

Dion's lips came down on mine. He kissed me until tingles of lust raced up and down my spine.

"I want the same thing." The timbre of Dion's voice was suddenly low, husky. The kind of tone that said he wanted to fuck. "That night, when you didn't let me get a condom…I was kind of hoping…"

"So was I." I stared up at him in amazement. How was it we were always not only on the same page, but the same sentence?

"You're the only woman I've ever felt that way about."

My heart pounded at the words. God, I was in love with this man. I was in the frying pan.

He pulled at the laces on the front of my shirt. They

had no practical purpose and were only for show. But the fact that he was starting to undress me had me already turned on.

"You want to hear something else?" he asked. He stared in confusion at my shirt.

"The laces are for show," I explained.

"What good is that?"

"To tease you."

"Torture is more like it." He pulled the shirt over my head and tossed it onto the floor.

"What were you saying?" I prompted.

"Oh." He covered my breasts with his palms. "Right." Through my bra, he ran his thumbs over my nipples.

I closed my eyes. "You were saying…"

"My mother always told me this would happen. That I would meet the right woman and fall in love instantly."

"Really?"

"Mmm-hmm. I want you to meet her."

"I would love to meet her."

Dion unsnapped my bra from behind. "I don't want to talk about my mother anymore."

"No?"

He tugged at my nipples. "No."

I gripped his shoulders and eased my head back as his lips found the underside of my jaw. He ran his tongue from there to my earlobe, then suckled my sensitive flesh. My lips parted in a moan.

Dion pushed the mounds of my breasts together until my nipples were only an inch apart. He swiped his hot tongue over one nipple, trailing a path to the other.

Then he took both nipples into his mouth at once, and waves of pleasure rushed through me.

"I want your pussy," Dion said, guiding me to the floor. "I want to eat you." He pushed my skirt up and pulled my panties down. "I want to eat you until you come in my mouth."

I whimpered at his words. "Not here," I said. "Not on the floor."

"The bedroom?" Dion asked.

"No. The armchair." Standing, I made my way over to the chair. I sat on the edge, stretched one leg slowly over one arm, then the other leg over the other arm.

Dion growled as he stared at my exposed pussy.

"Right here," I said—and stroked my clitoris. "Eat me right here."

Dion got onto the floor in front of me. I thought he would begin to eat me right away, but he simply looked at me. I felt sexy and desirable and adored.

I felt like a complete woman.

He ran the tip of his finger along the length of my folds, then traced the same path with the tip of his tongue. Spreading me, he dipped his tongue into my opening.

I closed my eyes and played with my nipples.

"Oh, yeah," Dion growled, lapping up my essence. "You're so wet. You taste so good."

He thrust a finger inside me, and I mewled. As he eased in another finger, he drew my clit into his mouth and suckled me.

Soon I was panting and coming. Coming hard, while

Dion sucked my clitoris so damn sweetly. "Oh, God!"
I cried, gripping the armrests. "Oh, baby…"

And then he was fucking me with his tongue, pushing it in and out of my pussy as deep as he could. His
thumb stroked my clit, relentlessly giving me pleasure.
He didn't let up. He continued to thrill me with his
tongue and his fingers until another orgasm was swell-
ing inside me.

This time I screamed as the force of my climax
tore through me, perhaps the sweetest one I had ever
experienced.

"I love you," I said, whimpering. "I love you, Dion.
I love you."

And when he thrust his cock inside of me, nestling
it deep, tears filled my eyes.

Happy tears.

Tears of love.

28

Dion's mother came over for dinner on Saturday night. She was an absolutely lovely woman. The kind I'd be lucky to have as a mother-in-law.

She was affable and sincere and overtly loving. It was easy to see where Dion had gotten his warm nature.

Where Treasure doubted our relationship, Dion's mother, Evelyn, accepted it. She embraced me fervently the moment she met me, as though I was already family.

All that mattered to her was that Dion loved me, and that I loved him.

The cancer treatment had left her bald, but a short Afro had grown back. From her exuberant nature, you'd never know she had ever been ill.

After she left and I was loading the dishwasher, my

cell phone rang. I hurried to get it—and my heart began to pound when I saw Robert's number.

I couldn't avoid him. And I didn't want to. We needed to resolve things immediately, where my business was concerned. With a heavy heart, I had shut the doors to the shop today and placed a sign in the window stating that the business would be temporarily closed.

Even though I wanted to talk to Robert, my stomach twisted as I answered my phone. "Hello?"

"Sorry to call you so late, Elsie, but we do need to talk."

"Yes," I said guardedly.

"Clear your schedule for tomorrow afternoon. It's time we get on with this divorce."

I was so stunned, I said nothing.

"There are details we need to hammer out. That's why I've arranged to have a mediator come to the house tomorrow, to help us with that."

Dion wandered into the kitchen. I met his gaze as I said, "A mediator?"

"Yes."

"Okay. I'll talk to my lawyer—"

"There's no need. The first thing people have to do is use a mediator to help come to an agreement. It's all set for tomorrow afternoon at one. I pulled a few strings to arrange it, so I hope you can make it."

"I'll be there. See you tomorrow."

Dion's eyes narrowed in question. "Who was that?" he asked, walking toward me.

From the expression on his face, I got the sense that he already knew. "Robert."

"He wants you to meet him tomorrow?"

"Yes. He's arranged for a mediator to go to his house so we can finally work on a separation agreement."

Dion was silent a moment, his brow furrowed in thought. "At his house? I've never heard of a mediator going to a person's house."

"For a man like Robert, that's the way he likes to get things done. He often had meetings with lawyers at home. There's a huge office in the house, even a boardroom…. Robert's the kind of guy who's not going to want be seen going into the local courthouse to deal with a divorce issue."

Dion nodded, but his expression remained wary.

"What?" I asked him.

"I guess I just don't like the idea of you going over there."

"Neither do I. But I had to close the doors to my shop today. Robert knows he's got the power to keep me out of business, because everything I have is in his name. If I have no money, I won't even be able to make next month's car payment on my lease."

"I'm not going to let you go without a car," Dion said.

"I know that. But I can't avoid Robert forever. And it sounds like maybe he's finally turned the corner." I stroked Dion's face. "This is a good sign. He's ready to proceed with our divorce. And as soon as I'm divorced…" I let my unfinished statement dangle between us.

"As soon as you're divorced, what?"

"You might have something you want to ask me," I said, grinning.

I turned back to the counter and lifted more plates to put in the dishwasher.

"You know, I can go with you," Dion suggested.

"Right. Like that would go over well."

"I could stay in the car."

The plates now in the dishwasher, I turned and faced him again. "And if Robert got wind that I was there with my boyfriend, how do you think he'd react? I know we're getting a divorce, but there's no reason to rub salt in his wound."

"Hey, it was worth a try." Dion bent forward and kissed my lips. "How long do you think you'll be?"

"I don't know. Maybe a couple of hours. Hopefully less."

"What time do you meet him?"

"One o'clock."

"All right. It's got to be done. Can't escape that. But you call me as soon as you leave there, or if you're there and things aren't going the way you want them to."

"You know I will."

The first thing I noticed when I got to Robert's house the next day was that there weren't any cars in the driveway. Not Olga's. And not one that should have belonged to a mediator.

But I went to the door nonetheless, figuring that the mediator hadn't arrived yet.

Robert opened the door before I could even ring the

doorbell, meaning he had been watching for my arrival. His face lit up in a warm smile. "Hello, Elsie."

"Hello, Robert."

He opened the door wide. "Come in."

I stepped into the house, noting the faint music playing and the smell of something cooking. Perhaps Olga's car was in the garage.

"Is Olga here?" I asked.

"I gave her the rest of the day off. I wanted privacy."

That was likely, given the circumstances, wasn't it? And yet a chill of alarm went down my spine. There were many rooms in the house where we could have privacy.

"I see," I told him.

"I've prepared lunch for us."

"Lunch?"

"I hope you haven't eaten."

"I haven't, but…when is the mediator coming?"

"Soon," Robert replied. "Please, let's go to the dining room."

As I followed him, I knew the reason I'd felt a chill. I wasn't thrilled about being here alone with Robert.

"Sit," he told me, gesturing to the grand and ornate dining room table.

It was set for two. A bottle of wine was chilling in a silver ice bucket. Bavarian crystal tumblers and wineglasses accompanied each setting.

"You cooked?" I asked in surprise.

"You know I enjoy preparing a good meal on occasion." Robert pulled out a chair for me next to the head of the table. "Please. Sit."

I sat. Robert poured me a glass of white wine. I lifted the glass, swirled the light-colored liquid around. I found myself studying its clarity.

And then I felt stupid. What did I think—that Robert had put something in the drink to knock me out or poison me?

I brought the glass to my lips and took a sip. "Very nice."

"I know how much you love red, but with the meal, I figured white would be better. It's Pomino. From Italy."

I offered him a guarded smile. "It's delicious."

"You stay and enjoy the music. I'll be fine getting everything together in the kitchen."

Classical music was playing on the sound system. Mozart. I recognized the piano concerto. It was among Robert's favorites.

He soon returned with a plate of food. It was salmon, lightly seasoned with butter and garlic, from the look and smell of it. Steamed broccoli and white rice were arranged artfully.

Robert set the plate on the table before me, went back to the kitchen and returned with his own meal. He sat beside me at the head of the table and lifted his fork and knife. "Bon appetit."

"Aren't you going to have some wine?" I asked, my pulse suddenly accelerating.

"Yes. Of course." He started to move his chair backward.

"I'll pour it for you," I said. I stood and lifted the wine bottle from the bucket, then filled his glass.

I watched Robert carefully, that feeling of wariness once again sweeping over me. I continued to watch him as I sank back into my seat.

Robert raised his glass. "How about a toast?" he suggested. "To remaining friends."

For a man who had been obsessed with the idea that I was leaving him for someone else, and who had tried to destroy my business, I couldn't imagine why he would want to be friends with me. It wasn't like he hadn't done things I couldn't forgive.

I suppose because I didn't speak, didn't even lift my glass, Robert decided to change his toast. "All right. How about toasting to leaving the bitterness behind us?"

I toyed with the stem of my glass for a moment before raising it. "I'll drink to that."

We both sipped the wine, and again I felt relief.

Pushing any worry from my mind, I lifted my cutlery and took a bite of fish.

Despite myself, I moaned a little when I tasted the exquisite flavor. I'd been too anxious to eat much breakfast, so I was hungry, and ate everything on my plate. I also finished my glass of wine, and even had another half glass.

I might as well be cordial, I decided. The more cordial, the more likely I would accomplish my goal for this visit.

Every so often, I glanced at my watch. Forty minutes and no mediator.

Robert led the conversation, talking about the changes within the company and how he might be ready to fully retire. He spoke about his son and daughter-in-law's recent trip to Japan, where the company was opening a new division.

He finished off the meal with a piece of warm apple pie. "I confess, Olga made the pie."

"Whoever made it, it's delicious." I had to admit to myself that this lunch with Robert had been quite amicable.

I glanced at my watch again. It was almost two. "Robert, when will the mediator be here?"

"Momentarily, I'm sure." His gaze wandered to the large window. "It's a lovely day. Remember that day you left, and I said it was a shame we didn't enjoy our home more?"

"I remember."

"I've been thinking a lot about that. It's the reason I'm ready to retire. No more crises with companies in Germany. I'm ready to spend the rest of my days enjoying the fruits of my labor." He held my gaze for a few seconds. "Maybe have a second chance at love."

"Robert—"

"Shhh," he said. "No more bitterness, remember?"

I nodded.

"You don't hate me, do you?" he asked. "I gave you a good life, didn't I?"

"No, Robert. I don't hate you. And this was never about you not giving me a good life. You gave me a world I never imagined I would experience."

Robert smiled. "Well, that's good to hear."

I finished off my apple pie, surprised at how much I'd eaten. I'd been famished.

I wiped the corners of my mouth with my napkin, then set it beside my plate. "Thank you for a lovely meal. I can help you clean up before—"

"How about you go out on the boat with me?"

The question caught me off guard. "The boat?"

"When was the last time we went out on the lake together?"

I shrugged. "I don't know."

"If this is going to be our last supper, if you will, then why not make it as pleasurable as possible?"

"But the mediat…" The words died on my lips. I got it.

"We don't need a mediator," Robert said softly. "Surely we can resolve everything without strangers telling us what to do."

I shook my head in disbelief. "If you wanted me to come over for a meal, why didn't you just say so?"

"Because you wouldn't have come." Robert smiled faintly. "Am I right?"

I didn't speak. I wasn't sure how to process this latest bit of news.

I thought of Spike's premonition, that Robert might actually hurt me.

"Elsie," Robert said softly.

I lifted my gaze. Looked at Robert.

"I know I haven't been pleasant through our…our problems. I'm getting older, Elsie. I didn't want to be alone. I wanted you to stay with me, but I see now that I went about it in the wrong way."

Robert paused, and I suspected that he wanted me to say something. But I remained silent.

"I'm sorry," he said, and held my eyes for several seconds. "I truly am. We started our marriage with so much hope. A great friendship. I didn't want it to end this way."

"Neither did I," I agreed.

"I've accepted that our marriage is over," Robert said, his voice heavy with resignation. "I know we can't go back. But what I'd like more than anything is for us to remain friends."

His words tugged at my heart. Robert had turned the corner. Finally, he was ready to move forward in a positive way.

"I'll always be grateful for the life we shared," I said. "I never wanted any bitterness. I'd like very much for us to remain friends."

An expression of regret passed over Robert's face. His smile was tinged with contrition. "Thank you, Elsie."

I got teary eyed. This was what I'd wanted. An amicable end to my marriage. "Thank *you*, Robert. Thank you for agreeing to put the ugliness behind us."

"You used to love the feel of the wind in your hair," Robert said, his eyes lighting up. "Remember how we would go out on the lake and stay there hours, reading novels together?"

I nodded. "Yes."

"And the way you would lie back and enjoy the feel of the sun on your face?"

"Yes." I remembered it all.

"One last ride on the boat," Robert said. "For old time's sake."

I found myself nodding. We would take a pleasant ride on the boat, a positive step in the direction of an amicable future. A future as friends with fond memories of our shared life.

"All right," I said. "Let's go for a ride."

29

I closed my eyes and enjoyed the feel of the wind on my face as Robert maneuvered the Baja speedboat over the lake's calm surface. There was something soothing about being out here on the water, almost as if the wind swept your problems off your shoulders and blew them away.

Robert was right. I'd missed this.

I felt both a sense of peace and nostalgia. Peace over the fact that Robert was finally being nice about letting me go. And nostalgia over the happy times we had shared. I found myself remembering how I had met and fallen for Robert. Remembering the romantic and charming man I'd thought the world of.

The engine sputtered, and the boat slowed. I opened my eyes. One glance around told me we were out very far on the lake. From here I could only see a thicket of trees, no houses.

I turned to face Robert. "Why did we stop?"

"Look at this place." He gestured around us. "The majesty of it."

"It's spectacular."

"Being out here reminds me that we're all a part of something so much bigger," Robert continued.

"Yes, I know what you mean."

"It also makes me realize how insignificant a person really is." Robert paused, locked eyes with mine. "You may be rich and powerful, but one wrong move and this lake will swallow you whole. Really show you who's boss."

I felt an odd tingling at the back of my neck. I wasn't sure where his train of thought was coming from—or where it was heading.

"It's almost incongruous that a place of such beauty and peace can turn into a grave. Know what I mean?"

The sun was bearing down on my skin, but a chill ran along my arms. I didn't answer Robert's question.

"A lot of people have drowned out here over the years. One just a few weeks ago."

The chill spread through my whole body as Spike's words sounded softly in my mind.

I got the feeling that he would hurt you...

Had I been stupid to trust Robert, to believe that he'd come to terms with our breakup? Had his goal been to play nice so that he could get me into this boat? And if so, what was he planning to do next?

"The young couple were renters from out of town.

Late one night, they borrowed the owner's boat and went for a joyride. You probably heard the story on the news. They were drinking, not wearing their life vests. The husband said his wife was standing up, dancing on top of the boat or something like that, and fell in."

"What are you getting at?" There was a defiant edge to my voice.

"Why do they do it?" Robert asked. "Something so foolish. Are people attracted to danger?"

I glanced around frantically. No one was in the vicinity. No one I could call out to for help.

No witnesses.

"I want to go back to shore," I insisted. I was wearing a life jacket, but God only knew what else Robert could do to me out here.

I got the feeling that he would hurt you...

"Is that what attracts you to Dion?" At my surprise, Robert's eyes lit up with amusement. "The danger?"

"Is that what this is about?" I asked. "This whole being-friendly charade? Because you know about Dion?"

"Of course I know about Dion," Robert snapped. He was no longer warm and friendly, but remote and frosty. "The question is, how well do you know him?"

"Well enough. Now take me back to the shore."

"I'm betting you don't know anything about his... well, his dangerous side," Robert went on, as though I hadn't spoken. "No, you know about the man who coaches college football. Who mentors kids."

"Take me back *now*, Robert."

"What you don't know is that your boyfriend, Dion,

has a past. Quite a colorful one. He's not just good in bed."

"I get it, Robert. You're mad because I'm fucking someone else. Can we go back to shore now?"

"You've had your fun, Elsie. I suppose it was bound to happen sooner or later. You are your mother's daughter, after all."

My jaw twitched.

"And I'm not heartless. I know I disappointed you with that whole baby business. I take my share of the blame. I'm ready to forgive you and start over again."

He couldn't be serious. "We're not going to have this conversation again. You can try to intimidate me with the talk about drownings, but I'm not go—"

"Intimidate you?" Robert chuckled, gave a "you've got to be kidding" laugh. "You're afraid of me?"

I didn't respond, just stared at him with an unwavering gaze.

"Dion's the one you need to be afraid of."

"If you don't take me back to shore, I'm going to jump out of this boat and get back on my own. And when I do, I'm calling the police." I'm not sure where the strength came from to say that, but I meant every word. I was tired of Robert thinking he could intimidate me. Control me. If I died trying to be free of him, then so be it.

Again, that chuckle. It pissed me off.

"You want to jump, jump. But know that what I say is true. Your boyfriend, Dion Barry, isn't who you think he is. In fact, his real name isn't Dion Barry. Gregory Williams is the name he was born with. I don't know where he told you he grew up, but he grew up in L.A. His street name was G-Boy, short for Green-Boy— because of his eye color."

A lump had lodged in my throat. I could hardly suck in air. Something about what Robert was saying had the ring of truth. Perhaps due to the easy confidence with which he was reciting these facts, or the reality that he knew as much as he was professing.

"When G-Boy was seventeen, he and his *crew* committed a series of armed robberies. A man was beaten and nearly died."

My back went rigid. I couldn't move.

"You might not want to believe what I'm saying, but you're smart, Elsie. You can find these facts on your own. Any good investigator can dig up dirt—even dirt people thought they long ago washed away with a new name and a new life."

Robert was silent for a long moment as he stared at me, giving me time to register his words.

"When Gregory was seventeen, he got into a knife fight with another gang member," Robert went on. "He was stabbed. Spent a week in hospital."

I gasped. Robert's words hit me like a sledgehammer to the gut.

His eyes registered understanding. "Ahh. Of course. He's got a scar. You've seen it."

I said nothing.

"Perhaps this is just a phase you're going through. Engaging in self-destructive behavior as a way to get back at me." Robert paused. "I might have been dishonest with you about the vasectomy," he went on, "but it can't be said that I lied to you about who I was. I've got the reports about Gregory back at the house. You can read the investigator's words with your own eyes."

I couldn't speak. My head was spinning. My heart was pounding.

"One last chance, Elsie. You say the word, and I'll forgive you. We resume our life together."

I heard Robert's words, but it was as if I was hearing them through a fog. All I could think about was Dion. That he had lied to me.

He had nearly killed someone…

God, no.

I whimpered, then gripped the leather arms of my seat as I tried to suck in air. My lungs weren't filling fast enough.

It felt like I was drowning. Drowning in a lake of confusion and fear.

I'd been stunned by Robert's words. Stunned at the truth he had revealed.

Dion had lied to me. He'd concocted a story about getting stabbed while defending his mother.

"Say the word, Elsie. We can leave the past in the past, move forward together."

A myriad of thoughts were rushing through my brain, but one took center stage. *It doesn't matter.*

It had been nearly two decades since Dion was a teenager. People made mistakes in their youth—sometimes big ones. If Dion had been involved in a gang as a teen, how could I hold that against him? Wasn't the point that he had risen above the mistakes of his past?

The man he was now was not the child he'd been

then. I would talk to him about what had happened, get his side of the story, but I wouldn't hold the past against him.

People could judge me because of my history—judge me for my parents' behavior—but that wouldn't be fair, either.

I loved Dion. We had connected. Nothing Robert said could change the reality of that fact.

"No," I said, slowly shaking my head. I was still gripping the armrests, my eyes closed as I tried to steady my breathing. "I love Dion. I love him."

I didn't sense the movement until it was too late. A pain suddenly pierced my temple, and my head jerked backward. My eyes popped open. It took me a good couple of seconds to realize that Robert had hit me.

I stared at him, confused. I registered the flashlight in his right hand. The vile expression on his face. And I knew, in an instant, that he was going to kill me.

I tried to move my body, but found I couldn't. The blow had stunned me.

"You're an ungrateful bitch." Robert wrapped both hands around my neck and began to squeeze. "You think I'm going to let you just walk away from me? Humiliate me with some other man?"

"Rob…ert…" His name was a choked cry from my lips. "Stop…"

"You're a whore, Elsie. A filthy, pathetic whore. You should have been grateful for the life I gave you. Not spreading your legs for every man like your mother."

Maybe it was Robert's words, but a surge of adrenaline suddenly shot through me. My survival instincts roared to life. I couldn't die like this. Couldn't let Robert murder me. He would dump me in the lake and tell the world I had drowned.

If they ever found my body.

I grabbed at his hands, scratched at them. He squeezed harder, but I wriggled violently, trying to free myself. His grip only tightened.

My lungs began to burn. They needed air.

I can't die like this…

With a grunt, I forced my knee into Robert's crotch with all the strength I had. I hit him good and hard, and he cried out, his fingers reflexively releasing me. Then he doubled over in pain, clutching his groin.

It took only a moment to gasp in much-needed air, then I shoved Robert backward and scrambled away from him. I ran straight to the edge of the boat, prepared to vault into the water. I had a life jacket on. I could make it to shore, no matter how long it took.

"Elsie…"

With one leg over the side of the boat, I glanced back. Saw Robert on his back on the vessel's floor. He was clasping at the life jacket over the left side of his chest.

"My—my chest. Elsie, help me. Please…"

I knew what he was doing. Playing possum so that I would go over to him. And then he would overpower me again, finish the task of killing me.

Robert had cried wolf too many times. I didn't believe for a second that he was having a real heart attack now.

I put my other leg over the edge of the boat.

"Elsie."

There was something in Robert's tone. Something that gave me pause. Made me turn once more. He was still on the ground, groaning and writhing.

"Oh, God," he gasped.

My eyes widened in alarm as I regarded him. He gripped at his life vest with one hand, clawed at his throat with the other.

Maybe he wasn't faking a heart attack.

"Please," he begged.

I swung my legs back onto the boat. Adrenaline was still rushing through my veins as I cautiously approached Robert. I looked down at him, saw a fear in his eyes I had never seen before.

He met my gaze. Held it as his eyes grew as huge as saucers. And then his eyelids fluttered shut.

"Robert?" His hands went slack. But I still couldn't be sure he wasn't faking this. "Robert?"

He didn't respond. Didn't move.

Dropping onto my knees beside him, I turned my ear over his face. With the light breeze, I couldn't tell if he was breathing.

"Robert?" I shook him by the shoulders. "Robert!"

No response.

I didn't know CPR. I didn't know how to help him. If Robert was going to have a chance of surviving, I needed to get back to land right away.

Hurrying to the helm of the boat, I dropped into the seat and started the engine. I guided the speedboat back to the shore as quickly as I could, glancing back over my shoulder at Robert several times.

He hadn't moved. No once.

When I got to the shore, I ran to the house to call 911.

But in my heart, I knew it was too late.

Robert was gone.

epilogue

The paramedics had attempted valiantly to resuscitate Robert when they got to the house. I had stood back and watched in a state of shock as they used a defibrillator on him to try and get his heart pumping. Then they loaded him onto a gurney and transported him to the waiting ambulance, all but running every step of the way.

Though the paramedics had gotten to the house within minutes of my emergency call, and though their efforts to save Robert had been exceptional, my husband was pronounced dead by the time he arrived at the hospital.

He'd had a heart attack, and then had stopped breathing. Given that he had gone without oxygen for several minutes, even if Robert had been resuscitated, he would have had brain damage.

It would have been no way to live, and there was comfort in knowing that Robert wouldn't have to spend the rest of his days in a vegetative state.

As for me, the nightmare was over. Robert would never bully me, harass me or make my life miserable again.

But I wasn't happy about what had happened. I'd never wanted Robert to die—at least not like this. I was, however, relieved. It would be a lie to say that I wasn't. I was relieved to know that I would be able to move on without any of Robert's vindictive threats hanging over my head.

Robert's death made me a widow, but I didn't stay single for long. Dion and I married two months later— just after I found out I was pregnant.

Minus the twenty percent that would go to charity and the matrimonial house Robert and I had shared, Robert's will was divided equally between me and his three children. They were all flabbergasted when I renounced my share. I told them that I thought it fair the money go into a trust fund for Robert's grandchildren. My husband's children and I hadn't been close during my marriage—they saw me as Wife Number Three, maybe even as a gold digger, and had mostly kept their distance. But I think I earned their respect when I made it clear I wasn't after Robert's money. All I asked for was my store and the million dollars I'd been promised in the prenuptial agreement. I would be more than fine with that.

Dion and I moved about five miles south to the community of Huntersville, where we bought an average-size family home. Huntersville was close enough to my shop, but far enough from the neighborhood where I'd lived with Robert.

In our new house, we promptly painted the baby's room blue—for the little boy we were expecting. We were happy and putting the pain of the past behind us.

Some days, I can't help looking back at my life with Robert, at how ugly and crazy things became. But I don't have any regrets. He was what I needed at the time. And I married him for the right reasons. And if I hadn't married him, I would never have opened the store I'd always wanted to.

And if I hadn't opened the store, I likely never would have met Dion.

But, perhaps I would have. Because I firmly believe that he is my soul mate. The one man in this world I was meant to be with.

And although sometimes it takes many years to find the person who you'll love with very fiber of your being, I do believe it happens eventually. And when you do, it's magic. It's always magic when it's right.

★ ★ ★ ★ ★

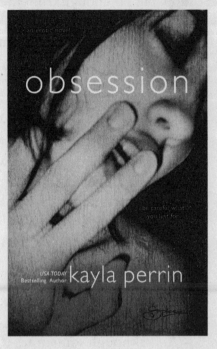

Her babydaddy's a deadbeat.
Her ex-boyfriend thinks
she's a booty call.
Her fiancé was cheating
on her—and his wife...
And now he's dead.

USA TODAY
BESTSELLING AUTHOR

KAYLA PERRIN

Her fiancé's hostile widow, who happens to own the hip South Beach condo Vanessa Cain and her young daughter shared with Eli, wants her out. Vanessa loves her home— but to keep it, she has to come up with money. Lots of it.

Which means bringing in big business for her boss's motivational speaking agency. So with a business plan and a bikini, Vanessa heads down to the Bahamas to convince Chaz Andersen—the biggest name in life coaching—to sign with her.

This single mama is about to get herself into a whole lot more drama!

single mama drama

"A writer that everyone
should watch."
—Eric Jerome Dickey

MIRA®

*Available wherever
trade paperback books are sold!*

www.MIRABooks.com

MKP2551TR

THE EDGY SEQUEL TO *SINGLE MAMA DRAMA*

KAYLA PERRIN

This single mama's been through hell—her cheating (and still married) fiancé is dead, her professional reputation is in tatters, the man she really loves walked out of her life and, worst of all, she's about to lose her fabulous South Beach condo to a conniving witch.

But it ain't over yet....

SINGLE MAMA'S GOT MORE DRAMA

"A writer that everyone should watch." —*New York Times* bestselling author Eric Jerome Dickey

Available the first week of January 2009 wherever books are sold!

www.MIRABooks.com

MIRA®

MKP2616TR